FALLING INTO BLUE

FALLING
INTO
BLUE

BARBARA BOUCHET

BLUE
ORB
PUBLISHING

SEATTLE, WASHINGTON

Published by:
  Blue Orb Publishing
  Seattle, WA

Requests for permission should be directed to
  permissions@BlueOrbPublishing.com

ISBN: 978-0-9824569-1-0
LCCN: 2013923026

Printed in the United States of America

AUTHOR'S NOTE

While some of the themes in this book are taken from my life, this is a work of fiction and should not be confused with a portrayal of my life or of any family members.

FALLING INTO BLUE

PROLOGUE

I'M almost thirteen years old and am still living at home. But I'm planning to be long gone in a few years. Then I can start doing everything I ever wanted.

I've tried to remember the most important things so far, starting with when I was really little. I know Rainbow Ghost wants me to. But I'm still not sure why. Maybe between now, which is 1965, and when I'm all grown up, I'll have so much to remember that it will all make sense.

1

BANSHEE
SIX YEARS AND FOUR YEARS

I REMEMBER the banshee from when I was little. It was after Mom came home from her breakdown and I saw my first movie at the theater. The banshee jumped out of the screen with her shiny blue and silvery white jolts that sparked out of her. She screamed forever with her witch magic, and you knew it would tear your skin off if you didn't close your eyes and plug up your ears all at once. I peeked just a little through my fingers.

That night after the movie, the banshee came in the girls' bedroom. I was almost asleep when she started screaming. Her shrieky screams grabbed my skin and shook me till my eyes popped open. I saw her there in the corner, waiting for me. Then I slammed my eyes shut. She threw out a big jab of lightning that went all the way through me. It was sharp inside my chest and made an achy thud.

I just had to look at her. So she wouldn't go anywhere else. So she wouldn't come over to me. She crouched in the corner and stayed put, except for a few streaks of lightning. Finally, I went to sleep. When I woke up the next morning, she was gone, but I knew that banshee was real, even though I could see it was just some wadded up sheets sitting in the corner. She came to get me every night for a long time. She jolted me sometimes and scared me so bad I almost wet the bed, but she never got me.

I didn't see another movie again for a long time. And it wasn't because I told anybody about the banshee because I wasn't that stupid. I'd never get to do anything again if they thought I was a crybaby

5

from watching a movie. I wasn't really was sure though, that I wanted to see another movie. That screen was too big, and it was so loud you couldn't make it stop if you tried.

But I wished I could go again at least to see the colors. They were so shiny bright. Not like any colors you see in real life. It's too bad that banshee blue was wasted on a banshee. Because it was the most beautiful blue I've ever seen. Anywhere. It wasn't like the sky or like water or even like blue Easter egg dye. It was so much shinier than real, I knew it came from some secret place that was more real than anything in my regular life. A place where lots of things hide.

It was like that shrieky lonely feeling that you get when everyone forgets you and it feels like you're just a big puff of nothing. That kind of thing happens all the time at our house. I felt it even before Mom had her breakdown.

The first time I had that shrieky feeling was when I was about four years old. It was the day they started digging the big hole for the new house.

The new house is on the other side of the driveway, across from the motel. Dad works on the new house all the time, but it's so big it might take forever for him to finish it. Till then, we have to keep living in our part of the motel. I just hope we get to move in before I grow up and leave home, so we can live like regular people for a while.

We had lots of company the day they dug the pit for the new house. So it was already like a holiday. Grandma Stoltz, Dad's Mom, was visiting, plus some aunts and uncles and a few of their kids. Everyone got up bright and early to start work. Dad, our uncles, and all the boys got to go outside. The girls had to stay inside and cook.

Flora, Mom's twin sister, gave me the potato peeler and an apple so I could help peel apples for pie. I didn't get to use the paring knife because I wasn't five yet, and you had to be five to use knives.

Mom made some buns from scratch while Grandma Stoltz made the pie crust. Usually Mom was the one who made the crust. I heard her whisper-hiss to Flora when no one else could hear, "There's no way

I'm going to compete with his Mother on something as sacred as her damn pies. I wasn't born yesterday."

All my older sisters helped the grown ups and took care of the babies, so they weren't underfoot. I was just old enough to not be underfoot. Georgina, my oldest sister, made the heavenly hash salad. It was everyone's favorite. Usually, we only got it at Thanksgiving and Christmas. It had fruit cocktail, mandarin oranges, bananas, marshmallows, and lots of whipped cream. I peeled the bananas.

All that cooking was supposed to be for the men who were outside digging the huge hole in the ground. Dad's brothers were all tall and strong like Dad. Uncle Frank was the handsomest but also the scariest because he got mad so easy. He was married to Flora, Mom's twin sister, and they had lots of kids too.

Finally, when it was time for lunch, I got to go outside and see what those guys had been doing all that time. Two men I'd never seen before were eating sandwiches by a big muddy bulldozer that was down inside the hole they were digging. I felt the ground rumble. A huge dump truck was driving down into the hole. Not even a speck of me was scared to go chase that truck. I ran behind it down into the hole.

The dump truck man was pulling out his lunch on the seat. I walked over to see what he was eating. He had his shirt off, and the muscle on his arm was as big as Daddy's, only tan. He looked even more handsome than Uncle Frank. He smiled at me and said, "How'd such a pretty girl get down here in all this dirt?"

"With my feet." I looked down at the fresh dirt that came half way up my legs. He smiled again, and I could tell he liked me even though he was a stranger. I said, "Can I come up?"

He said, "Sure," and reached down to swoosh me onto his lap. His stickery black mustache tickled the back of my neck, and I almost fell off his lap from giggling and being shaky excited. I hoped I wouldn't get in any trouble for sitting on his lap. I got to hold the brown shiny gear knob and put my hands on the black wheel the way my brothers did on our tractor. I was as strong as any boy! Maybe I'd even get to help him drive it when the truck got full again. Then he said, "You better get on down now. I need to get some things done before they start up again."

I said, "I'll help. I'm a good helper."

He said, "You can help by going back inside so I can get some work done."

"Please?" I looked right at his face. It was so big and close I could see the little holes in his skin.

"Naw, I don't want you to get hurt."

"I won't get hurt. I'll stay right here." I wiggled a little on his lap.

I was afraid he was going to get mad, but instead he just picked me up and plopped me down on the ground. I could smell the sweat from his arms. It was like Daddy. He said, "Why don't you save me a place right beside you at dinner?"

"Really?"

"Yeah. We'll be done in a few more hours."

"OK. I'll save you a spot. I promise." He was going to sit by **me** at dinner. But I still didn't want to go back inside.

Then Georgina hollered down to me to leave those guys alone and climb up out of there. I did, but it was real slow on the way up. When I got to the top, I lifted up my arms to her, and she scooped me up.

She said, "You know you're getting too big for me to carry you."

"I know. But just for now?" I sat on the edge of her hip and watched the bulldozer man start up the engine. Then Georgina carried me inside.

I told her, "The dump truck man likes me, and I get to sit by him at dinner."

She said, "Yeah, he's a cutie all right." I knew I did good.

It was a long time waiting for dinner to be ready. By the time my sisters started setting the table, I was yawning and rubbing my eyes. Mom told me, "You're tired. Why don't you go and take a nap before dinner starts. It's still going to be a while."

I said, "I don't need a nap, and I'm old enough, Mommy. I'll help you some more too."

"There's no telling how long it'll be before dinner. You go on and take a nap, and I'll wake you in time." She was saying it like she didn't want any monkey business from me. So I started walking to the bed.

As soon as Mom started talking to Flora, I ran as fast as I could into the coat closet in the kitchen. It had a long curtain to hide all the junk. Its floor was covered with piles of coats, sweaters, shoes, and old toys. I dug myself down into the pile, so only my head was sticking out.

I'd stay there until dinner was ready. That way I wouldn't miss anything. I peeked out and watched them put dishes, glasses, and silverware on the table. I could hardly wait! But it was **so** dark and warm inside the closet.

Next thing I knew I was waking up. It was dead quiet in the kitchen. I was yawning, and my stomach was rumbly from being hungry when I remembered the big dinner! I climbed out of the closet and saw the table. The dishes were dirty, the food was eaten, and it was almost dark outside. What happened? Where was everyone? I started screaming crying, "Where aaare you?"

Dean, my older brother, was walking through the kitchen and saw me. He came over, shoved me a little and said, "Where were you? I was looking all over for you before dinner."

I ran howling into the living room looking for Mom. Some of the kids were playing Monopoly on the floor. Mom was on the couch combing Maureen's hair and talking to Flora.

"Mommy, what happened to dinner?"

Mom looked over at me kind of sharp and said, "What is it?" She yanked through a tangle and Maureen, who was just a little older than me, yelped.

"Dinner, Mommy. It's all gone!" My voice was real loud.

"Well, of course it is. We ate it." She slapped Maureen on the bottom to say that her hair was done.

"But what about meeee?" I was starting to yell.

"What's gotten **into** you anyway?" She was getting mad at me.

"The dump truck man. Where is he?" I tried to not scream.

"Why, he's gone. They've all left."

"Him **too**?"

"What about him? I told you, everyone but family left a while ago." She turned away from me like she was going to talk to Flora again.

"You said you'd wake me! And now everything's gone!!" The sad and mad in me was exploding into sharp pieces of lightning. I wanted one of those pieces of lightning to come right out and kill Mom dead. See how she liked that! I screamed, "You promised! It's all gone!!"

Mom didn't die one bit. She just said, "You just settle down young lady. Or else. I'll not have you shrieking at me like that. You sound like a banshee."

The lightning jolts did settle down. Into hard little rockets that kept shooting around inside. I knew I better not let even one of them come out my mouth, or I'd get slapped. They could still come out my eyes though. But instead of being mean nasty rockets, they came out crying.

Flora tapped Mom's arm and whispered something in her ear.

Mom looked back at me and said, "It's too bad you missed dinner. I told one of the boys to go get you. I guess they didn't do it." I could tell she didn't care one bit.

"Couldn't you see I was gone?" I was scared before I even said it.

She sort of laughed, "I guess I didn't realize it until just now." Then she turned to Flora and said, "Does this kind of thing happen to you, too?" Flora laughed just a little.

Every last rocket was gone, and I started wailing from so far inside it scared me even more. Because something was gone inside. It made me shiver so hard I stopped crying. Then I looked up at Mom and saw the way she looked at me like I wasn't even there. Like I didn't feel one thing. Like she didn't even know who I was. And all I could do was try to hate her as hard as I could. And she probably didn't even notice that not one speck of me loved her anymore. I knew she'd forget. I knew! I started crying again and ran out of the living room.

I went outside to see if any of the work guys were still there. It was pitch black except for the lights by the tractor where Dad and his brothers were smoking and laughing in German.

I went back in the kitchen, looking for the heavenly hash bowl. It was empty. I licked some of the plates where there was still some whipped cream left. All that crying made it salty. Flora came in and told me, "Don't be doing that. You'll get God knows what kind of germs. If you stop blubbering for a while, I'll fix you something to eat."

She gave me some leftover mashed potatoes and gravy, which was too thick from being cold, some ham, which was OK, and peach pie, which tasted pretty good. But I couldn't stop blubbering. I asked Flora, "Didn't Mom even know I was gone?"

She patted me on the shoulder and said, "Your Mom has a lot on her mind, Tracie. She didn't mean to forget you. You'll understand some day. When you're older and have your own kids." Then she walked back into the living room.

I sat by myself and stared at how dark it was outside. The yellow curtains with little orange flowers grabbed my eyes and were too bright. I looked back at the black some more. I didn't want to go in the living room with everyone who didn't even know if I was there or not. Even the dump truck man didn't notice I was gone. And I thought he liked me! All I knew was that there wasn't one other person in the whole world who remembered me. Maybe I wasn't really there. Maybe that's why they forget you, because you're not really there anyway. Maybe you're made out of thin air, and that's all. Maybe you're just a ghost inside with a banshee swirling around you.

I went to sleep that night and wet the bed. I wasn't a bed wetter either, since I hadn't wet the bed since I was a baby. But I felt so cold when I woke up and that pee coming out of me was so warm I couldn't stop once I started. For just a second, I could see why someone would turn into a bed wetter. Because it felt so good. Then the bad feeling of the blackness outside the kitchen window came swooping back, and I knew there was nothing good about anyone who ever wet the bed. Now I was just like all my other bed wetter brothers and sisters. It got worse when the cold feeling came back into the bed.

All I could do was roll myself as tight as I could into my warm Indian blanket and try to make the shivers stop. They did. Kind of. But there was this feeling in my brain that made me dizzy. Then it's like I was falling down a tunnel that made me even dizzier. All that whooshing of wind blowing into my ears was so loud! I tried to cover them but couldn't because of falling too fast.

Finally, I landed. I must have fallen asleep. Everywhere I looked there was sunshine that was too bright and rainbows that were jaggy and jolty. They were leaping everywhere and shooting through me. I didn't like it at first, but after a while everything got softer. It was like I was a rainbow too. It was fun to spring and bounce through the air.

Then I saw someone who was completely rainbow. Her rainbows were soft and had more colors than you could ever imagine. She didn't look like a regular person at all. She was like a ghost made out of rainbows and was so beautiful that I wanted to swoop her inside me and never let her go. I couldn't do that though because even though I could see right through her, she was still a real person. And a real person can't live inside you. Only you can. She told me that, even though she didn't really say it out loud.

She came over to me and touched my shoulder. All of a sudden I wasn't alone anymore. It was like all along I'd been so lonely I could almost die from it and didn't remember how bad it was until right then. I started crying hard while she slowly wrapped me up in her rainbow self. Finally, I was all quiet inside.

Then the pee smell from my flannel nightgown floated up. I knew I was still icky, but she didn't seem to mind. She sent me the smell of some new flower. It was a smooth silky smell that was also kind of wet. After a while, it seemed like it was coming from my own skin. Nice, nice, nice!

That smell floated into the sound of wind chimes. The way they tinkle in the summer when the wind breezes over them. It was her way of talking. I couldn't tell what she was saying. Because they weren't words. I felt her hand on my chest. My heart was like a drum, and she was making it thump. Nice and slow. I could understand something. It was like she was saying, "Re-**mem**-ber, thump **thump**." So I'd remember something. And it was right in my heart. It made me strong too. She did it over and over again until I woke up.

The pee was even colder. But I had something inside me that made it so I could stand almost anything. I didn't know what it was, but I could feel it inside and promised I'd do just what Rainbow Ghost told me. Remember. Only I wasn't sure what. And I still had to figure out how to hide my wet bed so no one would find out.

It was Saturday morning so I could stay in bed with the covers pulled up until everyone else got up. Then I'd sneak out of bed and change my nightie before anyone smelled me. I wasn't sure what to do about the bed. Maybe I'd let Billy, my next youngest brother take a nap on my bed and then get mad when he wet it. I wouldn't get too mad though.

2

BREAKDOWN

SIX YEARS

WHEN all of us kids piled in through the back door from school, Mom was gone, and a stranger was standing over the stove, cooking macaroni. What was she doing in our kitchen?

Becky, my older sister, knew who she was. She said it was a friend of Mom's, named Mrs. Samuel.

Then she asked her, "Where's Mom?"

Mrs. Samuel looked up from the steaming macaroni and said, "She's at the hospital. Your Dad came home from work and took her." She didn't look at us while she said it.

"What's wrong with her?" asked Sonny.

"She's not feeling well. Why don't you little ones go on out and play now."

Since I was only in the first grade then, that meant me, Billy, who was about four and a half, and Maureen, who was in the second grade. The babies and Luann, who still acted like a baby, got to stay. They didn't know what was going on anyway. I said, "I want to know some things too."

But Sonny said, "Go on out, runt, you're too little to know anything." I stood right there and begged to Mrs. Samuel, "Can't I please stay? She's my Mom too."

"You'd best leave."

"It's not fair." I started to cry.

"Too bad, runt," Sonny said as he pushed me out the door.

We could hear them talking through the door, but it was just mumbly jumbly sounds that didn't tell you anything. Outside was cold. None of us played. Maureen stood there with her hands in her navy blue coat pockets, staring at the dirt, while Billy tried to take the metal part of the door apart.

When one of the chickens came pecking at my shoe, I stopped crying and screamed at that stupid chicken to stop it. Then I chased it until feathers flew out of its wings.

No one would tell me anything until dinnertime. Mrs. Samuel left, and Dad wasn't back yet. Becky said, "Mom's going to be gone a long time and might not come back unless we're all real good." She was in the seventh grade and was the oldest kid at home, ever since Georgina got sent away.

"What does she have? What's wrong with her?"

Becky said, "It's a nervous breakdown. Mom's really sick, but it isn't like throwing up or having the flu. It's from being too tired from having so many kids."

"Can we go visit her at the hospital?"

"You can't visit people with breakdowns, or they might get so tired from seeing you they'll get even sicker. Besides, she went to the state hospital, and it's about a hundred miles away."

I looked at Francie, who was just a little more than a month old. Maureen was feeding her a bottle. "Not even Francie gets to see her?"

"Nope," said Becky.

"Why would she want to see any of us anyway? She's probably glad to be somewhere else," Sonny said.

I hoped he was as wrong as he was mean and that right then she was missing me. I could sort of see her sitting in the hospital bed, putting a bite of chocolate pudding in her mouth and thinking about what a darlin' I was. She would wish she could give me a bite of her pudding and wouldn't think of anyone but me. When I looked up and saw Mom and Dad's empty places at the table, I felt kind of crumply. Maybe Sonny was right.

We were all pretty quiet except for Francie, who was crying because she hadn't burped yet. We passed the macaroni. I wasn't that hungry, even though Mrs. Samuel made it look beautiful on top with the parsley and red pepper on top. And even though it was nice and gooey with lots of cheese, it tasted dusty and salty. It made me think of holding on tight to Mom's arm during a dust storm and kissing her salty skin while the wind tore away at us.

Dad came home after I was in bed. He told Becky she had to stay home from school until Mom got back because there was no one else to take care of his babies. Becky was in charge of the whole family now and had to take care of our big sprawly motel too, even though she wasn't that old. Luckily, she knew how to do almost everything Mom did. In the morning, she didn't go on the bus with the rest of us. She took care of Francie, Nicky, Luann, and Billy while Dad went to work.

By Saturday, we didn't have much food left in the house. I knew, because I'd been helping Becky cook. Saturdays are when Mom would usually go grocery shopping. So when Dad got up to go to work again, I asked him, "Can I go with you to get groceries?"

"I'm going to work," he said.

"But we need groceries. And Becky can't drive."

"And we need money to buy the groceries. Why do you think I go to work goddammit?" He was yelling.

"But what if we don't have any more food? What are we going to eat?" I was scared to say anything when he was already mad, but I had to.

He started screaming at me, "How the hell do I know? We're all going to starve for all I know. We're all going to the goddamn poorhouse." He kicked one of the kitchen chairs. "Something had better change around here." He opened the refrigerator and then slammed it shut. I knew he might hit me if I said one more word. I didn't. I just sat there and tried hard to think of what needed to change.

When he sat down again, he lit a cigarette and poured some more coffee. I handed him canned milk for his coffee and tried to smile. He didn't look too mad anymore. I looked at his tan hand where the purple veins popped up on top. I remembered sitting on his lap at church when I was real little and holding one of his big fingers with one hand and pushing down on those veins with the other hand.

Finally, I said, "I'm sorry Daddy." He looked at me right in the eyes, and they were so blue and the black dots were so tiny and sharp, they poked all the way down into my belly.

Just when I thought he would either hit me or kiss me, he jumped up and said, "I've got work to do. You girls will have to cook with whatever's here." He walked out the door and in a couple of minutes his truck drove away.

I went into Mom and Dad's bedroom where Becky was feeding Francie. I told Becky, "We aren't going to get any groceries, and Dad says something had better change around here, or we're all going to the poorhouse." She looked kind of worried but just hugged Francie even closer and pushed her nose into her fuzzy baby head. I asked Becky, "Can I feed her for a while?"

She said, "OK."

"Becky, do you think there really is a poorhouse where you go to starve?"

"Probably. But Number 5 and 6 got rented last night, so that's good. I'll go clean them if you take good care of Francie. If she needs her diaper changed, remember to put your thumb where the pin will stick you and not her. And remember to burp her good." Then she got up and pushed her hand into her side and walked toward the living room the way Mom did when she was pregnant. She got to the doorway and turned around. She said, "And Nicky already got his bottle. He's asleep, but you know how he wakes up from gas."

I told her, "Don't worry. I'll take care of Nicky too. And I won't stick anyone." I was glad there weren't too many tenants at our motel, so we didn't have too many rooms to clean. But if we didn't have tenants then we didn't make enough money either. And if we didn't have money, Mom and Dad couldn't pay the Merlinos, and they'd come and take our property away and we'd have to go to the poorhouse for sure. I just couldn't worry about everything, so I burped Francie, changed her diaper and used four safety pins the way Mom taught us, so nothing could leak out.

Just then Billy, who was the next kid after me, came running into the house screaming, "It's Mama cat!! She's sick! She's bleeding in the garage!" His face was so red his freckles disappeared. I held Francie close to my shoulder while I ran after Billy to the garage. That was where Dad put all his junk. He stuffed the garage with old lumber, paneling, and two-by-fours. The workbench was piled with tools that no one but Dad knew how to use. There were boxes and sacks of nuts, bolts, nails, and screws all over. Machine and engine parts were lying on the dirt floor. It was cobwebby, dusty and greasy in there, and too dirty for a baby. So I put the burp and spit-up rag that was on my shoulder onto Francie's head. We went behind the stack of old tires where a rotten mattress was lying on the dirt.

Billy was pointing to Mama cat who was lying on her side with something that looked like guts hanging out of her bottom. None of us had seen her in a few months and now she was so fat she looked like she was going to pop. Billy reached over to pet her and she tried to bite him. She was making a low growling sound and then a gray-ish-black goopy ball slid out of her bottom. When it wiggled a little, you could see little ears and a tail. After Mama cat started licking it, it kicked its feet and rolled around. It was a baby kitten! Mama cat had gotten pregnant, and we didn't even know it.

Since Mom didn't believe in letting animals live inside, Mama cat only got to come into the house to catch mice. She'd hardly ever let you pet her, especially when she was pregnant or if she had new kittens. She was kind of wild and mean sometimes but was our only house cat. All the other cats were so wild you could never pet them. They were her grown up babies. None of them had names, and you couldn't even tell them apart. Mama cat was our biggest and fattest cat. And we never fed her once.

She had twelve kittens. The next day, Sunday, we went out and could only find four. We looked all over for the other kittens, but they were gone. When we told Dad, he came out to look. Mama cat let him pet her and even started purring. "She doesn't look so hungry now," he said.

"But where do you think the kittens went?" Maureen asked.

Dad looked at her and said, "How long since someone fed her?"

"We never feed her. Mom won't let us," I said.

"Well, she must have gotten pretty hungry because those kittens are all gone." He reached under Mama cat and pulled out part of a dead kitten head. We all about threw up while Mama cat licked herself. Dad said, "Bring her some milk every day for a while." There was no way I wanted to bring her anything if she ate her very own babies. But if we didn't, maybe she'd eat the rest. I hated her fat Mama cat self! No wonder we didn't have more cats, even though she had kittens all the time.

Billy said, "I bet it was the other wild cats who ate the babies."

"Yeah, sure, runt," said Sonny. "Mama cat wouldn't let those wild cats near her babies. She's a fighter. But do you see even one sign of a fight on her? Do you?" He and Dean smirked at each other.

Billy didn't say anything. He walked back to the house with his head down like he was crying. When we got inside we told Becky what happened, and she said, "That's why Mom doesn't allow animals in the house, because they act like wild animals."

The next Sunday we all missed church. I don't know why we didn't go, because we **always** went. That afternoon someone knocked on our kitchen door. A woman was standing there with a white dish full of food. It had little ridges that came up the side and had blue flowers in between the ridges. It must have been hot because she was wearing potholders. She was giving us food. And she didn't even know us. Why? Why would someone be that nice to us?

She said to Dad, "I heard about Fiona and wanted to help somehow." I was standing behind Dad looking at how pretty and clean she was. She was wearing nylons and smelled like soft powder. She looked down where I was standing, and smiled. My heart beat fast from feeling shy, and I tried to smile, but it wouldn't come out. She left without the dish. How would she ever get it back?

The food was as good as she was pretty. It was some kind of noodles with tuna in it. I was glad we weren't starving yet. Maybe someone else would bring us more food. That night after I went to sleep I woke up to pee. You had to go through the kitchen to get to the bathroom. That's where I saw Dad, at the kitchen table. He was all alone.

He was staring and didn't even notice me. I hid behind the door and couldn't help peeking at him. His eyes looked so sad and wild I wanted to cry but was too scared. He stared until I thought his eyeballs would start spinning, and he would jump up and smash something.

I tried to move but couldn't. Then his shoulders started to shake, and he pushed his face down into his hands. Big strangling sounds came out of him like an animal that's dying. When he pulled his head up, his face was stretched into a scarecrow face that wasn't my Dad anymore. His skin was wet, and he kept pushing his head down and then pulling it back up, over and over, making those scary sounds grown ups never make. I guess he was crying. I finally went back to bed and waited for everything to stop, so I could go to the bathroom and pee. I hoped I wouldn't fall asleep and wet the bed.

About two weeks after Mom left for her breakdown, Georgina came home from boarding school. The boarding school was run by nuns and was for delinquent girls. Georgina went there with our cousin who was Georgina's age, for the eighth grade.

I still wonder why Georgina got sent there. She hadn't made that much trouble yet, at least not any trouble that I knew about. And why did they call it a boarding school anyway? Every time I thought of Georgina at the boarding school, it seemed like she was in a prison where there were just hard boards for beds, and nothing but raggedy blankets to try to stay warm with. I asked her about it, and she said she had a regular mattress and plenty of blankets, but it didn't do her any good because she could hardly ever go all the way to sleep there. She hated it at the boarding school.

When Georgina came home, she and Becky were both in charge even though Georgina was the oldest. Georgina wasn't very nice to any of us, but she acted like she knew what was going on, which felt good to me. Becky was always kind of nice and did most of the work. She didn't get mad and screech at us the way Georgina did. But Georgina was trying to get us to be better kids so Mom would come back.

The third weekend after Georgina came home we all went to church. Afterward, we went to Mrs. Samuel's house. Dad, Georgina, Becky, Sonny, Dean, and of course Nicky and Francie all got to go inside while Maureen, me, Billy, and Luann had to stay out in the car, which wasn't fair. It was hot outside and even though we had the windows rolled down, the car was like an oven. We weren't supposed to get out of the car or make any noise and make the Samuels' neighbors think we were a bunch of monkeys with no manners.

We were good for a long time, but then Billy started picking at the upholstery in the car, and that made me grab his fingers to make him stop it. Then he yelled, so Maureen pinched me without any warning for making Billy yell. So I kicked Maureen for being such a snot and Luann accidentally got kicked too. So she started howling. I told Luann to be quiet, which of course she never would do, and she kept howling until I was screaming at the top of my lungs to just shut up!

Suddenly Georgina opened the car door and said, "You guys never learn, do you! You're the reason Mom left, and you're going to be the reason she never comes back!" We were all dead quiet now. I felt so bad about being a loud mouth that I didn't know anything anymore. Except that Georgina was probably right. And I was the worst.

Georgina said, "Mom might come home in about two weeks if you're good. But why would she want to come home if you're all acting like a bunch of little monsters?" For just a second, I was **sooo** glad that Mom might come home that I almost forgot about what a little monster I was.

"Now you kids stay out here and shut up, or else!" Georgina left the car to go back in the Samuels' house. I was as quiet as a mouse. I wondered how Mom would know if we were being good or not when she was still at the hospital and couldn't see us. I figured she probably did it like Santa Claus did.

I didn't know back then, that Santa was just everyone pretending. And even though I'm twelve now, I was only in the first grade then and didn't know lots of things. I only knew I'd better learn to shut my mouth if I ever wanted Mom to come back.

Mom was at the hospital almost seven weeks, and I never got to talk to her once, to tell her anything or to ask one question. I got kind of used to her being gone. I figured out how to do almost everything by myself. Even if it wasn't very good, I was still proud. When it was time for Mom to come back, I was a teeny bit scared. Maybe she wouldn't even remember that I was her darlin'.

It was Sunday afternoon when Mom came home. She kissed and hugged all of us, and I was happy to see her but started to feel kind of bad inside. She didn't look one bit tired or sick. Her skin was all pink, and she had on lipstick. With her hair curled, she looked kind of pretty. She looked better than I ever saw her. Why? Was it eating the yummy hospital food all that time? Or was it because she was so happy to be away from us kids?

Maybe Mom never missed me at all. Maybe she didn't miss any of us. Probably she liked it that she didn't have to look at us or listen to any of our stupid questions or help us get dressed in the morning. She could just sleep and sleep and sleep, and we would all disappear, maybe for forever.

It was like there was a big sledgehammer swinging around in my guts. I remembered what Georgina said about me being a monster. It wasn't Mom's fault that she wanted to forget me. I knew there was something wrong in me. Then the sledgehammer swung hard and told me there was something wrong with my whole family. It made me so jolty and dizzy I almost threw up.

That rocking and hammering finally slowed down when I fed Nicky his bottle that night. He was old enough to feed himself if he had to, but Mom thought it looked bad when babies had to hold their own bottle. She said it might give them a complex when they got older. That sounded bad, and I never wanted Nicky to have a complex. Anyway, I liked feeding him. After his bottle, I petted his silky blonde head, and he fell asleep on my shoulder. I fell asleep too, and dreamed about being outside the house and trying to get inside. I was locked out. And every time I touched a door or window I got shocked. But I kept trying even though I got jolted down to my shinbones.

Lots of little things were different after Mom came back. Dad was nicer to her. Mom wasn't as tired as she used to be, but was more floaty. Georgina said Mom had shock treatments when she was gone. She had twelve or thirteen of them. They were supposed to help her want to come home. It was like being electrocuted only you didn't die. I wondered if they felt like my dream did. I can't see how that would ever make someone want to come home.

After a few months, Mom started wearing her pregnant clothes again. Even though we already had ten kids we could always use one more baby! It was a nice fat feeling seeing Mom wear her big smocks. I hoped maybe we'd get twins. Mom still looked tired, but I knew she liked babies too, and she said it was God's will to give her another child. All I knew is I'd get to have another baby to take care of. It was like when summer comes again.

3

WHITEWASH

SIX YEARS

WHEN Mom was gone to the hospital for her breakdown, we didn't know if she'd ever come back for sure. Then it was just Dad and us kids. Dad never told us how to do things. But he yelled his head off when we didn't do it right. Like if we didn't clean or fix things the right way. Luckily he was gone working most of the time so he couldn't holler at us then.

But even when he was gone there was lots of screaming. Screaming, hollering kids, and more dirt than you could ever imagine. Even though no one taught me how to do things I still figured some stuff out.

Like the best day to wash diapers is Sunday. Even though you're not supposed to work on Sundays, I always did. It was the last day to wash those diapers before school on Monday. It wasn't my job to wash them in the washing machine. I was just supposed to wash the poop out of them. The pee was OK. It could go right into the washer. But the poop ones had to be washed by hand first. No one wanted poop in the washing machine. I'd do as many as I could stand on Sunday and then let the rest of them sit until the next Sunday.

It was always afternoon when I did diapers. A big pile would collect in the bathroom shower that was by the kitchen. We didn't use that shower anymore because it was broken, and we had three more bathrooms with showers we could use.

We lived in the first four units of the motel plus the utility room, and every one of the units had a front door, a living room, a kitchen, and a bathroom. They were all strung together in a line. Dad was so smart, he just cut a hole through the wall to the next unit when it got too crowded.

The shower in bathroom Number 1 was also the one closest to the kitchen, so it was easy to store a big sack of potatoes there. The diapers would sit across from the potatoes in the other corner of the shower. Usually, the two piles would stay apart, but there was always some slob who'd throw a diaper on the potatoes. Yuck! It always stunk in there. And there were about five hundred more flies than diapers, which was a lot, with three poopy babies.

The only interesting thing about diapers was the wormy maggots. They were everywhere. Even in the potatoes sometimes. I don't know how those white, crawly, skinny worms did it, but they turned into flies. First they got a brown hard shell. Then that maggot shell cracked open and a wet blob of fly came out. I even saw it once. It was so gross. But I put that fly on the windowsill and pretty soon it was nice and dry and flying around with all the other flies.

The poop in worm diapers just rolled out of the diaper. That's because it had already dried out a little. Fresh poop was too wet. It stuck to the diaper, and you had to push your hands all the way into the toilet to rinse it out. So it was better to leave the fresh diapers in the pile for at least a week. But if you let them sit too long, the maggots turned hard and the poop in those diapers got so dry it stuck like cement onto the diaper. Some of the poop would fall off, but you had to scrub the rest of it really hard. So it didn't take too many smarts to figure out that worm diapers were the best. Not too wet, not too dry.

I could never see why regular people would wash diapers every day, when you could do it just once a week. Sure, it stunk real bad, and you had to keep your tongue way in the back of your throat, but it wasn't as bad as doing the dishes. You had to do dishes every day and someone was always yelling at you. Diapers were bad, but everyone left me alone.

No one cared if I did all the diapers or not as long as there was no poop floating to the top of the washing machine, and there were enough diapers for all the babies. I know that everyone was glad I picked the diapers for my job because they were all weenies about it.

They knew if I didn't do it, one of them would have to, since they couldn't make me pick the same job over and over. All my brothers and sisters knew they were lucky, and I was doing them a favor.

I always washed my hands after doing the diapers too. Even if I didn't wash them too good, it was OK, since Mom told us we got resistance from having a few extra germs. That extra resistance made us stronger than most kids, especially those kids from houses that were too clean. Sunday diapers were good for that.

Monday mornings were real bad because I'd forget how to get ready for school over the weekend. First we had to eat something like oatmeal to stick to our ribs. I'd let some of it stick to the roof of my mouth until it formed a big mound and then let it slide to the back of my throat until I started gagging. I'd try to see how far back I could make it go and still keep from choking. This was also good practice for not gagging while washing diapers.

After breakfast, I'd have to find something clean to wear for school. That was impossible because no one washed the clothes when Mom was gone. I also needed to make a lunch and find my shoes and coat before the bus came. When we saw the bus on the highway coming from the big hill, we knew we had ten minutes. When it was at the little hill, we only had two minutes left. Then we had to get everything for school and run as fast as we could to the highway to catch the bus. If it was Lou, the nice bus driver, and he saw one of us running, he'd usually wait. Since there were so many kids, and we didn't all come at the same time, he'd usually wait a few minutes. But if it took too long, or he didn't see us, or if it was the substitute driver, the bus would leave. Then we had to walk to school, which was about five miles away. The last time I had to walk I got blisters.

One of the worst and the best days of my life was about a week or so after Mom left, and I wasn't even a little used to it yet. In the morning, I was running around as fast as I could because I couldn't find anything to wear, and the bus was already at the big hill. I finally went out to the dirty clothes pile and found three jumpers. I picked the one that smelled the best and put it on as fast as I could, but then I couldn't find my other shoe. I started shouting, "Where's my shoe? Who took my shoe? I can't find my shoe! Why won't anyone help me find my shoe? Where's the other shoe?" I stopped when Dean told me to shut up and look under my bed. I found my shoe.

But the bus was coming, and it was already at the little hill. I still didn't have a lunch. Oh no! I'd starve since I only ate two bites of oatmeal at breakfast. I started shrieking, "What can I have for lunch? Where's the bread? Where are the lunch sacks? The bus is coming! Oh no! What can I eat?"

Meanwhile, about four other kids are also yelling. "The bus is coming! It's almost here! The bus is almost here!"

I saw some bologna but knew that was only for Dad. Then I saw the mustard. Good. I could have a mustard sandwich. But the bus was here now. Kids were starting to pile out of the house and down the hill. I put mustard on the Wonder Bread, shouting, "Hold the bus! Hold the bus!" Some kids ran fast down the hill, and some went slower so Lou wouldn't leave before the late kids got out the door. Everyone else was on the bus, and I still hadn't found my coat.

Sonny, who was staying home sick said, "You're going to miss the bus, runt." I had my lunch but no coat. I knew I forgot some other things, but the bus was going to leave. I started crying, and that made it harder to run as fast as I could.

I tore out of the house, running, waving, and screaming, "Wait! Wait for me! I'm coming!" The bus was already moving. I stumbled and almost fell but kept running. Crying was making my eyes see fuzzy, but the bus stopped and waited. I ran up the steps of the bus and said, "Thanks." Lou smiled at me. He was the nicest driver in the whole world.

When I got to school, I wanted to go to sleep. I was looking down at the desk while Sister Jerome was talking to the class about how we never listened. My eyes were staring at patterns on the desk and the skin along the inside of my arms. Suddenly I saw the dirt patterns. Rings of dirt went all the way up to my elbows from when I washed my hands. The dirt crawled up my arms and stayed there. There were lots of rings of barely different colors, but all of it was brownish-tan, and it wasn't supposed to be there. I put spit on my finger and tried to rub the dirt away, but it got a lot worse. I started to cover my arms with my hands as slow as I could so no one would notice. It was like the dream I had where I was naked and locked out of the house.

Then I pushed away from my desk and looked down at my lap. The blue color in my wool jumper was so dark and quiet that even Sister's voice stopped for a while. I stared into my skirt until I saw a hole. A raggedy moth hole. Some lousy moth ate part of my skirt. I started to look for other holes. There was one big one and two other smaller ones. I hated those moths for wrecking everything! If I had a moth on my desk right then I'd rip its powdery wings right off.

Next thing I saw was that my jumper was all wrinkled, and it smelled weird too. I hated that stupid dirty clothes pile. I tried to wash my jumpers once a long time ago but shrunk them. And I didn't get to iron wool because little kids burnt wool too easy. I tried to cover the holes but couldn't cover my dirty arms and the moth holes at the same time. So I pulled my knees up to my chest. I covered almost everything. Only by now it was recess, and I had to go to the playground. It was a rule.

On the way out to the playground, I walked close to the wall and smiled but didn't look at anyone so they'd leave me alone. When I sat down on the warm blacktop, my knees were pushed close to my chest. Then Anastasia came along with her red kickball and wanted me to play. I told her no thanks. Just because I smiled didn't mean I wanted to play. I wasn't even looking at her anyway. Why did she want to play with me?

She sort of rolled the ball over to me, and before I knew it, I was standing up and rolling it back to her. Then I remembered my holes and dirt. Now she'd see! My face felt hot, like I had a fever. I had to make it so no one would see me. So I told her I didn't feel very good and walked around the corner of the school building where no one was playing and plopped myself back down on the blacktop. I hugged my knees again and closed my eyes hard. When I opened my eyes a little, I saw her peeking at me. That made me pull even harder on my skirt to hide the wrinkles. I hoped the sun would make me smell good.

By the time three o'clock came, it was time to go home, and the whole class stood up to pray. We all did the sign of the cross and were supposed to make up some prayer and send it up to God without talking out loud. Sister Jerome could always tell if you were really doing it or not. I didn't get in any trouble so I must have been doing it OK.

The bell rang five minutes later. Everyone was leaving to go home when this other nun, Sister Angelina, came into class. She whispered to Sister Jerome and pointed at me. I couldn't tell what they were saying. The white starchy things on their heads stuck out like cardboard and blocked their faces from the side. Those starchy walls reminded me of what they put on racehorses, so they don't see too much and get jumpy.

I felt scared and like I was going to pee when Sister Angelina motioned for me to come over to her. Luckily, she was nice and smiled down at me. She took my hand for me to come with her. Her fingernails went straight across. They were white on the tips, and her hand was soft. I wanted to brush it on my face. She said we were going to the convent. I thought no one but nuns could go there. Were they going to turn me into a nun?

The convent was right next door to the school. When we went through the big square door, I felt like peeing again. She might have been talking, but the hall was too big, and she was too tall for me to hear her.

She brought me to a big room that had a bathtub and a few sinks in it and told me I was going to get a bath. I had to take off all my clothes though. She must have known I was modest because she turned away while I undressed. There was already water in the tub. How did it get there? I went in it but didn't know what to do. I'd had showers before, but had never been in a bathtub before, even though I'd seen pictures.

She put her hands on my shoulders to sit me down in the water. I asked her where the bubbles were, like in the pictures. She brought some stuff that made bubbles. I could tell that they were only for special occasions. It was for me. It was my first time in a bathtub! Happiness was jumping up and down all over me when she started to wash my skin. I got to just sit there while she soaped me with a white rag that was steamy warm and smelled like perfume. It felt so slippery and slidey I started laughing. I wanted to lie down on her arms and hands forever. She even started to talk about some other little girl she knew. I could tell she liked me because I reminded her of the other little girl.

Then she pulled up my shoulders to stand me up. Some water had been getting hot in a pot. It looked like she was going to scald me with it, but then she mixed it with some cold water and let me feel it until it was just right. She poured the water all over me and rubbed my skin a little to get off the soap. Then she wrapped me up in a huge towel that was scratchy but smelled clean. My hair was still sopping wet. She took another towel and started to rub my head. She rubbed it so much I thought her arm would fall off. I asked her why she was doing that so much. She said she was drying my hair. That made no sense to me, but I liked it. She would rub, then brush it, rub it some more, then brush, until after about an hour it was dry. Maybe she was worried about a wet head the way my Mom used to be.

At the end, she put me in a clean uniform. I don't know where she got it, but she didn't have any underpants for me. She said it would be OK not to wear any this once but to put some clean ones on when I got home. That was OK with me because I liked the way it felt without any. She brought me some apple slices and milk before I left and showed me how to sit with my knees together. That's pretty important with no underpants. The last thing she did was bring me a mirror to show me how I looked. My hair was sticking out all poofy and fuzzy around my head. She said I looked like an angel. Maybe that's why she was called Sister Angelina.

One of the other nuns drove me home even though I wanted to stay with Sister Angelina. I didn't want to go home to no Mom and a scary Dad. I didn't want to wash any more diapers. I wanted a bathtub and someone to wash me until I sparkled. When I did get home no one cared if I looked like an angel. I looked for clean underpants and couldn't find any. That's when I started to throw up. I wasn't sick though. It was just my stomach telling me I was never going to feel as good as that bath ever again. I figured maybe I could be a nun when I grew up.

4

UH-OH
SIX YEARS

WHEN Dad left for work in the morning, he and Mom kissed smack on the mouth. That was like a rule with Mom. "You're not taking one step out of this house without giving me a kiss, Mister." Then she'd stand with both of her hands on her hips and make a baby pout face until he came over and kissed her. "That should last me through the day," she'd say, and then smile like she was shy.

When she wanted us to feel sorry for her she'd say, "I'm a delicate flower." But it didn't work because when she said that we all laughed like it was the biggest joke in the whole world. Except for Dad, who only laughed at her when she didn't know it. He didn't make fun of her so much after her breakdown, but before they got married he got in big trouble for it. When he brought her over to meet his whole family for the first time, he played a real mean trick on her, and she didn't think it was one bit funny.

His whole family spoke German and she didn't. So Dad told her how to say, "Hello. I'm pleased to meet you," in German, for when she met them the first time. She was kind of nervous about talking in German, but he kept saying it would be OK. Then when she met his Mom, she said what Dad told her to say and Grandma Stoltz started laughing like crazy.

Same thing with his Dad, his brothers and sisters and aunts and uncles. Mom thought she was saying it wrong and that's why they were all laughing. She was also mad at them for being so rude. But not as mad as she was at Dad, when she found out that what she'd really been saying in German was, "Hello. I am a big, hairy monkey." Even though Mom stayed mad at Dad for it and he still thought it was funny, they kissed at least two times every day.

The second time they kissed was at night when Dad came home from work. While they were kissing, us kids dive-bombed for his lunch pail. It was metal and shiny with a round top and could hold lots of food. Sometimes Dad didn't eat everything, and we got what was left. The best thing was a little can of mandarin oranges that only Dad got. He always got meat in his sandwiches too. Mom said that's because, "He's the breadwinner. And he's working hard to keep a roof over our heads."

After Dad and Mom finished hugging, kissing and whispering things to each other, he'd pick up one of the babies. He didn't pick me up any more after Mom's breakdown because I was already six years old and was no baby. He'd pick up Francie, who was wrapped in her newborn fuzzy blanket that already had lint balls on it, or Nicky, who was bigger, but was still a baby.

Luann, my little sister, got to sit on his shoulders while he walked into the kitchen to get a beer. One time I ran ahead and opened up the refrigerator to get the beer for him. I asked him, "Dad, why don't you drink the Hamm's beer that has the cute cartoon bear?"

Mom was stirring some split pea soup, and even though I wasn't talking to her she said, "That's exactly what they want you to think. They're turning a whole generation of you kids into alcoholics. You're all programmed to buy that stuff the minute you get old enough. You won't even remember why you want to buy the beer because you'll all be brainwashed by then. And it all started with what everyone thinks is a harmless cartoon." Dad didn't say anything. He just went into the living room to lie down on the couch and drink his beer. He only got one beer.

I wished I could lie down beside him and look at the hairs on his arms while he rested. I wouldn't move a muscle either, but Mom said to leave him alone until dinnertime. She told me to help Billy set the table. Billy was almost five years old and even though he was little, it's not like he was retarded or like it was that hard to remember that if we were having soup, you had to have soup bowls. He was just trying to get me to do his job by acting like a baby.

When dinner was ready, we rang the dinner bell. It looked like that big one with the crack in it that they have on half dollars. Everyone came running because they knew the good stuff would be gone in just a few minutes. Split pea soup was just plain yucky, but the ham hocks in it were good. And the red Jell-O with the bananas in it was yummy too. We said the dinner prayer and a Hail Mary.

Mom dished food for Dad first and then herself. After that, you had to be fast because if you were too slow there'd be just the gross food left. It was too bad if you were little and couldn't reach very far.

I was fast. I grabbed the soup ladle and got a big ham hock. But Dean and Sonny, my older brothers, stabbed it right off my plate. They divided it up and gave me just one bite. "Here, runt, eat up," Sonny said. So when the Jell-O, which we had to pass in a circle around the table, came to me, I took a whole bunch because I hated fuzzy pea soup and wanted something besides biscuits. Mom told me it was too much and made me put some back. Then I started to cry about how Dean and Sonny took most of my ham hock. She looked at their bowls and of course there wasn't any ham hock left because they ate it so fast from being such pigs and then I didn't have any proof. I was so mad I stole some Jell-O from Luann when she wasn't looking.

By then I didn't want to eat it because my stomach felt kind of icky and not that hungry. But I couldn't leave until Mom and Dad were done because we were supposed to stay and discuss things, like civilized people do. So I just cut the Jell-O into little squares that kept getting smaller and smaller until pretty soon it wasn't Jell-O anymore, just red, clear stuff you could feed to hummingbirds. But we didn't have hummingbirds, so it was just garbage.

Meanwhile, Mom and Dad were talking about how they had to go over to the Merlinos on Saturday to talk about money. Mom and Dad had to give the Merlinos money all the time because that's who they bought our property from. Mom hated going over there because she said she hated begging. I didn't understand what a mortgage was except that in the cartoons, the bad guy had the mortgage and a black mustache. He was the one who tied down the girl who screamed all the time. But she always got rescued even if she did have to beg a lot. Besides, the Merlinos were nice. They always gave us cookies and let us play outside while the grown ups talked.

On Saturday morning, Dad was outside working while Mom got the babies diapered and ready to go. Since I was feeding Francie her bottle, Mom let me stay in her bedroom with her while she got dressed. I watched while she put on her girdle. She always wore a girdle that went from top to bottom so it held up her bosoms like a bra on top, squished in the fat in the middle, and came down just past her crotch on the bottom. There were garters hanging off the bottom part of the girdle for her nylons. She didn't wear nylons around the house, but she always wore her girdle. There was no crotch on the girdle so she could pee right through it.

It was when she was peeing that she had that weird smell. I know everyone smelled it, but us kids never talked about it because it came from down there, and down there was no place to talk about. When she closed the door to pee, to get some peace and quiet, us kids hollered at her through the door because we knew she wasn't doing anything else except sitting there, and it was the best time to talk to her. Sometimes she'd let one or two kids in and then close the door. Usually, she'd just leave the door open because she said it was no use.

After she got on her girdle and nylons and was mostly dressed, she peed, and the smell was there again. I asked her, "Why do you smell that way when you pee?"

She said, "It's what happens when you grow up."

"Yeah, but why does it smell that way?"

"You and your questions," she said. Then she wiped herself, got up, and put some cold cream on her face. I carried Francie over to the toilet and sat on the seat so we could watch better while she rubbed the greasy cream around. Then she wiped it off with a Kleenex. After that, she patted on some powder. She looked as white and puffy as the Pillsbury dough boy. Then she stuffed the front of her girdle-bra with some fresh Kleenexes. That's where she stored them for runny noses, lipstick blots, and baby spit up. When she pinched her cheeks I said, "Why do you always pinch your cheeks like that?"

"Circulation." Then she pinched mine. "See how pink they are now? Men like that. The most important thing to remember when you grow up and get married is to take care of how you look. Nothing will drive away a man faster than looking haggard in the morning. Get up before he does, put on your face and comb your hair so he'll know he's married to someone who's worth something." I nodded and tried to remember it forever. I wasn't sure I wanted to grow up that much though, especially if I got a really bad pee smell from it.

Mom told me to make sure I got at least two good burps out of Francie, so I kept patting her on the back. Pretty soon Luann, Maureen, and Billy were calling for Mom. They were yelling, "Mommmmmm. Where are you, Mom?" She looked at me and said, "Shhhh." So no one would find us for a while. I helped her get peace and quiet and didn't say a word while she finished putting on red lipstick and rouge on her cheeks.

Then she took some Hershey's chocolate out of her bra front, where it was hiding between the Kleenexes. She squeezed off a melty piece of it, gave it to me, and popped the rest of it in her mouth. I hadn't seen her put that chocolate in there! So that's where she kept it! She went, "Shhhh," again, and I knew I'd better not tell anyone about it. Then she left the bathroom, and I stayed on the toilet with Francie, burping her and sucking the chocolate, which was so warm from being in Mom's girdle-bra.

On the way to the Merlinos Mom and Dad were kind of quiet, especially Mom who usually talked to Dad all the time. Mrs. Merlino gave us some orange Kool-Aid and told us we could have as many of their grapes as we wanted but not to waste any. They were fat and purple but had big seeds in them and thick skins that you had to spit out. When Mom and Dad came out from talking, Dad was laughing, but Mom looked mad. Then Mr. Merlino gave Dad two big boxes of grapes to take home. We all waved good-bye.

In the car, Billy told Dad that the grapes weren't that good. Dad said, "They're for wine."

Mom just looked at him kind of disgusted and said, "You don't know how to make wine. Mr. Merlino has been making wine for twenty years, and it still tastes like vinegar."

"Yeah, but he isn't me. I know I can make something real nice. You wait and see."

"I'll wait and see all right, like I have with this goddamn motel of yours that's making beggars of us." Us kids got real quiet. We all knew it was Dad's idea to buy the motel and Mom only went along with it because it was his dream. She thought it was Dad's fault that we were so poor because he promised her he'd give her nice things, and anyone could see that we only had about two nice things in the whole house.

Before I was born, Mom and Dad took care of an apartment house. Then Dad had his dream to build his own motel. So he bought our property which was which was about 300 miles away, and started building the motel by himself while Mom ran the apartment house and took care of the kids by herself. She already had five babies by then and was going to have another one – me! – pretty soon.

Dad drove back and forth every few weeks to see Mom, but mainly stayed at the motel while he built the first unit for Mom and the babies. He lived in the utility room, which was the only building there when he bought the property from the Merlinos. It was made of cement.

Mom said she'd rather run the apartment house alone than go live in some cement dungeon with five kids and no washing machine or dryer. When unit Number 1 was done and had a doorway to the utility room, Mom and the babies came to live with Dad again. He bought Mom a washer and dryer for an anniversary present that year. She didn't seem to think it was a very good present. But why not? It was what she wanted.

On the drive home, Mom and Dad kept yelling back and forth about lots of stuff that I didn't understand. I know she was mad at something he said to the Merlinos. She said, "You made me look like a goddamn fool." I was glad to get out of the car when we got home.

Sonny, who was about four and a half years older than me, and the oldest boy in our family, said, "I've scoped out the situation with Mom and Dad and you little kids better make yourselves scarce." I figured he was right so I stayed outside with Billy and Luann and we fed little rocks to the chickens for a while. They were so stupid they thought it was chicken feed and fell for it every time.

We thought maybe the coast was clear and came into the utility room. Dad was standing at the bottom of the steps. There were only three steps on the stairs, and Mom was on the top step with her hands on her hips. She looked taller than Dad.

His face was reddish-purple and he was screaming, "I can't do anything right around here. I'm sick to hell of it." He started stomping toward the door. Us kids ran toward our beds by the washer and dryer.

"Yeah, that's right, slink away like a coward." Mom sounded like poison.

He took two big steps back toward her but was still at the bottom of the stairs. "I'm not going to take this from you anymore. I'm leaving and there's not a goddamn thing you can do about it."

"If you take one step out of this house you can forget about **ever** coming back."

"I'll get a goddamn divorce then." He was spitting from screaming and talking at the same time.

"Go ahead, but I'm keeping the kids." The glass of milk she was squeezing in her hands was starting to shake.

"Like hell you will! You aren't fit to do it by yourself. What kind of mother can't even take care of her newborn? We'll just see what the judge has to say about you and your goddamn psychiatrist."

"You son of a bitch." Mom looked like he just slugged her in the stomach. Then she took the milk she was holding and threw it in his face. White drippy milk rolled all over his hair and face and ran down his shirt.

He swiped at his face and hair and sounded German, but the words were plain English. "You'll never see me again." He was like a cloud of smoking black fire when he grabbed the utility room door. It slammed hard behind him, and we heard the engine on his truck start to whine. We ran to the door and saw the truck spitting out gravel when he took off.

Mom kept saying, "Damn you, damn you..." She was crying too. After a bunch more damn yous and you son of a bitches, she stomped off into the bedroom. Me and Billy looked at each other. All ten of us kids were there, and even the babies heard everything. Mom and Dad never fought like that!

It was scary that night because I was afraid Dad was gone forever. We went to church on Sunday without him. I missed smelling his fresh shaven whiskers and his big hairy arms. And I remembered how sleepy I'd get when I leaned over on him when the priest was talking, and we had to sit for a long time.

Later in the afternoon, Mom's favorite priest, Father Laughlin came over to our house. He was the assistant priest, and Father Comstock was the head priest. Mom talked to Father Comstock lots of times about rules for being a Catholic. Catholic rules were different than the Protestant ones she had before she married Dad. Mom and Flora both got converted at the same time since they had to, if they were going to marry Catholics. Mom argued all the time with Father Comstock, but when she came back from seeing Father Laughlin she was almost always bright and sunshiny. Everyone knew she liked him the best.

It was weird to have Father Laughlin come to our house because usually Mom went to talk to the priests at the rectory where they lived. We didn't even know he was coming and hadn't even cleaned the house. Mom asked him to come into the kitchen where she could make him some coffee. Us kids were supposed to clear out and leave them alone. They talked in the kitchen for about two or three hours.

I know we weren't supposed to do it, but me and Becky, my second oldest sister, heard Mom crying and peeked in at them through the door, which we opened just a crack. There was Mom with Father Laughlin. He had his arms around her and was petting her head while she was crying. He looked like he loved her more than Dad ever did. Maybe he even wanted to kiss her. That was the only time I ever saw her look like a delicate flower, and it scared me almost as much as Dad being gone. Becky and I looked at each other and said, "Uh oh."

It was like a secret between Becky and me that didn't fit anywhere in the whole world. We never talked about it. But it didn't matter because Dad came back that night, and he wasn't mad anymore. He and Mom talked, kissed, hugged, and promised us kids that they wouldn't ever get a divorce. They promised God too. And Becky told me she heard Dad say he would change some things for Mom. I didn't know what that would be, but I hoped so.

5

SUNDAY MUSIC
ALMOST SEVEN YEARS

O N Sundays, we had music sometimes. But only if Dad was in a good mood. You never knew when that would be, but when he was feeling good, he went over to the Knights of Columbus building after church. Above its doorway there was a sign like a shield with a sword and ax crossed on it. And of course no windows so no one could peek. Only grown ups could go in, grown up men, like my Dad. Not one woman ever knew for sure what they did in there because it was all secret. I think I know what they did in there though.

They would dress up in armor with big red and white feathers on their helmets and look kind of dumb, but they weren't embarrassed. Then they'd all try to stab each other with their spears but not really kill anyone. The judge would say who's the best knight. He would also keep them from really killing each other in case someone lost their temper real bad the way Dad does sometimes. And since Dad always smiles when he comes out of there he must be the one who wins all the time. I'm not just making all this up either because when I asked Dad if that's what they did in there, he smiled at me and winked. So that says something.

They didn't have contests on Sunday mornings though. They did those just on Friday nights when they had their long meetings. I had no idea what they did in there on Sundays after church. Probably they just talked, but why did they have to go in the secret building to do that?

The first time we had music on Sunday was after Mom came back from the mental hospital. I was about almost seven years old. Dad went into the Knights of Columbus building and stayed for more than half an hour while the rest of us waited outside. Mom talked with the visiting priest underneath the sycamore tree. Us kids hung around the parking lot, picking loose paint off the car, kicking the dirt, and talking about what would happen to us if Mom and Dad died in a car accident.

Because if they both died at the same time, the Knights of Columbus would take us kids. They would adopt us and be like our parents. When I was real little, I thought that meant we'd have to live in the secret building and all those knights would be our parents and at least that way we could see what they did on Fridays. But what would really happen is we'd get adopted by the family of some knight. Only we didn't know who that would be. And neither did Mom or Dad. We knew some friends of Dad's who were knights with him, but they already had kids. They didn't want anymore.

Since there were so many of us, Mom said we'd all get sent to different families. We'd be like step kids then. You'd never know what kind of a family you'd get or who would want you. Would they be rich? Or poorer than us? Would we have to work like Cinderella?

Maybe you'd get a normal family and you'd start to be normal too. Like other kids who have clean houses and nice clothes. I said, "Maybe I'll get a nice sister and no brothers and we'll lie in bed and talk and laugh all night on the softest pillows in the whole world while my new parents talk in the other room about how glad they are that they adopted me." I could see me and my new sister, lying on satin sheets, tossing our heads back as though we didn't have one thing in the whole world to worry about. I threw my head back like I was already adopted.

Then Sonny, who was the exact reason why someone would never want a brother said, "What makes you think anyone in a family like that would want you? Why don't you wise up? You know there's not one person in this whole family who has a chance at a family like that. Including you, runt." Then he hit me in the arm hard enough to make sure it hurt. "Get it?" I knew he'd hit me again if I said one more thing. I didn't.

Becky said, "Even if one of us got into a really nice family how do you think you'd feel if the rest of us were treated like slaves in some family that was even worse than the one we have now."

"Not that bad, really." Dean was mumbling, but you could hear it clear enough.

Georgina said, "One thing's for sure. At least some of us would end up in real bad families. **And** we'd never be together again." Then she laughed and said, "Not that I'd miss any of you." We all laughed.

Maureen said, "Well, Mom and Dad aren't going to get in any accident anyway. We should all just be glad of that."

"Yeah, right," Sonny said sarcastically. He and Dean started punching each other in the stomach and laughing the way boys do when they're acting stupid.

Dad came out carrying a gray box that had a handle like a suitcase. Even Mom didn't know what it was. And Dad wouldn't say. He whistled all the way home while we tried to guess. When we ran out of ideas, Dad started talking to Luann, who was in the front seat with him, Mom and Nicky. "Do you know what I did when I was a little girl like you?" I hunched forward, hanging on the back of the front seat so I could hear better.

Luann was just staring at Dad. Finally, she said, "What?"

She was so stupid! "Luann! He wasn't a little girl," I said. She turned her head back at me and stared.

Dad said, "Oh yes I was."

Georgina, who was sitting beside me, just shook her head. The other kids weren't paying attention to the front seat.

"Daddy, you never wore dresses," I said.

"Little pink dresses with lacy white socks." He was grinning. Mom was smiling a little too.

"No you didn't. You can't be a girl and then a boy."

"Maybe you can't, but I did." I wondered if he really did.

"Were you born a girl?"

"Well, how could I be a little girl if I wasn't?"

"Yeah, well how could you be a boy now if you were born a girl?"

"It's amazing isn't it?"

I looked at Mom again and asked, "Mom, do you think Daddy's lying to us?"

"You'll have to ask him."

"Daddy, are you?"

We were just up the driveway when Dad announced, "We're home. I'll have to tell you some other time about what I did when I was a little girl."

When we got inside, he laid the box on its side and flipped the silver latches. Inside was a record player! I'd never seen one close up before. Mom asked, "Does it play 33's?

Dad said, "Just 78's."

"What are 33's?" Billy asked.

Mom said, "The 33 records are a lot bigger and go around slower than the 78's." Dad went into the bedroom and slid a box of records off the top shelf. He shuffled through a bunch of them until he found the one he wanted. He laid *Roll out the Barrel* onto the turntable.

It was like a party, only at **our** house. Dad picked up Luann and twirled her around the room while his feet kicked around like he had fleas. He was doing the polka. Then Mom came over and set Luann down onto the floor. She said, "I want the first dance." Dad started the record over again. Mom smiled, "And make the last dance a waltz for me." He grinned, lifted her hand and they started dancing. Her feet moved the way his did, but they were just regular feet. His had turned into some kind of jumpy liquid that made his whole body move like it was electric and smooth as satin all at once. It made you want to touch him. Or better yet, dance with him.

When Mom was done with her dance there were at least four of us begging to be next. She went in the kitchen to cook breakfast while Dad put on, *You are My Sunshine*. He picked up Nicky, who was just a baby then and tossed him into the air. Nicky cooed and giggled and threw up a little from getting bounced around. Then Dad picked up Luann again and I screamed, "It's my turn! You already got one!" I was almost crying. Dad looked at me and I thought he might get mad at me for throwing a fit, but instead he said, "Next song." I sat on the floor and watched him fling Luann into the air while his feet made more designs on the floor.

Then he changed the record to *The Tennessee Waltz*. It was slow. He lifted me up by the arms and swung me around in a circle. That part wasn't dancing. It was just for fun. Then he bounced me in the air, grabbed my waist and said, "Hold on." My legs wrapped tight around his waist and my arms around his neck. He held me snug with one of his hands and unglued one of my hands from his neck. He shook it a little until it was wobbly and I was giggly. Then he started to waltz me, real slow compared to the polka, but we were still moving all over the floor. The guy in the song was singing about how he lost his little darlin'. Inside myself, I promised right then that I would always be Daddy's little darlin'. Forever. My head flopped onto his shoulder and I knew that this was what forever was supposed to feel like. Then the song ended and all the other kids were screaming for their turn. I got down from Dad's arms.

When the little kids all had a turn, Mom called us in for breakfast. Dad looked tired but not the coming home from work kind of tired. More like happy tired. Georgina kept putting on records while we ate our Sunday scrambled eggs and special sausage made for us by Uncle Frank. Mom said, "And on the seventh day God rested." Just like us.

After breakfast, Dad got out his harmonica and started playing along with the music. We all loved it when he played his silver harmonica. It meant he was in a good mood for sure. But he was already in a good mood. How can you have two of them at the same time? It was weird, like one of those sins that you never know why it's a sin because it feels so good. But you can go to hell for it.

My stomach felt thick and kind of icky. I laid on my back on the floor and rocked my stomach from side to side while Daddy played his harmonica. I rolled on one side and looked at Dad. I liked him this way, but he didn't seem like his regular self. I rocked over onto my other side and looked at Becky, who was also watching Dad. She was chewing her lip. I asked her, "Where's Mom?"

"She's getting fixed up in the bathroom." Becky didn't look away from Dad.

Mom was putting her hair in rollers. The pink ones were already in rows on the top and sides of her head and she was rolling little blue ones at the bottom, by her neck.

"Whatcha doin', Mom?" I didn't really care what she was doing, I just wanted to ask, and watch her for a while.

"Well, I can't start the week looking like some fishwife. It's bad enough that I went to Mass today with my hair looking the way it did."

She got every little hair in the rollers. Then before I even thought about it I said, "Do you think Daddy will take us for a ride today?"

"I don't know. Why don't you ask him real nice?"

I went back to the living room where Dad was still sitting forward in his gray chair playing the harmonica. I came over and stood right by him. He patted his lap so I could sit on it. Then I could see up close how he moved that harmonica across his mouth while he breathed in and out kind of funny. How could his mouth tell where the sounds were so he could pull the music out of that thing?

When he was done playing that song, I asked, "Daddy, are we going for a ride today?"

"We'll see."

"Oh boy!" I jumped off his lap and started yelling, "We're going for a ride! We're going for a ride!" Dad started another song and that's how I knew we'd really get to go. I ran out of the house telling the other kids to get ready because we were going for a ride. Everything inside me was bouncing and rolling now.

It took a long time before everyone was ready to go. Mainly because Mom had to sit under the hair dryer while Dad taught Georgina how to polka. We tried pulling Dad's arm so he'd come out of the house and into the car. Georgina told us to knock it off because she didn't want any of us little brats to get in the way of her turn dancing with Dad. We kept pulling his arms, but he was so strong we couldn't get him to move one inch. He just laughed and started dancing with Georgina again.

Finally, everyone was in the car. We drove into the big long hills that rolled off into the distance behind our motel. It was almost an hour of flat highway and sagebrush before we got to the blonde hairy wheat fields. Then we saw our first really big hill.

We all said, "Faster! Faster!" at the same time. I wanted to go as fast as we could too, but it was also getting too lumpy inside my belly. When Dad speeded up and we zoomed down the hill it was like a roller coaster, even though I'd never been on one. He went even faster when we came up the other side. My stomach zoomed too. All the kids were laughing and saying "Faster, Daddy, faster!" Dad was grinning and looked like he never wanted to stop.

Mom warned Dad, "Be careful, Karl, or you're going to get all of us killed."

I could see us getting into a car crash. Dad driving right off the edge of the road with all of us screaming while the car smashed into a million bits and everyone dead, especially Mom and Dad. Only I could see us driving along regular, too, the way we really were. I closed my eyes, but I kept seeing the crash.

Pretty soon there was another big hill and we went so fast I burped. And up came a sour lump of sausage. I swallowed it back down and hoped it would stay there, but I wasn't so sure. I still didn't want to slow down and neither did Dad, no matter what Mom said. Maybe my stomach wanted to go slower though because it was feeling a little icky-pukey by then.

After about five more hills Mom said it was time to turn around to go home. All the kids whined at the same time, "No, Daddy! Farther!" Dad got that look in his eye and sped up for the next hill. Mom said, "I thought I was going to get to relax. And now I have to keep an eye on you too? That's all I need – one more kid." We all heard that and got quiet.

Dad went faster than ever. But I wasn't screaming to go faster anymore. I was trying to lie down on the seat even though there wasn't enough room. I squished into Becky a little and she didn't say anything. And Billy didn't care if I curled my legs under him as long as his legs got to stay on top.

The hills on the way back weren't too good because my stomach was rolling hard even when the hills weren't. I knew something was wrong. Mom was mad at Dad and he wasn't smiling anymore. His mouth made that straight line again. Who knew what he was going to do? Or what my stomach would do. Maybe I'd throw up. I'd get in big trouble for messing up the car. I sort of jolted when I thought of that and accidentally kicked Billy in the bottom. He yelped and howled, "She kicked me for no good reason."

Dad looked back at us from his mirror and yelled, "What the hell's going on back there?" He sounded the same as ever.

Mom turned around and looked right at me, "Well?"

"It was on an accident. Cause my stomach hurts."

"Are you going to throw up?" she asked.

"Maybe. I don't think so. I don't know."

Billy said, "She's faking it, Mom."

I didn't say anything. I just looked at Mom like I was begging.

She said, "Billy, you come up front here with me and Luann. Let her lie down." Now I could actually almost lie down. Becky let me put my head on her lap as long as I promised not to throw up on her.

Meanwhile, Mom and Dad were talking. Maybe they weren't going to fight. Dad said he'd return the record player that night after dinner. Mom said not until she got her last dance with him and he better not make her beg for it either. They needed to go to the Merlinos again about our mortgage. And one of the motel units needed a new stove. And the guy Dad did carpenter work for wasn't paying him enough. Then they talked about some of the guys in the Knights of Columbus. It was just grown up stuff. Stuff I didn't care about that made me feel sleepy. My stomach was feeling kind of floaty but OK now. Everything was moving nice and soft and the crash pictures in my brain were so far away they were like cartoons.

The other kids were either quiet or busy doing something that didn't get them into trouble. Then Sonny and Dean, who had been sitting in the seat farthest back and punching just each other, leaned forward to start teasing me. Dean asked, "Are you dead?" and stuck his finger in my side.

I said, "Mommm, they're making me almost throw up again."

Dad yelled at the boys, "Knock it off back there or you can get out and walk." He was growly. For me. Like I was his darlin' and he'd make all the bad go away forever. After a while, everything got melty again and I got even more sleepy. I remembered Daddy dancing me. We waltzed all over those golden wheat fields the rest of the way home.

6

Number Nine
ALMOST SEVEN YEARS

THE thing that never made any sense was that when Mom left for the mental hospital, for her breakdown, Butch, my grandmother, stopped coming down to our house. She and Grandpa lived on our property, and Butch usually came to our house all the time. But after Mom went to the hospital she never came to see us once. She just disappeared. It was like she was mad at us for something.

I knew Butch didn't want Mom having so many babies because of what she said when Francie was just a few days old, and Mom was in bed feeding her a bottle. I was lying on the bed too, waiting for my turn to hold our new baby. Mom was real tired and couldn't get out of bed very easy. She said Francie was a breech baby, and it was real hard when they came out bottom first.

Anyway, Butch barged right in without knocking and just stood there with her hands on her hips, looking at Mom. She hadn't even seen Francie yet or goo gooed at how cute she was. She just stood there staring at Mom. It was like she was waiting for Mom to say something or like Mom had done something wrong. Finally, Butch said, "Well, I hope you're proud of yourself."

"I **am** proud." Mom held Francie close. I could tell that Mom forgot I was there, and it didn't look like Butch even noticed me. I didn't say a word or move one muscle. I just melted into the covers on the bed.

"Are you proud that you almost bled to death? That she almost tore you apart? Is that all you're good for? To breed like an animal?"

"Mom, it's what I believe in. It's a matter of faith. If you were a Catholic, you'd understand."

"I understand all right." She was almost whispering now, but it sounded like a snake. "You and that husband of yours can't keep your hands off each other."

"We're married! It's sacred when it's done in the eyes of the Lord."

"Sacred!" She almost spit the word out. "You deserve everything you get! And don't come to me when he leaves you high and dry. Why would any man want to come home to you like this?"

Mom looked like she was trying to fight back but was too tired. I could tell she was losing. Her face turned kind of white. She finally whispered, "Please, Mom, try to understand. My faith is all I have. Maybe it will kill me, but maybe it will make me strong." She reached up her hand to try to touch Butch's.

Butch jerked her hand away and said in a real low growl, "Don't come to me with your filthy love." Then she walked out of the bedroom. I could see Mom was crying. And she wasn't holding Francie the right way. I was afraid maybe Francie would roll onto the bed and hurt her floppy newborn neck so I said to Mom, "Can I hold her?" She let me take her. She said, "Be careful with my baby girl." Then she laid on her side and cried some more.

A few weeks after that, Mom left for her breakdown. That's when Butch disappeared. I found out later, that she and Grandpa left on a trip but they never told us. It seemed like forever until they came back.

There were lots of strange things about Butch. Like the way she would go up to Number 9 and do things that made no sense. Number 9 was different than the other units because we never rented it. It was always locked, and not even the passkey to the other units opened it. Mom was supposed to be the only one who had a key. She used to go up there by herself to get peace and quiet. It was how she got rid of us for a while.

Mom said we had no business going in there. But Butch must have had some kind of business because we saw her coming out of Number 9 one time before Mom had her breakdown. Billy and me were playing tag and saw her locking the door on the way out. We ran over to Butch and asked her, "Whatcha doin', Butch?"

She kind of jumped and we saw she was hiding something underneath her sweater. She said, "I thought you kids were at school."

"Oh, they sent us all home early because of a bomb drill," I said.

"Well, don't come sneaking up on people. You scare the daylights out of a person that way." She started walking up to her house kind of fast and ignored us.

When Butch was gone, Billy and I just had to peek inside Number 9. I stood on Billy's shoulders and looked through the kitchen window. Then he got a turn standing on mine. There was a table and some chairs in the kitchen, and you could barely see a couch in the living room. Otherwise, it was plain and bare just like the other times we peeked. Only this time we **had** to go in and try to figure out what Butch was up to.

A few days later, me, Maureen, and Billy found some cement blocks that we hauled underneath Number 9's kitchen window. I don't know why Maureen did it with us because she never broke any commandments, especially, "Thou shalt not disobey your parents," but she did this time. Once we got the blocks stacked high enough, we climbed in through the window. Billy didn't come in because he was too scared. So he was our lookout.

It was my first time in Number 9 and the window was right over the kitchen sink. I crawled through the window and into the sink. When I jumped onto the floor the dust whooshed up into my nose. It was so quiet in there you had to make a little noise just to feel regular. Maureen and I whispered to each other.

The dust was so thick in some places you could see where the mice made little designs with their paws. The living room had people footprints. Right by the living room curtain where the dust was real thick, we saw a whole bunch of squiggly circles scratched onto the floor. You could tell they weren't made by mice.

There was some melted red wax on the floor in front of the couch. Where did that red wax come from? I never saw any red candles at our house. Maureen noticed that there were some really tiny seashells that went in a line along the wall. The line went from the dust circles, all the way around the living room and into the bedroom. The seashells were like the ones from Aruba that Butch had saved in a big glass fishbowl. Lots of them were cracked, and some of them were smashed into powder.

We went into the bedroom. It was dark in there because there was only one little window with a dark blue curtain covering it. It was so sad and spooky in that room. You could imagine someone laying down on the bed and feeling so bad that they'd never get up again. They'd lie there and cry so hard you'd think their baby died or that they were a baby and were going to die. And then they did die, and all you had left was ghosts.

Without any warning Maureen turned on the light and I about jumped out of my skin. There were more red wax drips on the white bedspread. It looked like blood, but it was just wax. There were a lot of little feathers on the bed too. In the middle of the bed was a crucifix. There were feathers on Jesus' feet. We looked to see if the pillow was shedding feathers, but it wasn't. It was too weird. Maureen and I looked at each other and all of a sudden we both started screaming and laughing all at once. We crawled back out of the window as fast as rabbits. Billy screamed, "What's wrong?" We just ran.

We didn't talk about it with anyone. None of it made any sense. Was Butch the one who left that stuff there or Mom? Probably the crucifix was Mom's. Because Butch wasn't Catholic. But Butch could still have a crucifix. What was going on in there? And what was Butch hiding under her sweater when we surprised her? It reminded me of Butch's stories about Aruba, which is some island by Venezuela, where the natives did Voodoo, and weird stuff happened all the time.

Mom and her twin sister Flora lived in Aruba with Butch and Grandpa when they were just girls. Those natives didn't like white people one bit. Because they were bad luck. And twins were **really** bad luck. So Mom and Flora had to be extra careful when they walked home after going into town. Otherwise, some of those wild natives might catch them and chop them up with their machetes. They tried to look different than each other by wearing different hairstyles and different clothes. But it didn't fool those natives. They were full of Voodoo but were still really smart.

I had to find out more about Number 9. The next time I went up there was when Mom was in the hospital with her breakdown. It was a rainy day, and I couldn't stand being stuck inside our house with so many kids and icky feelings. Georgina and Becky kept the keys to the motel, since they were in charge of everything while Mom was gone. It was easy to swipe the key from them. I went up to Number 9 alone.

I came in through the front door when I was sure no one was looking. It was dry inside except for where I dripped mud. And spooky. The shells and feathers were scattered, and there was still red wax on the living room floor. But in the bedroom the sheets were stripped off the bed, and there was dried vomit on the floor. You could see it in streaks where someone sort of wiped it up. But it got smeared thick underneath the bed. While I was looking under the bed, I found a little white pill that had a black design on it. It wasn't aspirin. I put it in my pocket for keeps.

I sure had a lot of questions about Number 9, but since I wasn't supposed to be going up there in the first place, I had to be real careful what questions I asked.

After Mom came back from her nervous breakdown, she didn't go into Number 9 anymore. And didn't want to talk about Number 9. She said, "It makes me shudder just to think about it." I asked her, "Why do you shudder at Number 9?" She sort of floated away. I squeezed her big freckled arm and said, "Mommm, what are you doing?"

"I was just thinking," she said.

"What about?"

"About Mrs. Schneider and those dark blue curtains she put up in Number 22. That woman must be depressed. Horribly depressed." Then she walked into the bedroom and took a nap.

Becky was still in charge of cooking, even after Mom came back. She taught me how to cook too, and I could do almost everything she could, except use the big knife and the pressure cooker. If I didn't act like too much of a baby she'd ask me to taste things like soup, spaghetti sauce and potato salad to see if they needed anything. Sometimes she'd tell me things while we were cooking.

One night we were making dinner and I was standing on a stool, stirring the pudding. It took a long time. She was cutting up carrots and celery for the soup. We were talking about Mom's shock treatments and Becky said, "You know what Dad told me?"

"What?" I was all ears.

"What the Doctor told Dad."

"Yeah, what?"

"That Mom wouldn't ever come home unless he changed. That he had to treat her better, and not make her work so hard or he'd never see her again."

"I thought it was because of us kids. That she wouldn't come back because of us."

"Maybe so, but Dad also had to promise the Doctor that he wouldn't let Butch be mean to Mom. He's not supposed to let Butch come over unless Mom says it's OK."

The pudding wasn't even starting to get thick. I turned up the heat. I wondered why Dad told Becky all those things. But I guess it was because she was almost a teenager. I wondered what Dad did to Mom that would be worse than what us kids did. He did yell a lot louder. He was even louder than me.

I knew that Becky was telling me a lot of secret stuff, so I told her all about when Maureen and I went into Number 9. She acted like none of it was any big deal. I asked her, "Who do you think left the crucifix?"

"I have no idea. You're probably too little to understand anyway. That's why you shouldn't be going up there. It just mixes you up." She pulled the celery stalks apart and chopped off the dirty parts.

"I can figure things out though," I said.

"No, you can't. No one can figure out anything with Butch and Mom. You just have to do what Mom says. Because that's the only way it makes sense."

"Yeah, but what about all that weird stuff?"

"You're too little for all that! That's why you weren't supposed to go up there! Don't you know that much by now?" Becky was scowling, but I didn't care.

I yelled, "No! I want to know everything! I told you my stuff so now you have to tell me."

"No, I don't." Becky was peeling the carrots fast now. Those floppy orange strips were going all over the counter. "But I'll tell you something anyway."

"OK, what?" I was listening hard. The pudding was getting a little stuck on the bottom of the pan and still wasn't any kind of thick at all. I turned down the gas even though I'd have to stir longer.

"It's confusing because Mom says there's no such thing as Voodoo, but it still scares her. And Butch thinks Voodoo is real, but she says she'd never do it. And Mom is Catholic, but Butch hates Catholics. You know how they fight all the time and how Mom thinks Butch is always trying to make her think she's crazy when she doesn't think she is? But maybe Mom **is** kind of crazy because now she has to see a psychiatrist every week because of her breakdown."

"Yeah." This was all news to me, and I wasn't sure what half of it meant. My forehead was starting to hurt from listening so hard and trying to figure it all out so fast. And I had no idea what a psychiatrist was, but I wasn't going to ask any stupid questions. Because Becky was telling me more stuff than she had in my whole life.

"Well," She bit her lip while she sliced the paring knife through the carrot and against her thumb. "I think they were fighting with each other about which is stronger, Voodoo or Catholics."

"What does that have to do with Number 9?" I was kind of mad that she wasn't going to explain anything.

"I knew you wouldn't understand."

"Yeah, I do," I lied, "but who do you think left the crucifix?"

"It doesn't matter. If it was Mom, it was to make herself stronger. If it was Butch, it was to scare Mom."

"Why would they do that?"

Becky yelled at me, "See what I said? You're too little or too stupid to understand one thing." Then she cut her thumb from pushing too hard. She stuck it in her mouth.

"I'm sorry, Becky," I said real nice. "If I get you a Band-Aid will you tell me just one more thing?

"Maybe."

I ran to get her a Band-Aid from the bathroom. When I got back, she was running cold water on her finger. First, I stirred the pudding quick and then held the Band-Aid on the cut part while she pushed down the sticky ends.

I got back up on the stool to stir some more and pulled the white pill with the design on it out of my pocket. I asked her, "Why do you think this little pill was in Number 9?"

"You went up there again?"

"Yeah, when Mom was in the hospital."

"You know you weren't supposed to go up there."

"Why not?"

"Because."

"But why not? I already saw everything."

"What did you see?"

"The throw up on the floor."

"Oh."

"Becky, do you know what happened up there? You can tell me. Just tell me. I'll figure it out anyway."

"I doubt that." She looked like she was thinking again. She was still cutting the carrots the same way. Only now if she sliced too hard the Band-Aid would get cut, not her. "Do you promise you won't say one word to anyone, especially not Mom or Dad? Because the little kids aren't supposed to know."

"I promise." I crossed my heart. "Stick a needle in my eye."

"Number 9 is where Mom tried to kill herself."

I stopped stirring and looked right at her. "What do you mean?"

"I mean she tried to commit suicide. So she'd be dead."

"Dead? Why would she try to be dead?"

"I don't know why. She just did, and she almost died."

"What made her almost die?"

"It was those little pills like the one you found. They're like sleeping pills. If you take enough, they'll kill you."

It was like something slammed me in the head. I was dizzy. Becky didn't look so nice to me anymore. She looked mean. Why was she making fun of me in such a scary way? But I wasn't going to act like I was scared.

I told her, "She wasn't trying to kill herself. I bet she just took too many pills by accident."

"It wasn't some accident. They even had to call an ambulance."

Why was Becky saying those mean things about Mom? Usually, she was nice and did everything the way she was supposed to. And now she was acting like nothing was good anymore. She looked weird to me, like her face was changing. It was too sharp in my head. Maybe it was true. Maybe it was Mom's way to get away from us kids for good. All the peace and quiet she'd ever want. Was that why Mom shuddered when she thought of Number 9?

The pudding started to look kind of strange and wavy to me. Even it was trying to scare me. I stared down into it until it pulled me in, and I was a little wavy bubble that was going to get bubbled up and then pop into thin air. I imagined Mom being dead forever. It was the creepiest scariest thing ever. And it was crawling up my neck. Maybe I'd go away forever too. Even if I didn't want to.

It was like someone was hitting my head with an ax and cracking me right down the middle. That's when I knew that Becky was lying. Because Mom would never kill herself and leave us all alone forever on purpose. Just like she'd never sell us. Not even for a million dollars. She loved us. And if you added up all the kids, it had to be enough love.

Then I remembered that I was supposed to stir the pudding. I did, and it was thick now but stuck on the bottom. It tasted burnt. I asked Becky if I should throw it out. She said no, because we didn't have the makings for another batch. That it would be OK because it didn't taste that bad.

I knew she was being nice to me, and I was sorry, but I told her anyway, "I know you're lying about Mom."

She looked at me and rolled her eyes. She said, "I sure wish you were right."

I ignored her and poured the pudding into bowls. I put extra in Mom's bowl and made a face design with the last drips. It was like Mom's face. Smiling at me. A weird smile.

7

BLUE BLOOD
SEVEN YEARS

W HEN we ran out of every game in the world and there was nothing else to do, we could always walk up to see Butch, my grandmother, and Grandpa at the top of the hill, and count our money. Butch saved our money for us in tin cans with our name on the can.

When Grandpa saw us coming, he didn't like it one bit. He looked out at us through his thick glasses and mumbled through his pipe, "Why do you kids come on up here and heckle us like this? You're more than just a few you know." Yeah, I guess we knew that. But what did that have to do with anything? Besides, we didn't go up there to heckle him. We came to heckle Butch, and she liked us. When one of us walked in the door he always grumbled and you could hear him swearing. Then he went down into the basement with his *Popular Mechanics* magazine and hammered on pipes. He was a real grouch.

Butch liked me the most. She was going to take every one of us on a trip some day. I was going to go with her to Hawaii where I could hula dance with live flowers around my neck. Or maybe Paris where I would learn French and go places that Little Madeleine went. She'd take Billy, who was my next youngest brother, to Africa where he could kill lions. Maureen, my next oldest sister, would go with her to the Holy Land and do something boring. Each kid got their own trip with just Butch and no one else, not even Grandpa. We talked over and over again about where we would go and what we would do. We even saved some of our money for it. It was hard to save though, when we could buy perfectly good candy with that money. That's why Butch saved it for us, so we wouldn't blow it all.

When we asked Butch how long before we'd go on our trip, she said, "When my ship comes in."

"What ship?"

She just laughed so you could see the top of her false teeth where the pink part of the plastic ended and said, "Before you know it."

We asked Mom when Butch's ship was coming in. Mom said, "She doesn't have a ship. That's what people say when they aren't ever going to have enough money to take you any of those places they promised. Don't get your hopes up."

Then we told Butch what Mom said. Butch said real serious, "You have to believe. That's the way things come true. If you believe anything hard enough, it'll be real." I knew she was right.

But I wasn't sure I wanted to save **all** my money for our trip. I had fifty cents and wanted a Big Hunk and Sugar Daddy as bad as anything. They were five cents each. When I told her I wanted to take out ten cents for candy she said, "Girl, that money is burning a hole right through your pocket. You keep thinking about that money and it'll keep right on burning."

I could feel my pants pocket getting hot. "Don't worry, Butch. I'll save the rest. I won't spend it all, like some other kids I know." I looked at Billy, who I knew would take out all but about five cents, and then gloat in front of me when he got all his candy.

"I'm not worried. It's up to you. You can waste every last cent for all I care," Butch said, shaking her head. She turned away from me, so all I could see was the back of her head, which still had black hair even though she was kind of old. I counted out ten cents and then put my savings can back in the kitchen cupboard where she stored it. Taking that money felt like peeing in front of a stranger. I just hoped she didn't notice.

Billy and I left and walked along the highway down to the store to get our candy. When we got back home, we took our sacks of candy outside where the sun was warm. We flopped down on the weeds and dirt, stuck our knees in the air, and watched the puffy white clouds breeze around. That sun made my Sugar Daddy smell even sweeter and stick to the teeny little hairs above my mouth.

It lasted a **long** time when you just licked it and didn't chew. Licking the candy was kind of like saving it. Only you got to have it and save it at the same time. That candy was sure better than ten cents in a tin can any day.

We watched the clouds and licked. Or gobbled, like Billy. When one of the clouds got in the way of the sun, it seemed like everything in the whole world went gray and icky. Luckily the sun and clouds chased each other really fast, so we didn't have to stay in the icky very long. We got the pretty again after just a few seconds when the clouds were moving fast. We looked at the big hill that was about five miles away to see if they had the icky or the pretty. The worst thing was if they had the pretty and we had the icky. Next worst was if we both had the icky. It was OK if we both had the pretty. But the very best thing was if we had the pretty and they had the icky. We played the *Icky-Pretty* game for a long time.

I wanted to take my money and spend all of it on candy. But I also wanted to save it all, in case Butch was right, and so I'd still be her favorite. I thought about it a lot while we played the *Icky-Pretty* game. Trying to decide if I was going to be a spender or a saver was a real problem. Like when a twig is going down a stream and gets caught between other rocks and bigger twigs. It gets snagged and then other stuff starts collecting on it.

One thing I could do was buy Necco Wafers. Then, if Billy bought some too, we could take turns playing communion. If I went first, I'd kneel down, close my eyes, and stick out my tongue. Then Billy would act real serious and holy, the way the priest did, and lay the Necco Wafer down on my tongue. It tasted better than the body and blood of Christ any day. And I didn't have to worry about part of Jesus getting stuck in one of my cavities. Necco Wafers were one way to get candy and be good at the same time. Only Neccos didn't taste as good as other candy. All the other kids thought the same thing.

Or I could **find** some money, buy candy with it, and not save any of it. Butch wouldn't care about that because she wouldn't even know. We could walk along the highway and look for pop bottles, beer bottles, and money on the side of the road. Maybe I'd find a nickel or even a quarter. But even if I didn't find any money I'd only need five beer bottles or two pop bottles for another candy bar. Then again, I might not find anything for all that looking.

I got sick of thinking about how to spend and save at the same time. My stomach started to hurt too, even though we had the pretty more than the big hill did.

I walked inside our house and it was definitely the icky in there. It was dark and gray and sort of quiet. I saw my two older sisters ironing shirts, folding diapers and watching the babies. I could tell they were in some kind of trouble with Mom since they didn't have the TV or radio on and weren't saying one word. Mom was probably in the bedroom. I knew right off I better not stay inside.

There was nothing else to do but walk up to Butch's. I told Billy, "I'm going back up to Butch's and you can't come." I was sick of everything by now, including him, even though he hadn't done anything wrong except have lots of candy left. And I only had a little.

Billy said, "I want to go too. I want some fun too."

"No way. Not unless you give me some of your candy."

"I don't have to. I bought it with my own money."

"And I don't have to let you go anywhere with me. So get lost and leave me alone." I started waking away.

"It's not fair you being so mean," he said and started to cry.

I turned around and yelled at him, "And it's not fair for you to be such a hog with your candy." I knew I was being a brat for no good reason. I felt bad about it, but I knew I couldn't be nice even if I wanted to right then. I just got madder at him for making me feel bad.

I kept walking and ignoring him. I could see that Grandpa's car was gone. Maybe he went into town alone. I hoped. When I got to the door, I knocked. Even if Butch was alone, she might not let me in since I'd already been there once that day. But Butch opened the door and asked me, "Are there any other kids straggling along?"

"Nope. Just me. Can I come in?" I sure was glad I ditched Billy.

"OK, but don't you tell the others or there'll be no end to it around here. And you better scoot when Gerald comes back." I got to come inside. The sun came in too. It was pretty where the light bounced off her pink table and onto the wall.

Butch was making Jell-O. The green kind Mom put cottage cheese into. That's all Mom would eat for dinner when she was going on a diet. I hated green Jell-O, but it made me think of yummy things. Because it seemed like when she was on her green Jell-O diet, everyone, especially Mom, got lots of ice cream or cookies after dinner.

So I asked Butch, "Are you going to make something yummy to go with it?"

"Like what?"

"Maybe some red Jell-O with pineapple in it?" I hoped.

"Why, that's a very good idea. You can make it and I'll teach you how. But you have to promise not to complain."

"I promise." I loved it when she taught me things, especially when it was just me.

She measured some hot water from the faucet and poured it into a bowl. I got to pour the powder from the box into it. And stir. And stir. And not complain. Even though my arm was killing me from all that stirring.

I stared into the red swirls and asked her, "Why did your Mother ever name you Butch? That's a boy's name."

"It's just a nickname. I got it from a woman friend in Aruba. It just stuck."

"Yeah, but it's a boy's name."

"It suits me just fine."

"Me too." I was glad it was just her and me. But the Jell-O was taking forever. I asked, "How long will it take to mix? "

Butch said, "As long as it takes. You remember what you promised. It isn't becoming to royalty to whine and complain."

"What's royalty?"

"Those folks with blue blood. Like us." She said it like I already knew what she was talking about.

"Who's got blue blood?"

"Me, your Mom, every one of you kids, and all your cousins on my side. Everyone in my line, your Mom's line." I didn't know what all that stuff about lines was about.

"So everyone in our family has it?"

"Not your Dad or anyone in his line. They're all peasant stock."

"Why not Dad too?"

"You don't just get blue blood. You can't earn it either. You're born with it."

"How did us kids get born with it? "

"You better slow down with your questions and keep working that Jell-O." I had accidentally stopped stirring. Hardly any of the little grains had dissolved. I was tired of the Jell-O idea but wanted to know a lot more about blue blood.

"Is it really blue instead of red?"

"Yes. It's really blue."

"But it's red when I get cut."

"Yes, but it's blue when it's inside you and that's what counts. Look at your veins, see how blue they are?" I did and they were blue.

"But everyone's veins look blue on the outside."

"But yours are blue on the inside."

"Butch, it doesn't make any sense!" I was mixed up and feeling kind of mad again but only a teeny bit.

"Lots of things don't make sense. But they're still true. You have blue blood and that's all there is to it."

"So what if I have blue blood? It looks just like everyone else's." I knew she didn't want me to argue, but I couldn't stop. It was like feeling mean and not being able to do anything about it.

"Listen, girl, it'll do you more good in the long run than any other thing you've got. It means you're royal and that sets you apart from others no matter what."

"But Buuutch, what does royal mean? I don't know what you're talking about." I was almost whining and begging.

"OK. I'll tell you." She carried the bowl of Jell-O over to the table so it would be easier for her to sit while I kept stirring.

"A long time ago, your great, great, great, great grandfather, the King of England was doing his business with the Queen's Lady in waiting. The Lady in waiting, your great, great, great, great grand-mother, got pregnant and had his baby. Now this baby was royal because his father was the King. But it was a terrible scandal. Even so, that baby was rolled in gold to prove he was royal even though he was illegitimate. But then the Queen got pregnant and her baby was legitimate and the lawful heir to the throne. They couldn't have any other royal babies around, so the King and Queen found a husband for the Lady in waiting, and sent them both off to the New World with the royal baby.

"They all made a deal. It was this. The King and Queen gave them money to get started in the New World and gave them the title to some land near the palace. In return, the Lady and her new husband would raise the royal baby as a commoner and never let him make any claim to the throne of England. They could give him the title to the land and he could claim that but nothing else.

"This was a pretty good deal since the King and Queen could have chopped off their heads. So they agreed and came to America and you are a direct descendant of that royal baby. He was your great, great, great grandfather. That's why you have blue blood."

It was the most exciting thing I'd ever heard. So that's what royal was! I asked to be sure, "The King of England is my grandfather?"

"Yes, the King from a long time ago, not the one living now." Butch looked glowy happy. I felt glowy too, like I had gold inside me and all the pretty you could ever want. The red Jell-O was dissolved too and the sun shining in through the window made me feel even more royal.

"Why don't we live in a castle and wear crowns and things?"

"Because we're an illegitimate line. Because the baby wasn't the Queen's. But we are direct descendants and that's something you should never forget. Now let's get that Jell-O into the refrigerator."

After she put it away, she poured some lemonade for me and some coffee for her. I had so many questions I'd already forgotten most of them and wanted to ask the rest before I forgot them all. But I could tell she had more to tell me. I sat still and smeared the drops on the outside of the glass into little swirls while I sipped the lemonade.

"The thing is, no one has ever claimed the land that we were given title to. We still have that title and the land is worth a lot of money. Only we have to find a way to get a hold of it." She looked like she was thinking hard.

"Why don't we just say we want it?"

"It's not that easy. You see it's right in the heart of London. About a quarter square mile. London is a real big city. And other people have been building and living on it for hundreds of years already."

"How can they do that when it's ours?"

"Well, they think it's theirs and we'll have to prove it's ours."

"We can do that, can't we?"

"That's what the title should do. Prove it's ours. But there'll still be a big fight."

"But if it's ours what right do they have acting like it's theirs?"

"That's right, girl. We need someone like you who'll go over there and give them a run for their money." She smiled at me and showed her teeth where a little lipstick was stuck. Her black hair was combed straight back and shiny in the sunlight. Then she said, "Only there's something you ought to know."

"What's that, Butch?" I felt proud and grown up.

"About thirty years ago the family hired a lawyer to go over there and get our land. The only problem was, he never came back. No one has heard from him since. Not even his own family."

"What happened to him?"

"No one knows. He was either bought off, murdered or had some kind of accident."

"Why would they kill him and what is bought off?"

"Being bought off is like being bribed. Like if they offered to give him fifty or a hundred thousand dollars, he'd agree to go away and never breathe a word of it to anyone. Or they could just kill him. He'd never breathe a word that way either." She made a weird kind of smile.

"Why would they give him so much money?"

"Like I told you, that land is worth a lot of money, maybe several billion dollars. A few thousand dollars would be like a drop in the bucket to them to keep the land. Each one of you kids would be a millionaire with all that money."

"Really? Me? A millionaire **and** royal?" This was definitely the best news in my whole life.

"Yes. Only someone will have to go there and fight to get it back. And it has to be someone from the family, who can't be bought off."

"Maybe I'll go over there when I grow up."

"Maybe you will. You'll grow up and look as royal as your blood. But you have to grow up first. Get ready for all that money you'll have some day. And get tough and smart enough so no one will trick you. And come back alive."

"Yeah. They'll never buy me off." It was like promising to never make a certain kind of sin. I could do that! "And if they try to kill me, I'll kill them back." It wasn't a sin to kill someone if they tried to do it to you first. I'd get all our money back. And everyone would know I was the best kid in the family. On top of that, I'd be practically the richest person in the world. "And I'll buy a whole room full of candy. No, I'll buy one whole room just for licorice. Then lots of other rooms full of other kinds of candy."

"You don't want to waste your fortune on candy, do you?" One of her eyebrows went higher than the other. I **did** want to spend all my money on candy. What else would you want to spend money on?

I didn't say that though. Instead, I said, "I guess not."

"Remember, you're not like other folks. Your blue blood gives you something others don't have. When you're a blue blood you don't have to spend all your money because you know you have more than you can ever spend."

This made no sense to me, but it made me think anyway. "So, I don't have to save any more money either because when I grow up I'll be a millionaire?"

She looked at me hard. "Of course you still have to save. Blue bloods save all the time and don't need to spend a cent. They know they're better than the others and that's all they need."

"Kind of like they have the pretty and keep it all to themselves?"

"Yes. Like that." I could hear Grandpa's car coming up the driveway. Butch said, "He's back. It's time for you to go now."

I left before Grandpa got out of his car. I waved at him and he barely nodded his grouchy head at me. He obviously didn't know I was royal yet. I looked at my veins and saw the blue again and again. Proof! I'd been royal all this time and didn't even know it!

By the time I got back to our house I was feeling **very** royal and had to tell someone. I found Maureen in the bedroom trying to find some clean clothes to wear after her shower. I told her about how I was a blue blood and how she had to start treating me nice or I wouldn't give her any of my money when I got to be a millionaire.

She acted like it was no big deal and then said, "Butch told me about us being royal a long time ago." She looked at me just to be snide. "Just remember, every one of us kids is royal. And if you and I were princesses, guess which one of us would be queen?"

"Who?" I was scared to guess.

"Me, because I'm older. So there." She smirked at me. I wanted to smash her in the face but didn't have one thing to say back.

Maureen kept talking, "And maybe I'll go over there and get the land before you, too." I hated her so much it felt like poison in my mouth. Not one word came out.

I'd forgotten about **all** of us being blue bloods. What good was it to be a blue blood when everyone in our whole family was too? And they could take the pretty away just like that! I sat down on my bed and pulled my candy out from under the covers where I'd hid it for safekeeping. I started licking on my Big Hunk. The more I thought about Maureen and how she already knew about being a blue blood and didn't tell me and now she was gloating about being older, the more I licked.

And Butch made it sound like she wanted me to go over there and get the land, but Maureen thought she was going to do it first. I started chewing whole bites of the Big Hunk and didn't care if it was going to be gone too soon.

Then on my last bite of candy I figured out how Maureen must have tricked me again the way she always did. I bet she didn't know one thing about blue blood until I told her. And I could fight those guys in London better than Maureen any day. Butch knew what a good fighter I was. I was her best grandkid. Even so, I made up my mind right then that I was going up to Butch's again the next day. I wouldn't say one word to her. I'd reach my hand into my savings can and take out twenty cents. For more candy. And it wasn't going to be Necco Wafers either.

8

Concoctions
ALMOST EIGHT YEARS

SONNY was pounding on my arm with his fist almost as hard as he could. My skinny-as-a-bird arm hurt so bad I tried to slug him back, but he grabbed my fist quick, twisted my whole arm behind my back and pinned me against myself. His arm muscles were almost as big as Dad's and he was **so** much bigger than me. The only way I could get back at him was to call him a fat pig. He **was** one too, but he didn't like anyone calling him that, so he pounded me even harder. It started to hurt worse than ever and I knew he wouldn't stop until I stopped saying bratty things. So now that I was almost ready to throw up from it hurting so bad, I'd have to give. The thought of it brought tears into my eyes that felt like blisters. I tried to stab him with my mind, but it didn't do any good. And giving in felt like stabbing my own self, but I knew I'd have to do it to get this fat pig of a big brother off me.

"Have you had enough, runt?" he growled. I wanted to spit at his sweaty face but didn't. "Do you give? Or do you want some more?" He slammed me with his fist again.

I was dizzy by now and said it as quiet as I could, "OK."

"What was that? Do you want some more?" He wanted me stabbed all the way down into the ground.

Finally, I said it the way he wanted. "OK, I give."

I wasn't crying anymore. I was staring at the stitches on my saddle shoes. He let go of me and when I looked up at him, he was smiling out at me through his mean happy eyes.

That night just before dinner I told Mom, "Sonny pounded on me again." I showed her my arm, which was red and swollen as big as two skinny-bird arms now. Under the skin, I could see big blackish bruises starting to show. She barely looked at it because she was busy dishing up the soup bone and noodle soup. I hated the bone fat that was always mixed with the gray scum at the top.

She told me, "Sonny only does it to you because he likes you. It's your own fault for giving him so much satisfaction. It's because of all your yelling, crying, and screaming. That's all he wants. And you shouldn't give it to him if you want him to stop. It's up to you." It wasn't fair that he wouldn't get in trouble for being so mean.

Then she started yelling, "Dinner's ready! Come and get it or we'll feed it to the pigs!" We didn't have any pigs anymore except for my brothers, so this was just a way to get us to hurry up. Besides, I didn't really care if she did feed it to the pigs. It was slop anyway.

That night when I went to bed, I cuddled my stuffed lion. I knew that at least Lion loved me. It was like a secret between us that I loved him more than anyone, anywhere. I promised him that even if there was a fire or an atomic war, I'd save him before anyone else, even before my little brothers or sisters or the family Bible. His golden fuzzy fur cuddled me back and the cold, mad, scared feeling inside turned into the soft sleepy one.

In the morning, I kissed Lion and asked him to help me. I knew this was wrong because we were only supposed to ask God for help. But I loved Lion more than God, which was also wrong. So I was already not on such good terms with God. Lion and I tried to figure out what I should do to keep from getting pounded on. We would go over it a thousand times and I never could figure it out. We always agreed on one thing: don't give. Lion's long brown eyelashes brushed my neck.

Since it was Saturday, we could play for part of the day or lie in bed for a long time if we wanted. I stayed in bed and thought about my birthday coming up in about a month. Of course, I couldn't have that feeling for even a minute without thinking of Luann. I think birthdays should be for just one person at a time, but Luann was born on my birthday when I was only three and was too little to do anything about it.

Mom said she was the most beautiful baby she ever had. Luann's eyes were kind of greenish-brown. "Hazel," Mom said, "like mine." Her eyelashes and hair were straight and brown like Mom's too. Luann's hair was thick, and that was nice but other than that she was not anything beautiful to me. Finally, after too much of the Luann feeling, I got out of bed and put Lion under the covers so no one could find him.

At breakfast, me and Billy were making art with the Shredded Wheat, Cheerios, and sugar. He made buildings in his bowl and I made faces in mine. The sugar made good cheekbones on the faces. After a while, Mom left for town, and we got the sneaky idea to make a concoction and give it to Luann just to see if she'd still fall for it.

Concoctions were our specialty and Luann was a born sucker. Anyone could be fooled the first time, especially if they were little enough. But Luann got suckered two different times into drinking a concoction. She should have been able to figure it out after the first or second time she drank a concoction, but since she never did, she deserved it all the more. It was her fault for being so stupid. And even if we were mean, she just asked for it with her *I'm the most beautiful baby ever* attitude.

Anyone could make a concoction, but I usually did it with Billy, and sometimes Dean, who was three years older. We started the concoction with some white vinegar in a quart jar. We added enough black pepper to make it thick with speckles. The speckles kept sinking to the bottom of the jar so we made it thicker with some ketchup and mustard. Then we added Worcestershire sauce, which we all agreed was the worst thing ever invented. Even so, it never seemed bad enough for a really good concoction. We put in soy sauce, about an inch of regular salt and some garlic and onion salt. Sometimes we put in some brown spices that smelled strong. It always seemed like we forgot the best part until the very end and then remembered. Cayenne pepper!! We always put in just a spoon of that, since we didn't know if it would burn your guts out if you got too much.

Every concoction was different. It just depended on what was the worst thing you could think of that was still sort of food. Sometimes we put in food coloring, and it never tasted like anything, but it did color your mouth. One time we wanted to put some dirt in, but were afraid of the germs since the dirt came from outside. And you never knew if chickens had pooped on that dirt. We knew that heat killed germs so we put the dirt in a pan and stuck it in the oven. We turned it on full blast, but after about ten minutes it smelled so horrible we thought it might be poison and threw it away.

When we were busy making our concoction, someone had to keep our 'suspect' busy in another room so they wouldn't know what was going on. Usually, it was Dean who did that part. He would tell the suspect that we were making a surprise and that they'd get some of it if they didn't bother us. When we were ready he'd bring the suspect into the kitchen where we waited with big smiles on our faces, saying, "We have something so delicious we wanted to give you some. You can have as much as you want. You can take a big gulp if you want."

When we tried this on Luann for the third time, it was a Saturday. I was almost eight and she was almost five. We said the thing about how this was better than a milk shake and it was all for her. The cup was metal and painted with a shiny purple color so she couldn't see through it. Even so, we said she couldn't have any unless she closed her eyes. When she closed her eyes and smiled as though she was going to get something real nice, I started to feel sorry for her. So I concentrated real hard and when I stopped feeling everything except the cold metal in my hand, I gave her the drink.

She brought it up to her mouth but then yanked her head back, probably because it stunk. Dean was covering her eyes so she couldn't peek. "It smells like a concoction," she said.

I could see she was starting to cry even though her eyes were still covered. I told her that even though it smelled bad, it tasted real good, but the trick was to get a big mouthful to get the whole flavor. If you took just one sip, it might taste bad. This made sense to her, but just to be sure she said for us to try it first. I took the glass and pretended to taste it and made yummy sounds. Dean did the same. Then he gave it back to Luann.

She took a whole big mouthful. About a second later, she looked like she'd just eaten a rat. Her face twisted up and her whole body started wiggling while she was jumping up and down. We started laughing so hard we could hardly see. After about another second, she spit it on the floor and tried to run to the sink to get some water. Dean blocked the sink. She was screaming and crying now. I acted like I was sorry and gave her a glass of what was supposed to be water but was really another glass of concoction. She gulped it into her mouth and accidentally swallowed some of it. We got pains in our sides and were rolling on the floor from laughing so hard. She was choking and crying about how she thought it was water and wanted some water. Then she got kind of quiet. We asked her what was wrong, did she want some more? She held her stomach and started to get a grayish-white color in her face right before she threw up. She did it right on us and then tried to run to the toilet. But the throw up was faster and probably smarter than her. There was throw up all over the kitchen floor and into the bathroom. It was worse than the concoction ever was.

We were kind of sorry about her throwing up and afraid we'd get in serious trouble if Mom came back and found out we'd done something almost as bad as making someone bleed. That was where she drew the line. No blood. No broken bones.

Now it all had to get cleaned up somehow. We tried to make Luann do it since it was her throw up, not ours. She got real stubborn. She wasn't going to wash off any of it because we were the ones who made her throw up in the first place. I wiped up the mess in the kitchen, but there was still a lot in the bathroom and all over her. She wouldn't wash any of it off since she was saving it as proof of what we did. What if Mom came home and saw it? I started screaming at her to clean herself up or I'd pull her hair out. She didn't care. Her head was tough and she had hair to spare. I knew she was going to get even with us and be her usual tattletale self if I didn't do something soon.

Billy and I both got the idea at the same time. We dragged her by the arms and feet out of the kitchen, down the stairs and outside onto the dirt. I held her with her back to my chest while Billy got the hose and started squirting her in the face and all over. He got me too, but that was OK. We just wanted all the throw up gone. Then she got her arm a little loose, pulled it forward, and jammed her elbow into my stomach. It made me lose my grip on her. She ran back into the house through the kitchen and into the throw up bathroom before I could catch her. Then she locked the door from the inside and said she was going to stay there until Mom came home, HA HA.

I was so mad I started kicking the bathroom door and telling her I'd kill her if she didn't come out right now. She kept laughing at me until I went outside and got a ladder to reach the bathroom window from the outside. I whispered to Billy to turn the hose on as far as he could and fold the hose to make it stop and not unfold it until I said so. He nodded. I climbed up the ladder telling Luann I just wanted to talk. When I got to the top, she threw a glass of water in my face and started saying, "Youuu caaan't get me."

She had no idea. I lifted the hose up, motioned to Billy to unfold the hose and blasted her in the face with it through the screen. There was no place for her to hide. She tried to close the window, but it stuck. She couldn't go in the shower because it was never used for a shower anyway. It was the one where we stored the dirty diapers and potatoes. I kept squirting her as hard as I could until she was laying on her side on the floor blubbering. Then I said, "Are you sorry? Do you give?"

Finally, she said, "OK." I told her to unlock the door. Then I turned the hose away and started to climb down the ladder. My hands were shaking from holding the hose so hard. My legs were getting trembly too, from fighting so much and from the really bad feeling creeping in on me.

I knew I was in for it when I came in the kitchen and saw where the water from the bathroom had flooded out. It was everywhere. The bathroom was horrible. Water was dripping from the ceiling and you could see some paint melting. The potatoes were mixing with the diapers and everything would get maggots now. The towels stored in the big shelves behind the door were all wet, along with the big box of Kotex. Whatever those things were for, they were no good now. My arms and chest felt like thick glue. Dean came in and said we were really going to catch hell. He asked Luann if she was OK. She said yeah.

Mom was due back any time. Dean told us to start hauling the wet paper stuff out to the incinerator so no one would find it. We also threw out the potatoes. The dirty diapers just stayed in a soggy pile, leaking out brown water. We used the wet towels to mop up the floors.

At least the floor would get cleaned. Maybe Mom would be glad that we cleaned it and not get so mad.

We heard the gravelly sound of the car coming up the driveway. There was still a thick layer of water on the bathroom and kitchen floor and trails of water all over the house. Billy had thrown the wet towels right into the dirty clothes pile. Now all the clothes would probably get mildew. It was maybe the worst mess we'd ever made in one afternoon.

Mom walked in with her arms full of groceries. Maureen was with her. Maureen wasn't even trying to hide the smirk on her face. She always thought she was more pure than the rest of us. You'd never find her making any concoctions. She was too busy trying to be like the Virgin Mary. I wonder if the Virgin Mary was as big a snot as my sister. Luann ran up to Mom and began blabbing the whole story. It was no use saying anything.

Us older ones got a whipping with the strap. Dean got it the worst because he was the oldest and should know better. Mom kept hitting and hitting him like she wanted something from him. He wasn't going to give it to her though. He never would cry when she strapped him. I felt really bad for him because I knew I was the worst, not him. He wasn't even around for the hose part. Billy and I got it the second worst. We always cried. Luann, who was of course the one who told on us to save her hide, got to watch after she found the strap for Mom. Maureen got to watch everything too, while she changed Francie's diapers, which were soaked from sitting in the hose water. Then she fed my littlest brother Jason, who was still a baby. But he didn't want to eat because he was crying too hard with me and Billy.

That night when I was talking to Lion I kept wondering why I got the strap for being mean to Luann, and Sonny never got it for being mean to me. Lion and me never figured that out either. We only knew that I was really bad. It was nothing you could ever say in confession either. It was the kind of bad that was worse than sins because you knew you'd never give it up, even for Lent, even for Jesus hanging on the cross with a crown of thorns that dripped blood into his eyes. Lion knew there was no cure for this kind of bad. The bad was all the way in me, no matter what.

The next morning we were all still mad at Luann for telling on us. We were standing over the furnace in the floor trying to get heated up. When the air blows up, it goes toasty warm right under your nightgown or PJ's and into your legs. But if you have a bed wetter there, you get stunk out real bad from the smell of cooked pee. Even though you can get used to it if you hold your breath, who wants to do that with a tattletale bed wetter like Luann? We told her she was a stink bomb and to go away until her nightgown was dry.

9

BULLY BOY
ALMOST EIGHT YEARS

SOME of the dark red blood water splashed on my ankle when I accidentally kicked the milk bucket. It was filled with liver. Quivery beef liver that was brownish-purple and like nothing you'd ever want to eat. We had to eat it though, fried with onions. The onions weren't that bad. But even though the liver was cooked it still quivered in my stomach every time I took a bite. The only way I could get rid of it was to sneak one piece at a time onto my sister's plate when she wasn't looking. Or chop it up fine, mix it with butter and stick little globs of it underneath the table. The butter was what made it stick.

We always ate liver the day we butchered. There was also the tongue, the heart, and the brains, but they kept longer. Tongue and heart were just salted and boiled for sandwiches. The brains and some other parts were made into head cheese. Dad loved it. Lucky for him no one else could even stand to think about head cheese, let alone put some of it in their own head. But he was used to eating that kind of stuff from when he grew up back on the farm.

Maybe head cheese was like candy he got for killing the bull. Mom said Dad hated to kill animals, but he never said that. He sat at the kitchen table and didn't say one word when he cleaned and loaded the rifle. His face was white and his mouth made a thin straight line while he took the .22 apart. He wiped each piece with a towel and laid it down onto the Formica table. The wooden part of the rifle was a smooth and golden-brown. It fit right into the black metal part. None of us kids got to touch anything. Dad didn't want any kids around when he was getting ready to kill. It seemed like he hated us then.

Finally, he'd get up and walk to the pasture where Molly, the Mama cow, was mooing nonstop. She had long legs but never galloped except before butchering. Every two years she had a calf. If it was a boy calf, we always named it Bully Boy, and by the time it was two years old we butchered it. Somehow, Molly always knew we were going to butcher before it happened. She started to moo the night before, mooed all the next day, and didn't stop until the day after that. We never could figure out how she knew beforehand. I didn't really like her mooing, but those moos told me she loved her calf and that she was smart for a cow. Dad hated it. He didn't sleep the night before butchering. He always walked around the house like there was something he needed real bad and couldn't find.

When it was time to shoot, Dad came outside with the rifle. This was the signal to the boys to tie Bully Boy up to one of the stanchions by the barn so Dad could get a good aim. After they tied him up, they were supposed to go behind the fence with the rest of us kids and watch. Dad would shoot from just a few feet away. He used the fence post to hold the rifle steady.

This one year Molly was really upset and was mooing so hard that Bully Boy (our fourth Bully Boy) knew he had to break free. He started kicking, pawing the ground, and pulling at the rope with his thick neck. I thought he was going to strangle himself. But he didn't. Somehow the rope broke. He tore loose and took off. Molly was close by and both of them started galloping to the far end of the field.

Dad started hollering at the boys, "Who in the hell's idea of a knot is that, goddammit!"

My two older brothers just stared at Dad with their mouths open and didn't blink until he screamed, "What are you looking at? Go get the goddamn bull!"

He was yelling so loud the veins on his neck were sticking out and I thought he would start swearing in German. Whenever he was screaming in German, we knew it was swear words.

Dean and Sonny started running toward Bully Boy, who had slowed down by now. But the minute he saw them waving their hands and yelling at him, he took off again. Meanwhile, Dad was yelling orders to them from the gate.

The rest of us kids started to yell too, just like Dad. I accidentally kicked Billy, my little brother, but he thought it was on purpose so he pushed me. It wasn't too hard, but I fell down. On the way down, I grabbed his corduroy pant leg, tripped him, and mooed. He tickled my stomach and mooed back. Then we both were on the ground on our hands and knees yelling, mooing, and laughing like maniacs for no good reason. Pretty soon all the little kids were mooing and yelling too.

Meanwhile, Dad was still yelling and the older boys were still running after the bull. Molly's moo started to sound like a growl. Her horns were pointed down and she charged at the boys when they got too close to her calf. They chased Bully Boy and got chased by Molly for about fifteen minutes while everyone else was screaming directions and mooing.

Dad walked away without saying a word. This was not a good sign. It wasn't like him to suddenly stop yelling. We got really quiet, waiting for what he'd do next. Even the little kids were quiet. Finally, Dad came out with another rope and told everyone to stay the hell still. He started walking toward Bully Boy, motioned with his head to the boys to get out of the way, goddammit, and began talking really quiet to Bully Boy. After another fifteen minutes, he had him roped and ready to be shot. Everyone stayed quiet except Molly, who was in the far corner of the field. She was still mooing but now it sounded like she had laryngitis.

We all got behind the fence while Dad aimed his rifle. The muscles on his arm looked tan and strong just like the wood on the rifle, but I saw his hand shaking. He set the gun down, kicked the dirt, lit a cigarette, and walked around in a circle a few times. Then he threw the cigarette to the ground like it had a disease and kicked it. Finally, he picked up the gun again. This time he aimed and shot. Just one shot.

Bully Boy's front feet buckled. First he fell onto his knees and then onto his side. Then nothing. Until Dad came over to him with his big knife and cut his throat wide open. Then he started to kick. All four feet kicked while the blood from his neck gushed out on the ground. My oldest brother, Sonny, said Bully Boy wasn't alive. That it was just his nerves doing all that kicking. Mom came out with a cup of hot coffee for Dad. They talked real quiet while Bully Boy bled. It took another fifteen minutes, maybe more, before Bully Boy was done bleeding.

Then Dad cut a hole between the tendon and the anklebone above both of the back hooves. He pushed a hook through each hole. The hook was attached to a rope, which was attached to a pulley. The pulley was on a huge metal frame that looked like a really big swing set, only with two pulleys instead of swings. We all had to help pull the ropes so the beef – it was beef now – could hang and not be in the dirt while they skinned it.

My oldest sister, Georgina, got to help with the skinning. Dad cussed at her when she cut into the meat instead of staying in the fat layer between the skin and the meat. He didn't swear very loud though and didn't make her stop skinning. I knew she was feeling proud.

I went inside for most of that part, to watch cartoons and hold my stomach. It wasn't the skinning I couldn't stand, it was the eyes on the bull's head, its gashed neck, and the huge pile of intestines all sitting in a heap below the carcass. The smell of blood mixed with fresh manure gave me a sick feeling. I went to sleep from the feeling even though I knew I'd be missing a lot of stuff.

When I woke up, the liver was in the bucket on the kitchen floor. My older sisters were peeling and chopping onions. I watched from the doorway because the onions were so bad they made me cry. Mom dumped even more onions on the kitchen table. So we'd have enough of something no one wanted to eat anyway. Then she pulled the liver bucket over by the sink and reached her hands down into the blood water. She lifted that big liver up and plopped it on the drain board. It was wiggling like it was still alive. My stomach felt as sour as my eyes.

By bedtime, I was tired but not very sleepy. The smell in our bedroom didn't help either. It was from the butchering rags that were in the laundry sink. Because our bedroom was also the laundry room. I couldn't get that icky blood and bones smell out of my nose. After a while of trying to sleep, I gave up and opened up my eyes.

Then I saw it. The carcass. It was hanging from a pulley right there on the bedroom door. I tried to figure out if it was really there because it was supposed to still be hanging outside and waiting to be quartered the next day.

I heard Billy, who slept in the bed next to me, make crying sounds. Instead of asking him why he was acting like such a crybaby, I asked him if he saw the carcass too. He did. That's why he was crying. The more we stared at the door, the more we both saw it. He crawled into my bed with me and we both closed our eyes to try to make it go away. When I finally got to sleep I dreamt about a chicken with its head cut off running around underneath the house. I woke up. Now I was crying and the carcass was still there, but Billy was asleep.

In the morning, it was gone. There was just a long bloodstained butchering sheet hanging from the door, waiting to be washed. I went outside and saw the carcass hanging from the metal frame, where it was supposed to be. How did they get it back outside? I was too sleepy and hungry to try to figure that part out.

I walked into the kitchen where I smelled food. There was a cooked tongue lying on the drain board. It was steaming and fogging the kitchen window. When it was cool, we'd skin it and have it for lunch.

10

ATOMIC WORKS
EIGHT YEARS

OUR whole town practiced for the atomic bomb. At school, we hid under our desks for the duck and cover drill. Or we'd go in the hall and squat while we covered our heads for the squat and cover drill. We also had the drill where we had to leave the classroom and go somewhere else before the bomb dropped. There were sirens that told us how long we had. The short siren said we had about an hour before the bomb dropped. The long siren gave you three hours to get to a bomb shelter.

Since we lived in the country and it took about an hour to get home on the bus, we wanted the long siren. Then we'd have time to get into our own bomb shelter at home. If we heard the short siren and were at school, we'd have to find someone in town to go home with. No one would want a whole bunch of kids coming to their house so I couldn't go with any of my brothers or sisters. I'd have to go on my own and find someone who'd let me come to their house. But I never knew who I would ask, or if they'd want me or let me come into their bomb shelter or if their bomb shelter would be good enough to keep us from dying even if they let me in.

Our bomb shelter was a good one. Dad built it in the basement of our new house. The new house still isn't done and might never be. But the bomb shelter is. Its walls are about a foot thick. I know because I was there when they poured the concrete. The door is thick and heavy, with a rubber seal around it. Dad got it from a meat locker. The door had a hole cut out of it at the very top. That's where he put the air filter.

I asked Mom if it would keep out the radioactive air. I already knew that radioactive air would be everywhere and it would kill you easy. But you'd be sick and get sores all over and throw up a lot before you died. Mom looked worried for a second and then turned on her sharp eyes that told me she was sick of my stupid questions and said, "That's going to be the least of your problems."

The bomb shelter wasn't that big. It was about the size of our living room and had lots of shelves with books, food, water, clothes, blankets, and medical stuff. We would use flashlights for light. Mom made sure we had enough water and canned food for about two or three weeks. We kept homemade canned cherries there too. They were everyone's favorite dessert. We canned about 250 quarts each summer, but by the time winter was almost over we'd run out. The only ones left were in the bomb shelter. So we hoped there wouldn't be a bomb soon or we'd get no dessert in addition to being radioactive.

Mom was sure there'd be a bomb sooner or later. "Those atheist communists won't stop until everyone's dead," she'd say when she watched the news. We all knew they would make us slaves and torture us for being Catholics unless we said we didn't believe in God. And if you didn't proclaim your faith you'd go to hell. That's why we had to stop the communists.

Sometimes after the news we'd all have to stop and pray for them to be converted and become Catholics. I didn't think it would do much good. Our only chance was the bomb shelter. No one else seemed too worried about it, but I could see a lot of problems with that shelter even if it was the best one around.

Like the lock on the door. When we first got the door, Dad put the lock on the inside. So that when the bomb dropped we could keep out strangers who wanted to come in our shelter. But after we started playing in there Mom got worried that one of the little kids would get locked in and wouldn't be able to get out. Then we'd have to knock a monster hole in the concrete wall to rescue that kid.

Mom and Dad talked about this with all of us at dinner and everyone agreed that the lock was a problem. I especially agreed and said, "It might be even worse, maybe we wouldn't notice someone missing and they'd die in there before anyone remembered."

Mom said I was exaggerating and that we never forgot anyone for more than a day and no one would die in a day anyway.

They decided to take the lock off the door. Now if we had a bomb we'd have no lock to keep people besides our family out. Mom said we couldn't let anyone else in, not even our neighbors. "If they want a bomb shelter they can build their own," she said.

I asked, "But what if they're screaming and crying and begging?"

She looked right at me and said, "Would you rather have **them** screaming and begging, or sacrifice your family? Because if you let anyone else in, we'll all die. So you have to choose. It's part of growing up. Your baby brothers and sisters are counting on you to not take food out of their mouths and put it in the mouths of strangers."

I felt like a grown up and knew we really needed that lock on the door. I also knew that by the time we heard the siren, there wouldn't be enough time to put it back on. And if they dropped the bomb really close to us we'd be dead so fast the lock would be a joke.

It was hard to imagine what it would be like to know you were going to die the next second. Once I saw a movie of a woman who was shot by a firing squad. She had long black hair that she kept swishing around like a horse's tail. She was so dopey, as though the worst thing they were going to do was to cut her hair. She didn't scream or anything. Then bang, dead. What a stupid movie. I knew it would be a lot worse than that right before you died.

A few weeks after I saw that movie, my cousin Lyle killed himself with a gun in his head and he was only fourteen years old. The funeral was going to be an open casket and you'd be able to see where the bullet went. That's why I didn't get to go. Mom said, "You're too young to see the tragedy of suicide." But Georgina and Becky went.

When they came back from the funeral, Georgina sat on the bed in the girls' bedroom painting her toenails and talked to Becky about why he'd do such a thing while Becky ironed a blouse. I sat on the floor, listened, and tried to figure it out with them. I also wanted some of the bright red toe polish on my toes.

Lyle shot himself on purpose. He had curly blonde hair and was cute but real quiet. No one knew why he did it. He shot himself in a closet. Why a closet? Georgina wondered out loud, "What do you think Lyle would have done if a bomb siren went off right when he was going to shoot himself? Would he shoot or run into his family's bomb shelter?"

It was a good question. I wondered what it would feel like to have the last thing you'd ever feel be the feeling that you were going to be so dead you wouldn't even feel it. We talked about it for so long I got some red toes out of it from Georgina. Then I got tired and went down to play in the bomb shelter.

When we played in the bomb shelter, we pretended all kinds of things. Mom didn't care because then she got some peace and quiet. She always said, "Blessed silence," when the house stopped being noisy, which was almost never. Not only was the bomb shelter soundproofed, but it was also pitch black when the door was closed. You couldn't even see your hand or one tiny speck of light. It was so black it made you dizzy from looking so hard for light that wasn't there. We pretended we were blind. We made tents with the blankets and played hide and seek in the dark. My brothers made machine gun sounds at each other. They'd be soldiers and I'd be the nurse for everyone when they gunned each other to death.

Sometimes we stole from the food shelf, which was wrong, but we only did it when we couldn't help it. The canned corned beef was good because it had its own little can opener. You could scoop the meat out with your fingers and get rid of the can real easy. We wondered what it would be like if this was our last can of food and pretty soon we'd have to leave the bomb shelter.

We'd have to go out and see how everything was broken and glowing radioactive. Anyone who was still alive would be more dangerous than you can imagine. Especially men if you happened to be a girl. That's why Mom said the first thing to do is cut off your hair and never let them see how you pee.

The most interesting thing in the bomb shelter was the medical books that Mom put down there. Before she met Dad, she worked for a doctor she really liked and from then on she collected all kinds of disease books. We looked at them with flashlights and were careful not to get any food spots on them from our fingers. One book showed naked people with weird things growing where they weren't supposed to. One guy had a penis that went all the way down to his knees. And it had lumps all over it. We wondered how he could stand to have his picture taken. Was he in the book because his penis was so long or because it had the lumps? We knew it was a sin to look at naked people, but since they were so disgusting, we figured the sin wouldn't be that bad. That was our favorite book to look at. But there was another one that we only looked at if we wanted to throw up.

It showed pictures of diseases people got on their skin. There were purple blotches, red blisters, black spots and pink bumps on more nasty looking skin than you ever wanted to see. I looked especially for skin that was radioactive but never found it.

We kept wondering where all those people in the books lived because we never saw anyone in real life as weird or ugly as them. Billy said, "I bet the book people just made up all those diseases."

I said, "Maybe, but they look real to me. Maybe there's a whole town where only disease people live and then they don't have to feel so bad because everyone else is just as gross. Maybe that's why they don't care if someone takes their picture. They think it's normal." We wondered what a whole town of radioactive people would be like.

They did radioactive experiments on animals in the town where we lived, so I knew it could do weird things to you. We thought there might be a radioactive alligator in the swamp in front of our house. Georgina said she saw some man from the Atomic Engineers Project get out of his truck and let the alligator go right into the swamp. She could have been lying, but we always looked for that alligator. All I ever saw was green slimy mosquito beds.

Both of our guinea pigs were definitely part radioactive. We got them from a friend of Mom and Dad's who was an atomic scientist. He said their parents were radioactive and he wasn't sure how it would affect the babies. Well, for one thing those guinea pigs never grew up. The whole time we had them they stayed the size of little kittens. Their hair stayed soft and fuzzy like kittens too. We named them Jack and Jill. Jack was white with black spots. Jill was white with brown spots. They had little teeth that didn't hurt if they tried to bite you.

Since Jack and Jill couldn't hurt a fly, the whole family played with them, even the really little kids. The only problem was they got dropped a lot, especially by the little kids. But even when I was holding one of them and being real careful, it would suddenly jump out of my hands and then fall on its head. Billy thought it was funny that they didn't land on their feet like cats do, so he'd drop them on purpose. I told him, "Stop being so mean to them! They can't help how they land!"

He said, "It's just an experiment. And besides, it doesn't hurt them. They're used to it." I slugged him in the arm until he finally left them alone.

After about a year, Jack started jumping in the air and then running as fast as he could until he ran into a wall or something hard enough to stop him. It looked weird and a little funny. When we showed Mom, she said, "He probably has brain damage because of the radioactive experiments."

Dad said, "Like hell, more like brain damage from being dropped on its head so many times."

Jack ran into the wall about once a week in the beginning. Then it was every day. When he died, he was doing it almost all the time. After he slammed into one thing, he'd get up and run right into something else. We could tell he was going to die from it. We just hoped Jill would be normal, but she started doing the same thing and died about two months after Jack. There was no way to keep them from bashing their brains out. Is that how Lyle's family felt about him before he died?

When Jill died, I promised I'd give her the best funeral ever. It would be for Jack too, even though he was already buried. We put her into a shoe box with part of an old brownish gold towel that was a rag now. It matched the color of her spots. I picked dandelions and a baby carrot and put them in the box with her. I curled some red ribbon and tied it around her little neck. She looked as bright as she could for being dead.

Billy, Luann, and even Nicky all wanted to be part of the funeral. I said, "OK. But we're going to have a procession and if you want to be in it, you have to follow me. You also have to do exactly what I do, and say what I say, or you can't be in it." They all promised they would.

We all got scarves to wrap around our forehead and tie in the back like gypsies. I told them they had to hold their hands straight up over their heads when we walked. I picked up the shoe box casket and held it up over my head. The other kids got into a line behind me and we started to walk in a big circle around the motel and the pasture.

I started saying Catholic prayers, but after a while I was feeling the scariest saddest feeling ever. All I could think of was Jack and Jill being dead, and the atomic war we were going to have, and how it would feel right before we all died. I pushed Jill up even higher into the air and started praying with words that weren't even words. I was making sounds that felt like there was a hole in the world and we were all being sucked right through it.

The other kids started to whine about not wanting to do this anymore. I turned around and screamed that Jack would go to hell and burn forever, and kill himself in the head for infinity, if they didn't make the sounds exactly like I did. I was screaming so strong at them that they knew I was telling the truth. So we all started walking again, with our hands up, making such loud, shrieky, sad sounds that I started crying. But it felt OK, almost good.

When I ran out of sounds, we stopped and dug a hole for Jill in the pasture. I said a prayer of words that weren't words and we all did the sign of the cross. We covered her up with dirt and went inside. I was tired and didn't want to play with anyone, so I told the other kids to leave me alone. I went into the bomb shelter, closed the door, and went to sleep.

11

VOODOO
EIGHT YEARS

M Y Grandmother, Butch, didn't talk that much about Voodoo. She said it was black magic and that even though people killed each other with it, "You shouldn't fill your mind with the likes of such."

I didn't even know what black magic was, except that it was marked on a plastic bag for the dirt she used for potting her plants. It said 'Black Magic' as plain as could be. I asked her what it was for. She said it helped the plants to grow.

When I walked up the hill from our house to Butch's, I always got the feeling of something new. It took almost five minutes if you were walking real slow and kicking gravel at the same time. In the summer it made you hotter to walk to her house, but once you got inside it was always cool. That's because she and Grandpa had a fan. They had a lot of stuff that we didn't have. They had a collection of Cracker Jack prizes that filled five huge pickle jars. When Butch gave us Cracker Jacks, we got the prize. But only if she didn't need it for her collection.

Grandpa got a machete when they lived in Aruba. But he was a grouch and never talked about anything. He didn't like any of us grandkids. Butch did though and told us all about Aruba. The stories about Aruba always had Voodoo or black magic in them. She wouldn't answer any of my questions so I never knew exactly what Voodoo was, but I could tell when she was talking about it because she got a shiny look that covered her whole face. The red rouge on her cheeks got even redder and she gave me even more of the feeling that something might happen.

Butch said most of the natives on Aruba did Voodoo and some of them were cannibals. She once knew another white family that lived there who had a native woman for their cook. For dinner one Sunday, the cook served some juicy slices of roast that everyone thought was the best meat they'd ever eaten. They thought it tasted like pork, but a lot better, and no one could figure out what it really was. When they asked the cook, she thought they already knew. She told them it was a baby and showed them its head in the kitchen! They had eaten a baby! The cook thought they'd be happy, but I guess she got fired instead. I always wondered whose baby they ate. Was it theirs? Butch wouldn't tell me.

Grandpa and Butch had the biggest and nicest bathroom I'd ever seen. The floor was mostly pink with gold speckles. In the middle of it was a huge diamond shape made out of black with even more of the gold speckles. That diamond shape would pop right out and look like it wasn't flat anymore when you looked at it long enough. I loved to sit on the toilet and stare at that diamond. It was the most sparkly beautiful shape I'd ever seen.

One time when I was about six or seven I took a shower in that bathroom. It was after I got soaked helping Butch wash clothes with her wringer washer. My job was to push the clothes through the rollers while Butch caught them coming out the other side. When I pushed the squishy wet clothes through the rollers, a lot of the water squirted onto me. So I got real soppy wet and she made me take a shower.

When I was done washing myself, she came in to dry me off. I asked her about the diamond on the floor. I asked her if it was black magic that made it pop out at me that way. She said, "Lordy, where do you get such ideas?" Then she started rubbing me real hard with the towel and told me, "You always remember to be careful with men, girl, because they aren't to be trusted."

She told me about a man she knew who cut up a little girl with a knife. She rubbed my face real hard and told me how he cut up the girl's face. Then she rubbed my bottom just as hard and told me how he cut her up down there too. And the little girl was just about my age. I was getting colder and colder the longer she rubbed. Finally, she stopped rubbing and started to touch me nice all over, especially where the bad man did all the cuts and told me how much she loved me. I was still cold.

Butch told me lots of special things that I knew not to tell anyone else. She gave me so much of the feeling of new stuff that I knew she loved me more than any of her other grandkids. I knew not to say anything when she got her Voodoo voice. I just listened and tried not to look at her black hair or where her red lipstick leaked out on the wrinkles around her mouth. I tried **really** hard not to look at her eyes. They were too shiny and strong. I looked at the wall instead and tried to see everything she was saying. Her voice was spooky, but it was easier to see things when she talked like that. But sometimes I was so scared I thought I'd break apart and start on fire.

Mom was always worrying about things going in and out of our brains. She thought Butch was sort of crazy and that she was trying to brainwash us kids. It was hard to tell who was crazy because Butch thought Mom was crazy too. I knew I was special to Butch and wasn't to Mom, but Mom was still my Mom even if she didn't love me as much as Butch did. I also knew to be on the lookout for brainwashing. But it never happened to me once. My brain was always full of stuff.

Butch always had more to teach me. She taught me how to save money in my tin can bank and not be a miser like Dean, who wanted to count his money ten times a day. And to not be a spendthrift like Billy. She taught me how to thread a needle and sew squares for a quilt, and how to file her fingernails. She thought I'd be a good manicurist when I grew up. I also learned about folding egg whites and angel food cakes. Butch said I was like a sprawly newborn calf that wants to start running right away, the way I always wanted to learn new stuff.

I only got to stay overnight at Butch and Grandpa's house a few times, since Grandpa didn't like us little vermin. I never wet the bed and that was one of the main reasons why they let me stay overnight and not any of the other kids. One time I stayed over and drank a whole glass of lemonade before bed. Then I had to get up and pee in the night. So I tiptoed into the bathroom. It was full of candles. They were all in a circle around the big diamond on the floor. The diamond sparkled when I peed. Then I looked up and saw Grandpa standing in the doorway holding his machete. He said, "What are you doing up?"

"Just to pee," I said.

Then he said, "You get on back to bed." I ran as fast as I could.

In the morning, I asked Butch what the candles were for. She said, "Oh Lordy, I've never seen a girl the likes of you." She wouldn't tell me what Grandpa was using the machete for either.

Butch never talked much about Grandpa. They didn't say much to each other either. Grandpa mostly just sat in his leather chair and smoked his pipe. He lit it with matches all the time and dropped them into his brown ashtray, which was big enough for his other pipes to sit in too. None of us kids were supposed to touch his ashtray. Grandpa said we'd get everything dirty with our grubby little mitts if we did. But that ashtray was see-through and smooth and made you want to touch it anyway. It sat by his chair where the magazines were.

The only thing he ever did besides smoke and read magazines was work in his shop down in their basement. That's where he kept his machete. It had a hole in its handle and hung on a nail on the wall for safekeeping.

I went down there once after I stayed overnight and asked him if I could chop something with it. He was sharpening his saw with a tiny file and didn't look at me. He said, "You go ask Butch. I'm not the one that decides anything around here and I don't want your Mom to come yelling at me about God knows what."

I came over closer to look at those teeny saw teeth. You could see them getting sharper every second. I said, "Can I help do that?"

"No, you can go upstairs now and stop bugging me. This is no place for little girls." Then he started coughing hard and had to bend over his shop sink and made that scratchy sound to spit something out. He pushed his hand toward the door and said, "Get on now!" His voice was rough and croaky.

I went back upstairs and asked Butch about chopping with the machete. She said, "When you're older."

"How old?"

"Old enough. Now it's time for you to go back home or Fiona will get worried."

Grandpa always coughed, but none of us knew he was sick. Not even Mom. Because we just thought it was from smoking. Us kids wondered why he was getting so skinny and asked Mom. She said she wondered too, and if he wasn't so damn stubborn, he'd go see a doctor like she said he should.

We knew for sure that something was wrong when he went to the hospital. I only saw him there once. It was about a week before he died. Butch was already there. He didn't look one bit like Grandpa. For one thing, he had long tubes stuck up his nose. I asked Mom what they were for. "To give him air," she said. For another thing, he was wearing a short nightie. "A hospital gown," Mom said. I could tell he was real sick or he'd never let anyone put that nightgown on him.

You could see his wrinkles everywhere, not just on his face. They were even on his legs and arms. There were so many wrinkles that they laid on top of each other.

He was staring at the wall, even when we were in front of it. He wasn't looking at any of us. But was staring at something. It was something the rest of us couldn't see. Butch said that people do that before they die. They look at the spirits on the other side and find out who's on their side and who isn't. That way they know who they have to fight after they die. She thought Grandpa would be OK because he was a good fighter when he had to be.

Butch said that he also had her to help him. I asked her, "How can you help when you aren't even there?" She smiled a sneaky smile and said, "I know my way around. You know, here and there aren't that far apart."

"But how do you do it?"

"It's kind of like praying. But without prayer words."

It didn't look like Grandpa was praying. Then Mom put a rosary in his hands. Now he was praying whether he liked it or not. Butch grabbed the rosary out of Grandpa's hands, but Mom grabbed it back. Then she looked at Butch and said we **all** had to kneel and start saying the rosary. Butch was spitting mad and left. She didn't come back.

You had to say one prayer for every one of those beads. I always wondered why you couldn't just say one Hail Mary and then say, "times fifty" instead of saying the Hail Mary fifty times. The same with the Our Fathers. But they weren't so bad since there were only five of them.

I never would have asked to come to visit Grandpa if I knew I'd have to do the rosary! Even if he was dying! I prayed for as long as I could, kneeling by the side of his hospital bed. Then I noticed a silver pedal on the side of the bed. I pressed down on it with my hand. It didn't move. Then I pushed hard with my knee and Grandpa's feet started to go up in the air. And the rest of him was just lying there. I stopped pushing that pedal right away, but his feet kept going up. He looked right at me and made a growling sound. Mom's eyes popped open. She looked at his feet and said, "That's it! Go stand outside until we're done! Both of you!" That meant me and Luann. At least we wouldn't have to finish the rosary.

We went out in the hall. Mom said, "Now stay **put!**" and closed the door.

Luann was standing there with her mouth hanging open. She said, "What made his feet go up?"

"Magic," I said. "Black magic."

12

CONVERSION

EIGHT YEARS

AFTER Grandpa died it was like a big party at our house for almost a week because Uncle Frank, Aunt Flora, and all of their kids came for the funeral. They came to our house a few days before the funeral because there was a lot of stuff to do. When you added up the eleven kids in our family with the ten in theirs, we had 21 kids total.

Every time Mom or Flora got pregnant the other one got pregnant too. They would have had exactly the same number of kids, except one of Flora's died when it was a baby. They did it that way without even talking about it. How did they know? And what was it that got them pregnant anyway? I knew it had something to do with a man's sperm swimming inside the woman, but how did those sperm get inside? And how did Dad and Uncle Frank's sperm know to go swimming at the same time? No one would tell me.

And since Mom and Flora are twins and Dad and Frank are brothers their kids are all even closer to us than double cousins. We're almost like brothers and sisters except that we're still way different. They're bigger slobs than us, for one thing, and Dad is real nice compared with Frank. We're lucky to have a Dad who doesn't go all the way crazy when he loses his temper. Sure he hits us, but none of us have scars on our backs or legs.

Anyway, one big gang of us hung around together that whole week. In our family it was: Sonny, who was twelve and a half, Dean, who was eleven, Maureen, who was nine and a half, me, who was eight, and Billy who was six and a half. Their family was: Mickey, who was thirteen, Martin, who was eleven and a half, Elsie, who was nine, Dale, who was seven and a half, and Theresa, who was six.

Mickey was the meanest. Dale was closest to my age, but since he was kind of holy and wanted to go into the seminary, Maureen played with him. So I played with Elsie, who had her own pony at their house.

I know we were supposed to be sad because of Grandpa, but how can you be gloomy when it's more fun than your birthday for a whole week? Frank and Flora brought sausage, ham, and blueberry peach pies. We had at least one yummy thing to eat every day and no one was watching us, or telling us when to go to bed. Because Mom got to talk the whole time with Flora, and Dad had Frank to go do things with. Everything was bright and shiny new. How can you be sad when colors jump right out at you and smile? And you get the tingle feeling that shoots in and out of you like dancing sparks.

Mom and Flora were sad though. And Butch didn't say much. Her face was white and she didn't shine one bit. It looked like she forgot her rouge. The three of them had to do a bunch of stuff before the funeral. I helped them a little.

I was at Butch's house showing Flora the quilt squares I sewed with Butch a couple of weeks before Grandpa went into the hospital. All of the squares had bright patterns, but the background was always black. We were alone in the sewing area for a few minutes and I asked Flora, "Why do you think Butch always makes her quilts with all that black?"

Flora said, "It's the way her mind works. Black is just part of it. She likes it that way."

Later on, Mom, Flora, and Butch were sorting through Grandpa's pipes. They were going to bury him with one of his pipes in his hand and had to decide which one. I came over to help and picked up his clean brown ashtray. It was cool against my nose and forehead and made the whole world look golden dark. I set it down and pulled open the drawer underneath his ashtray.

There was a whole box full of tobacco. Some of it was the kind we always gave him for Christmas. The sweet kind. The kind that Santa Claus would smoke if he was real and smoked a pipe. But Grandpa wasn't one bit like Santa. He wouldn't even try the sweet kind. His tobacco was the sharp kind that smelled brownish-green. It was like getting your nose stabbed with stinkweed milk. No wonder Grandpa died from it.

I lifted up a pack of the sweet kind and said, "Butch, how come he wouldn't try the good kind?"

She ignored me.

"Why did he just smoke the icky sourpuss kind?"

Butch looked up from the pipes and said, "You show respect for the dead. They can hear everything."

I looked down and said, "I didn't say **he** was a sourpuss."

Butch glared at me and said, "You think it's a joke?"

I smiled a little and said, "Kind of. Because he's dead and he can't do anything anyway, and besides, why would he care about anything I said?" I was glad Mom was there. I knew she wasn't going to make me shut up.

Butch was starting to shine a little. Her voice came like smooth knives, "The dead care all right. They care about more than you know or ever want to know. And when you talk about them, you ask them to come close. You best stay on the good side of spirits or keep your mouth shut."

Mom said, "Don't start scaring her."

Flora turned to me and said, "Your Grandpa isn't going anywhere. He's already with Christ."

Butch shook her head. I could tell she was mad at all of us. Her knife voice was stabbing a little. She looked at me and said, "You're a smart girl. So listen to me. They can breathe on you. On the back of your neck, down your spine and…."

"That's **enough**." Now Mom was fed up with Butch. She grabbed my arm and said, "We're leaving this instant!"

Flora said quietly to Mom, "I'll stay here a few more minutes and finish this up." We left.

Well, that shut me up, but Mom was still hopping mad and talked the whole time we walked back to our house. She told me how Grandpa had jumped on her all the time for her faith. Just like Butch did. He thought she was stupid for becoming a Catholic and even more stupid for having all those kids. But right before he died, he begged to be baptized and became a Catholic.

I was glad he wasn't going to limbo or to hell but wondered if he was breathing down on Mom's neck right then. I brushed away the cobwebby feeling on the back of my neck and told Mom, "See you at home." I ran so hard the wind blew, all the way back to the house.

When Mom came inside, she was nibbling on some chocolate. She made a grocery list and bit another piece off of the bar she was hiding in her dress. I was drooling for that chocolate. I knew I'd never get a bite if I begged. About ten minutes later Flora came back and they decided to go into town and get groceries.

I asked if I could come along and bring my little brother Jason too and I'd take care of him the whole time and that way he'd get a real good nap and they could talk all they wanted. Mom said OK I could go, but I had to be quiet as a mouse and not be asking questions every two minutes while she was trying to drive.

I laid in the back seat with Jason. He was a little over a year old. I fed him his bottle even though he could hold it by himself. I knew we needed a new baby before Jason got too much older. He was tired after his bottle and was wiggling around like a crabby little worm. I just held onto him real nice while he kicked and pushed at me. That way he'd take a nap for sure and not be howling all afternoon and making everyone miserable.

After he settled down a little, Mom handed me a piece of chocolate. I held Jason, got to listen to Flora and Mom talk, and licked at the chocolate, all at the same time.

"What a relief that he joined the Church before it was too late," Flora said. She sounded tired.

"And a Glory to God." Mom sounded even more tired.

"Truly, it was a miracle. He was **so** set against it. What do you suppose made it possible?" Flora had that wavery wispy way of asking a question.

"He ran out of excuses. And with death staring him in the face there was nowhere to turn but to God Almighty," Mom said.

"I'm surprised Butch didn't interfere," Flora said.

"Butch was nowhere to be found during those last few days. I have no idea where she was. All I know is she wasn't at our house. And certainly wasn't with her husband in his time of need." Mom sounded like she was telling on Butch. It made me wonder what Butch **was** doing during Grandpa's time of need. And what he would need anyway, since he was already dying.

"She probably just couldn't face it all," Flora added.

"Well maybe she could have, if she wasn't so busy thinking she was the one in charge rather than God. As if she can deal with all of life's mysteries on her own, with her twisted magic and Godforsaken ideas." Now Mom was making it sound like Butch was rotten and pathetic all at the same time. But being in charge and knowing all about magic sounded pretty good to me.

"She has no idea what it's like to have the Lord's protection," Flora said.

"She may not think she has to account for anything, but she'll have her time of reckoning when she comes face to face with her Maker." I hated it when Mom got that holy sound. It made you hope she'd never get the idea to pray for you. The warm chocolate that was melting all over my tongue, turned bitter-sour for a minute.

"Did Dad, did he really ask for the priest?" Flora asked. I wondered about that too – why he'd ask for the priest when he thought they were all so stupid.

"In so many words, he did ask. At the very end. Before that it was a fight. He didn't want to be baptized, but the more we talked, the more he opened up. It was really the promise of peace that comes with the Last Rites that he craved. And of course no priest would give the Last Rites unless the person was baptized first. He knew that.

"It was something about the rosary, you know, the one that the Pope blessed, that changed everything. Dad was so thin and pale in the hospital bed. And when I put the rosary in his hand, he had such a look of peace that came over him. His hands clung to the rosary even when it was time for me to go. So I kissed the crucifix and told him it was his." Mom sighed like it was the best thing you could ever give someone.

"That was such a wonderful gift." Flora sighed too, like she was smiling.

"The last time I came to visit him, he'd been coughing so hard there was blood on his gown and his face was blue. I put the rosary into his hand again and asked him if it was finally time to call the priest. He coughed hard again and nodded yes. And that's when he was baptized and received the Last Rites.

"Flora, I can't begin to describe the look on his face after the sacraments. It was like the battle was over. You could feel it in the air, that he was ready to die. And would be delivered into the hand of the Lord." Mom was wiping her eyes with Kleenex.

"I wished I could have been there," Flora said.

"I do too, Sis." Mom reached out her hand and squeezed Flora's. They both cried a little. I just snuggled Jason closer but made sure not to wake him up. I liked listening to Mom and Flora when they talked like that, saying things maybe they'd only say to each other because they forgot I was there. But even so, all that talk about crucifixes, sacraments, and dying reminded me too much of church and ghosts, and I started to get sleepy.

"Hmmm," Flora was almost humming. "Maybe it's just as well Butch wasn't there with her pagan views at the end, to muddy the waters for him."

"You know, there's always hope for her too."

Flora hummed some more and said, "Let's bury Dad with that rosary you gave him."

"I'd like that. If Butch doesn't make a scene about it."

"We'll see."

"Yeah. We'll see."

I could barely understand the rest of what they said because it was all blurring together the way everything does when you almost fall asleep.

13

DEFILING

EIGHT YEARS

TWO days before Grandpa's funeral Sonny, Dean, Maureen, me, and Billy, along with our cousins, Mickey, Martin, Elsie, and Dale, all got kicked out of the house for a whole day. We'd been running, laughing, screaming, teasing, crying, and howling like wild monkeys all morning. After one of us kicked over the milk bucket, three kids slipped and fell and milk got tracked all over the house. Mom and Flora told us to stay the hell outside with the other wild animals until it was time for dinner. And if we tried to come back in before then, we could spend the night outside too.

We walked out to the far end of the pasture where the cows were chewing their cuds. That's where the irrigation ditch leaked and it was always muddy. We could take off our shoes and dig holes in the black slimy mud or just ooze it through our toes.

On the way, our cousins started bragging about how they had a real farm with horses and this was nothing compared to how much land they had. They had a real creek going by their house too, not just an irrigation ditch. But we had a train that came by three times a day and a motel and our house was cleaner and we were closer to the city.

They had featherbeds though, and we just had blankets. But those featherbeds weren't just for fun. They needed thick featherbeds because rats came into their bedrooms at night and tried to chew through the quilts and on their feet. Our cousins knew how to kick rats in their sleep. They were all bragging about it. So what? I could learn to do that too. We all could. Except for maybe the babies.

Then they told us about the big hole in their bathroom floor. It had rats that came up from underneath the house and you could fall in the hole if you didn't watch out. I didn't much like the idea of falling down a scummy rat hole in the middle of the night just because I wanted to pee and not wet my bed.

Their house was rotting apart, but it was huge. Ours wasn't even a house and we were crammed in like sardines, but we had four bathrooms with no holes in the floor. Best and worst were hard to tell apart and if it wasn't for Uncle Frank's German temper, which was a hundred times worse than Dad's, I might have even wanted to switch families for a while.

The mud in the pasture was too cold to squish our feet into and no one felt like getting caught in a water fight because we didn't have any way to get dry clothes. Clouds were coming and going fast with the breeze. They were perfect for the *Icky-Pretty* game. But no one wanted to sit outside that long. It was sunny but too cold. And we were getting hungry.

We had some figuring to do. Sonny got Dean to sneak inside the house and steal us some food. Then we figured out how to hide, stay warm, and show our cousins the motel all at the same time. It was simple. Number 9. It was my idea and it wasn't a bad one, but it made me feel dry and scooped out inside. We took off for Number 9. Billy stayed by the house to tell Dean where we went.

We stopped to get a drink from the hose underneath Number 9's kitchen window. Then it was time. Sonny went first. He climbed onto the cement blocks that went up to the window, opened it, and we all crawled in. I hadn't been in there since Mom's breakdown. It was as dusty and mice poopy as ever. The dust gagged my throat and made it scratchy.

The green couch in the living room was still there and in front of it, in the middle of the living room, was Grandpa's golden-brown ashtray with a pile of ashes in it. The ashes were barely crumpled. It looked like they were made from burnt paper. Dean poked at the ashes and they broke apart. Little white bones were buried under the ash in the bottom of the dish. The bones looked burned and were a lot smaller than chicken bones.

"What kind of bones are they?" I said. "They're so little."

My cousin Martin said, "Maybe they're kitten bones."

"Or rat bones," Dean said.

Sonny said, "Or little tiny baby bones." They all laughed.

I ignored them. I picked up one of the long bones and blew the ash off it. It was so white. Maybe it was just a ghost of nothing bone. It reminded me of the white pill I found in there two years ago. I hid that pill for a long time and then when no one was around, I went into Mom's medicine cabinet and compared it with the ones in her bottles. It was called Miltown. I never did know what it was for, but sometimes she'd say, "Oh I forgot to take my Miltown."

I put the white bone in my pocket and looked around. I didn't see any shells in the living room, but there were still a few feathers. Maybe they were the ones from two years ago that just kept swirling and never got caught. Maybe they were new.

Dean and Billy came in through the window with a monster block of cheese and three boxes of crackers. Sonny used his pocketknife to cut the cheese and every time he did, one of the other boys made fart sounds because he was *cutting the cheese*. Like it was a new joke every time. What did cutting the cheese ever have to do with farts anyway? And why are boys such pigs?

I ate a little of the yellow cheese. The end of it was dry and greasy, the way cheese gets when you leave it in a mousetrap for too long. I whispered to Maureen, "Who do you think is leaving all this weird stuff in here?"

She said, "Probably one of the tenants. They sneak in here at night when we aren't looking."

I said, "How? How could any of them even get in here?"

"Well, it wasn't anyone in **our** family, so who, pray tell, could it be, other than tenants?"

"I don't know, but that's the stupidest idea I ever heard." Maureen started talking to Dale. She was no use anyway. I could figure it out by myself.

While everyone else was sitting in the living room flicking mouse poop at each other, telling dumb jokes, and showing off, I went with my cousin Elsie into the bedroom. I was looking for clues to something.

But I had no idea what. The bedroom was like a lure. And even though I didn't want to be lured, I also didn't want to miss something that might be there. My head felt fuzzy except for the sharp feeling right in the middle of it.

The bed in the bedroom was gone. We opened the closet. I'd never looked in there before. It was bigger than any closet in our house or any of the other units. How come? Then I remembered that it was where Grandpa and Butch lived before their house got built. Grandpa helped build Number 9 and since it was an end unit, they could make it different. They made a lot of things different in Number 9.

There were about eight or ten old hat boxes on the closet floor. Some of them were half opened. And the thing is, those boxes had almost no dust on them. And no cobwebs. Clean boxes. Where did they come from? Elsie and I checked every one of them. But they were all empty.

Something tickled the top of my head. I jumped and my guts lurched too. I jerked my neck up and saw that it was just the string hanging down from a light bulb. Not a spirit. Then my stomach burped up a thick glob of oily cheese. I swallowed and hoped it would stay put this time.

Elsie pulled on the light bulb string. The light showed dusty cobwebs hanging off those grayish-green walls. Especially in the corners. One end of the closet went farther than the other one. We walked toward the long end and pushed the hat boxes out of our way.

The wall at the end looked just regular until you got close. Then you could see a little brown latch that was almost in the corner. I turned it and pulled. The whole end of the closet was really a door that I swung open. There were three empty shelves behind the door. That must have been where the boxes came from. Secret boxes.

My head was jolting with one question then another. But they all stayed inside my brain. I thought hard about Butch and Grandpa while I rubbed the smooth bone in my pocket. Elsie didn't say much. She just wanted to go back in the other room where the other kids were because Number 9 was giving her the creeps.

We went back in the living room and the other kids were getting ready to go back outside. They left a few Ritz crackers on the couch. I decided to feed the mice before we left. I crushed the rest of the crackers with my foot. Then I scooped them up, went around the edge of the room, and sprinkled where the Aruba shells were from a long time ago. I sprinkled them and said:

Mouse and rat
Skinny or fat
I've got a treat
So come to eat
Be my spy
And tell me why

I didn't think when I was saying it. The words just rolled out and my insides weren't so sour anymore. I made my initials in the dust and hurried to catch up with the rest of the kids who were all out the window by now. I didn't know if I wanted to leave yet, but no way did I want to be in Number 9 by myself.

It wasn't time to go back home yet and we had to figure out what next. We stood around, shivered, and kicked little rocks at each other until someone got an idea. This time it was Billy. He wanted to try out Grandpa's machete. He'd been trying to get his hands on that machete for a long time. We all had. And now Grandpa was dead, Butch was at the funeral parlor, and that machete was all alone, hanging in the basement with all of his other tools we never got to touch.

The basement door squeaked when it opened. Some sunshine came in right on Grandpa's workbench and right beside it was the machete, hanging from its nail. Sonny said we couldn't turn on any power tools and to make sure and put things back so we didn't get caught later on. Then everyone started picking up cool stuff.

My oldest boy cousin, Mickey, went straight to the machete and snatched it off the nail. He slashed it around like he was a mean ugly pirate. I watched him and he stared at me like I was supposed to act scared and look away. I didn't. He started slashing the machete at my legs and I jumped. He laughed and I stuck my tongue out at him. He lifted the machete close to my neck and moved it real slow, like he was going to slice my head off. He was grinning like a maniac and I remembered what Butch said about men and knives. My legs started to shake. I hoped the machete wasn't too sharp.

I knew Mickey did worse stuff to Elsie than Sonny ever did to me. But he did it in private and he wouldn't really cut me in front of everyone, would he? I had to think fast. Then I remembered the way Mom said men like to be heroes. Then I did a totally disgusting girl thing that I hope I never do again.

I stared at Mickey and whined real loud, "Sonnnnyyyy, Mickey's trying to kill me." I heard Sonny walk over. He slugged Mickey in the arm and took the machete away. Mom was right! I smiled real snotty at Mickey while Sonny hung the machete back on the nail. Then Mickey slugged me in the arm. But just once.

Billy came over and grabbed the machete. I yanked it away from him and told him to be careful because I was the Queen of the Amazons now, and he was just a pygmy scab. He found a scythe and we played swords. I wouldn't let him have a turn until he promised to be a good slave for me after dinner that night and to cross his heart and stick a needle in his eye if he didn't. He was never a good slave, but I gave him the machete anyway. My arm was tired.

Billy was grunting and swinging his head like a goat that ate too many tin cans. The machete was whizzing. I told him to be careful. He told me to help him get some wood so he could chop, like in the jungle. So we got a long two by four and balanced it on top of an anvil, which happened to already be sitting on the floor.

Before I knew what was happening, he lifted the machete way up in the air and screamed, "Hiiii-Yaaa!!!" The machete slammed down into one end of the two by four and the other end of the board flew up and cracked him on the head. He fell over, onto the machete blade, which was stuck in the wood, and all of a sudden there was red blood. A lot of it. From the back part of his thigh. I had no idea the blade was **that** sharp.

Billy started screaming, "Mommmmyyyyyy, I'm **bleeeeeding!**" Everyone came over to look at the gash. It was bad. The skin was hanging open so you could see the bloody muscle underneath like when you butcher. Now we'd all get in trouble for sure.

Sonny said, "Way to go, runt," and put Billy on his back.

Maureen told him to hold on. Then Sonny said, "Don't let him bleed on me." I found a rag that looked clean and tried to sop up the blood. I held the rag close to Billy's leg while we hurried back to the house.

Dean ran ahead and told Mom that Billy got hurt. She and Flora were both waiting for us at the door. Mom told Sonny to put him on the kitchen table. She felt the bump on his head while Flora looked close at his slashed leg. Mom said, "Put him in the car. He's going to have to see the Doctor. Sis, will you come along? Sonny, we need you to carry him. And Maureen, you come too and get a few diapers so he doesn't bleed on the car seat." Why did Maureen get to go when I was the best nurse?

After they left, the rest of us huddled in the living room and took turns guessing what kind of trouble we were in. That's when Butch came back from the funeral parlor. She'd been gone a long time and wanted to know where Mom and Flora were. Dean told her about Billy and she wanted to know where the machete was. I said, "In the basement."

"You come with me right now, Tracie."

I sat in Butch's clean car in the front seat, where I'd never been before. I was so skittery sorry I didn't know what to do. I chewed my knuckle. It only took a minute to get to her house. Everything was fizzy inside. Butch looked like she meant business. Bitter sharp business. What was she going to do when she saw the tools lying all over and the machete on the floor? I walked behind her into the basement. She whirled around and said in a soft hissy voice, "How could you do this to your Grandfather? You know all of this was his. You defile him when you defile what's his."

Defile? What was that? It sounded bad. I said through my knuckle, "We were just playing with it. We weren't defiling."

She turned and looked right at me, holding my wrist hard in her hands. "You **were** defiling. Don't lie to me or I'll slap your lying face. I thought I could trust you. Of all people."

It stung worse than any slap. The fizzies inside all popped and I started crying, "I just thought since he was dead..."

"Haven't you been listening to me? The dead aren't dead. They never rest. They're all around, busy with things you know nothing about." She grabbed my chin and pulled it up so I saw right up her nose. "If you aren't careful, you start things you don't know how to finish. Are you listening to me?" Her eyes were too much like knives. I looked at the hairs in her nose. She yanked my chin again and this time her voice cut all the way in, "Tracie, do you understand me?"

I looked at her eyes for only a second and said what she wanted me to. "Yes."

Then she kissed me on each cheek. Her hands were soft again and she pulled me real close. Her hands petted my face and then my back. She hugged and kissed me until I was like warm dough that you could push your fist through. I closed my eyes and let the icky sweet dough wrap over everything. Butch pulled me closer and I could feel the bone from Number 9 in my pocket. I still didn't understand, but after a while, I didn't care and all my questions were gone.

14

FUZZY FAITH

EIGHT YEARS

AT the funeral home the afternoon before Grandpa's funeral, they propped up the top half of the casket so everyone could take turns staring at him. He looked like a wrinkly old baby in his bassinet with all that white satin and frilly lace. His gray head looked dead, but his hands didn't. The rosary Mom gave him was looped into one of his hands and a fancy pipe was in the other. His hands were folded on top of each other and looked like they were ready to get up and do a wiggle dance all over his dead body.

I kept an eye on those hands even when I looked at his mouth and nose and eyes. I don't know why, but my hand reached out to barely touch his forehead. That's when one of his fingers moved. That finger said, "You try to touch me again and I'll show you *all about* spirits." I pulled my hand away fast.

Georgina pushed me to keep going so the other people in line could see how dead he was too. I took a few steps and when I was almost past the casket, I looked back. One of his eyes opened for a second like he was winking to make everything a scary joke. When I got back to my seat, I could only see the silvery side of the casket. Nothing else moved except for the people in line.

Then we had to say the whole rosary. It wasn't as bad as usual because they had thick reddish-purple pads on the kneelers. That's because it was a mostly Protestant funeral home. Mom said those kneelers told you a lot about Protestants and their faith. That they wouldn't think of offering up something as minuscule as sore prayer bones, which is what she called our knees, as a sacrifice for Jesus. Those Protestants just **had** to have padded kneelers.

Afterwards, everyone came to Butch's house for a big party. The ladies from the church brought food. They also got the idea that Butch was going to become a Catholic too, because Grandpa converted right before he died. Butch said she thought Mom tricked Grandpa when he could hardly talk or think straight. And those church ladies were like flies buzzing around that she'd just as soon hit with a fly swatter. But she knew she had to act like she had manners.

I ate a lot of the German potato salad, chicken noodle casserole, and red Jell-o with baby marshmallows as fast as I could, and then ran outside to play with the other kids until it got dark. Billy got to be referee because he had stitches and wasn't supposed to be running or getting hit. But everyone ignored him because he was too little to know anything. Even though it was cold outside, we were all running so hard playing *Red Rover, Red Light-Green Light,* and *Tag* that it didn't matter.

We waited for *Dog Pile* until after Mom told us the first time to all come in and Flora yelled the second time that she wasn't going to say it again! Then everyone except Billy crashed into a pile on top of each other and started tickling. You'd do anything to keep from getting stuck on the bottom. So there was a lot of tickling, hitting, kicking, and screaming. Usually, one of the little kids got squished and we'd call them a crybaby and everyone would go inside. This time there were three crybabies because there were too many kids, but I wasn't one of them.

Maureen, Elsie, and me were laughing when we walked inside because Elsie's brother, Dale, got his pants almost pulled off in the dog pile. We were still giggling when we flopped on the floor in the living room. Elsie rolled over to grab a pillow while I was lying on part of her shirt. Her shirt pulled part way off her shoulder like she was a teenage glamour girl. I pulled my shirt down off my shoulder too and we looked at each. Then we both busted out laughing. Maureen wasn't quite sure what we were laughing about, but it was contagious. After a while, we were all rolling on the floor with stomachaches and drooling from laughing so hard. All we had to do was look at each other and it was hysterics.

Sonny and Mickey came in and shuffled their feet like they were going to kick us in the sides for laughing on the floor like idiots. Maureen started to try and say something, but it came out so silly we were like hyenas all over again. Sonny and Mickey got sick of us and walked out. We laughed so hard it was almost like crying. When we were finally done, we didn't even know what was so funny. But we were nicer to each other afterward. Even Maureen and me.

The next day was the Requiem Mass for Grandpa. It's a good thing I got to laugh the day before because a Requiem Mass is just black, black, black. Grandpa's casket was closed and had a black shroud on it with a big gold cross on top. Butch was whispering and spitting through her red lipstick to Mom when they were walking to the pews. She was mad that it was a Catholic funeral, but Mom said it's what Grandpa wanted and that it was his dying wish. Butch said he wasn't in his right mind or he'd never let a priest even touch him. Then they sat down.

Frank, Dad, Mom, Flora, and Butch all sat together. I didn't want to sit next to any of them so I got stuck in between Maureen and Luann. On one side of the altar was a statue of Mary with Baby Jesus. On the other side was Grown Up Jesus with his stabbed side and his heart bleeding from thorns stuck in it. The windows were yellowish-brown so you couldn't look outside. They started burning the incense so much it made cloud layers all the way up to the ceiling. My throat got thick inside from it. I stared up at the incense clouds and wished I was a cloud and could float right out the window where it was blue and cool.

Then out of nowhere a whoosh of wind came in one of the top windows. It turned the smoke into ghosts. One of them had fangs and another had a witch face with skin rotting off. I closed my eyes, but they were there inside my eyes too. A boy ghost came screaming at me with a machete. They were all swooping down on me. I opened my eyes again and they were gone. But I was still shaking and wondered where those ghosts came from.

After a few minutes, the shaky feeling was mostly in my stomach. I was real tired and knew that the smoke was just incense smoke again. It looked greenish-brown and smelled like Grandpa's pipe. Then I remembered some of the nice things Grandpa did for me. Like taking me along on a trip once with just Butch and him to see Frank and Flora and my cousins. And buying me a Coke. And stopping the car when I had to pee and not yelling at me for it.

I felt a soft floaty feeling on the back of my neck that didn't scare me now. It felt good, like Grandpa when he was nice, which was almost never but was, sometimes. I closed my eyes again and prayed to him to make all the bad ghosts go away. I promised I'd believe in him from then on if he did. Then I saw him inside my eyes. And he wasn't dead. He looked just like himself, only better and stronger. He gave me a grouchy smile and nodded. The rest of the Mass wasn't too bad.

Two days later, Frank, Flora, and all their kids left. It was a weird kind of empty. There was nothing to do at our house and I felt like a cold soggy sock, dangling there with no foot to make me go. Then Mom came out of her bedroom with a bunch of cleaning supplies. She had on work pants and a red scarf around her head. Mom was going to do some work! She looked around the kitchen table where a few of us kids were sitting and asked me, "I'm going to clean out Number 9. Tracie, do you want to help?"

I jumped a mile in the air. "Just me?"

"Yeah."

I looked around at everyone else and smiled. She asked me because everyone knew I was the best helper. And now we'd get to be alone together and I could talk to her the whole time we cleaned. I could see she was in a good mood. That's the way she always was after being with Flora. They were like ice cream for each other.

She was whistling as we walked. I asked, "Why are we cleaning Number 9?"

"Because it's time to rent it out."

"Why wasn't it time before?"

"Because I was too tired."

"Why aren't you too tired now?"

"Because."

I knew better than to ask 'because why.' Then I remembered the weird stuff in Number 9. All those big questions about Mom and Butch and Voodoo jumped up from my brain and slammed into each other. Even though everything was buzzing and my stomach was already jumping, I knew this was my best chance so far to find out some things. I said, "Mom, how long has it been since you went up to Number 9?"

"A long time."

"Does anyone else get to go up there?"

"No one else has a key. Why?"

"I dunno, I was just wondering if anyone else had a passkey or ever got to go in there because I **know** us kids aren't supposed to."

She turned her head to look at me like I was suspicious. I was scared she'd ask me another question and then I might end up in big trouble whether I lied or not. We were walking up the steps to Number 9 and she stopped for a minute. Now I knew she wasn't going to ask me anything. She had her eyes closed and I could see she was praying. Then she used the passkey to open the door. It was nice not crawling through the window.

The living room was dark, the way it always was. Then Mom pulled the drapes and some tiny feathers whooshed up. I'd never been in there with the drapes open. You could see everything. It was light and even dustier than ever. The couch was a golden-green color now but still ugly.

Then I saw the Ritz crackers I sprinkled! I'd forgotten all about them. A lot of them were gone, but you could still see the circle. And my initials!! I walked over to where you could still see TS and wiggled my feet. I hoped Mom didn't notice. I pointed to the ashes and burned bones and said, "What's that?"

She crouched down, ran her fingers over the edge of the ashtray and picked up one of the bones. Then she tilted her head and looked up at the ceiling. I looked up too. There was a chalky, light blue circle on the ceiling. It was so light you might not even notice it if the drapes were closed. I said, "What is it?"

"I'm not sure, but it has all the markings of   and her pagan hand-iwork." It was weird to hear Mom say it out loud.

"Butch?" I asked it like I never once thought of it myself.

"I'll never understand her. That chalk circle looks harmless enough and the cracker circle isn't like her at all but these ashes and bones... in Dad's ashtray..."

"Yeah, do you think they're Voodoo?"

"Don't believe everything you hear, Tracie. It's all just the workings of a superstitious mind. It's only when the mind gets twisted that..."

"What then?"

"Then you have to get rid of what's warped." She stood up, got the broom and told me to get the garbage can and wastebasket. It took only a couple of minutes to whisk the bones, ash, and crackers into the garbage. She stashed the ashtray with the cleaning supplies and smiled. She said, "Well, that's that." I was glad that was that.

We walked into the kitchen and she started writing things on a piece of paper. "What are you writing?" I asked.

"Things we need to buy before we can rent it out. Let me know if you think of anything as we go."

We went into the bathroom next and just looked around. I gave her my ideas for towels, and toilet paper. Everything was OK until we went into the bedroom.

I remembered how maybe Mom tried to kill herself in this same room. And now here she was, bright and sunny and we were clean-ing things up. Together. Only something howling sad was still there in that bedroom and it pushed into me. I remembered the Miltown I found on the floor after Mom left for her breakdown and remem-bered being so little and yucky with Mom gone and no one would tell me anything.

Mom yanked at the dark blue curtains on the bedroom window. They snagged and tore a little. She said, "Damn curtains."

"I hate those curtains too, Mom."

"Now I'll have to make new ones, dammit. And you know how I hate sewing." Then she jerked really hard and pulled them all the way down. They laid in a pile at her feet. "It's about time we got some light in here."

I could tell her good mood was gone. Her voice had sharp edges splintered all the way through it again. She opened up the closet and pulled the light on. The door to the secret shelves was still open and the boxes were scattered everywhere. I asked, "Do you think those boxes are Butch's too and what was in them and why did she need secret shelves and…."

"Tracie, just stop with the questions. I've had enough right now." Her hands were shaking a little and her face had that sucked in look again. She was looking for something. Her hands reached around in her pants pockets and came out empty. She seemed worried when she didn't find it in her blouse pocket either. I asked, "What is it you can't find, Mom?"

Her voice was shaky, "Would you be a real darlin' and run back to the house and get my rosary? I must have left it on my nightstand. And come back as fast as you can."

"OK, Mom. As fast as I can."

I ran to the house and found a rosary on the floor beside her bed. It was her glow-in-the-dark one that was light as a feather. I tore back to Number 9 and when I went into the bedroom, she was slouched onto the floor. I gave her the rosary. "Is this the right one?"

She smiled a sad sweet smile. "Thanks darlin'," she whispered. I sat down beside her and she put her hand on mine. I couldn't tell what anything was. She was never nice and sad at the same time.

"Are you OK, Mom?"

"I'll be OK. I just got shaken up there."

"I hope you won't take a bunch of Miltown again."

"What do you know about that?"

"Just that that's why you had to go away. From taking too much Miltown." I didn't say the part about her maybe trying to kill herself.

"I'm sorry you had to know anything about that. I was so depressed and…" Tears were dribbling out of her eyes. She didn't even try to get rid of them. After a minute or so she shook her shoulders and arms and said, "You have to fight depression. You can't give in to it. It's like a hole you have to dig yourself out of, and if you don't, no one else will. Remember that."

"Is that what you do?"

"It's what I try to do. And sometimes I just get too tired. But you have to get up anyway. No matter how tired you are. And sometimes the only thing you have is your faith." She squeezed the rosary.

I thought hard about everything she said. We just sat there with our backs against the wall, our legs on the dirty floor, and our arms pressed against each other.

"Mom?"

"What is it?"

"What about when people around you don't have faith. What do you do then?"

"You have to pray for them."

"What if they don't want you to pray for them?

"They just don't know that they want you to."

I wondered about that, but my brain got too fuzzy trying to figure out how someone could actually want you to pray for them when they were practically screaming at the top of their lungs that they really hated it when you did. I got nowhere.

Then there was this bad stink smell in the air. I asked Mom, "Did you do that?"

"Not me." But I could see her smile a little the way she always did when she did it and you knew she did and she knew you knew, but she still wouldn't admit it.

"Me neither. I wonder who it could have been."

"Maybe it was a little ghost." Mom always said that when she was teasing.

"Maybe it was Grandpa."

"Maybe so. Maybe so."

15

Indulgences

ALMOST NINE YEARS

IT was Good Friday and this was the day you could get a plenary indulgence the easy way, just by going to Benediction and saying five Hail Mary's and the Apostle's Creed. Benediction was a snap. It was at noon and only lasted about twenty minutes. Just the right amount of time to say your plenary indulgence prayers, sing the best songs they ever had in church, and still not have your knees hurt too bad from kneeling.

I needed the plenary indulgence real bad because all my sins from the last year were stacked up on my soul. Even though when you went to confession you got your sins forgiven, you still had to go to purgatory for those same sins if you died. Purgatory was just like hell, only you didn't have to stay there forever. I sure didn't want to go there for even a day if I died because the fire there would cook your skin until it looked like fried pork rinds, which taste pretty good but not when it's your own skin. And they'd torture you worse than the communists ever would and you'd scream and scream and no one would lift a finger until you paid good for those sins, which weren't even that much fun to commit anyway, but sometimes you couldn't help it.

In one of the books we got at catechism, it listed all the prayers you could say, and how much indulgence you got for each prayer. Indulgence was how many days you got taken off your purgatory time for saying that prayer. Like for a Hail Mary, you got 120 days off of purgatory, and for the Our Father you got 180 days. The Apostle's

Creed, which was really long, was only about 60 days. That wasn't exactly a bargain.

My next youngest brother, Billy, and I used to see how many days we could collect by saying the shortest prayers with the most indulgences as fast as we could. I collected about 3,000 days once and he had almost as much. Then he said, "Now we probably have so many days we can do some sins for free because we probably have extra." That sounded good, but what if we still didn't have **enough** indulgences? Because they never gave a list of all the sins you could commit and how much purgatory you got for each one. Maybe it'd be a thousand years of purgatory just for pulling your sister's hair.

Then we learned about plenary indulgences. They were the best thing ever invented. One plenary indulgence wiped out all the purgatory time for every sin you ever committed. All those other indulgences were like nickels and dimes next to a bazillion dollar bill. It was like a miracle.

Even though you could give indulgences away, why would anyone do that? I kept them all to myself, especially if I got a plenary indulgence. Because I needed it worse than anyone else I knew. And it was the only for sure way to get your soul completely clean.

So I actually **wanted** to go to Benediction even though it was sunny outside and murky inside the church. We all kneeled. Since I knew it wouldn't last too long I tried to kneel the way you were supposed to, with your back straight up and your knees hard on the wood kneeler where it gave you knee bruises. Not sitting on your heels, not pushing your butt back against the seat, not hunched over the pew, and not wiggling around.

We sang "O Salutaris Hostia" and the priest took the host out of the tabernacle, which was like a little tent where the host lived. The host was flat, round, and was made out of just flour and water. But after it was blessed, it was a host and that made it the body and blood of Jesus Christ. Us Catholics believed it really was his body and blood and not just pretend like the Protestants. Mom said it was like a mystery that you never could figure out and shouldn't even try.

The priest put the host into the middle of this huge beautiful gold thing that was also flat and round and looked like the sun with all of its rays pouring out all over the whole world. My big sister, Becky, said it was called the Monstrance. That seemed like a pretty awful name for the only nice thing to look at in the whole church, except for the baby angels that flew around Mary's head and feet. All those gold rays in the Monstrance were supposed to make you think about how God's love poured out that way. But the sun made me feel like it loved me more than Jesus ever did. God never felt as good as the sun.

Anyway, the Monstrance always reminded me of the sun and that the sun was outside and I wasn't and in just a few more minutes I'd have no more purgatory left and then I could go out and jump around again. Of course, that's when I did my worst sins, when I was feeling good, so I'd have to be careful and make my clean soul last a little while.

Once the host was inside the Monstrance, the altar boys started the incense. There were about five or six altar boys, since it was Good Friday. They walked around swinging the gold incense burners that weren't really made of gold. The burners hung from long chains that were looped around the altar boys' hands. That way the boys could swing and rock those incense burners and get the smoke everywhere.

I always liked the first whiff of incense until it got so strong I knew I never wanted to smell frankincense again. Even though it was supposed to be a big deal present for the Baby Jesus from one of those kings, I bet he didn't like it either.

They burnt so much incense that pretty soon you could hear people coughing and everything was hazy. Those altar boys never knew when to stop. But the smoke sort of glowed where the sun came in the window and looked like that picture of the Mormon guy who was in a forest standing in a smoky sunbeam when God talked to him. Then he started the Mormon Church.

We sang *Tantum Ergo* while the priest covered his hands with a fancy cape and lifted up the Monstrance. You were supposed to think about how Jesus was being tortured. And how he was being whipped with a whip that had little sharp nails on the end of it that dug all the way into the muscles in his back.

Just when you couldn't stand another second of torture or smoke, we started to sing *Holy God We Praise Thy Name*. And you knew

Benediction was almost over. It gave you the feeling of something good because you knew that pretty soon, you could run outside again. And on Good Friday, if you got a plenary indulgence, you knew you could die right then and not have to worry about one thing.

It was sunny outside and the sky was so blue you could fly right into it. But it was still Good Friday and you knew Jesus was hanging on the cross right then and would be dead at around three o'clock. So on the way out of the church another priest was waiting at the door to put ashes on your forehead so you wouldn't forget. And you weren't supposed to wash those ashes off either.

At dinner that night we all still had our ashes. Mom and the little kids had come to Benediction too. But on the little kids you couldn't tell what was dirt and what was ash smudge. Mom and Dad were fasting from solids until Easter Sunday, so they just drank coffee. The rest of us got Bisquick biscuits and pea soup. It didn't have any ham hocks because of no meat on Friday, especially Good Friday. Mom looked kind of serious and holy and I felt like I had a secret happiness inside that I knew I better not show anyone. But it snuck out anyway.

Luann and Francie, who were younger than me, were tickling each other and fell off the bench where they were sitting. Neither of them was hurt, but I think Mom wanted them to feel bad enough to start crying. Since they didn't, she said, "You know, Jesus died on this very day for all of our sins and the least you could do is show him some respect."

I said, "I don't think he died for mine."

"And why is that, Miss Sassy Pants?" Mom asked. Now I was in for it. But I didn't know for what.

"Because I did a plenary indulgence today." I said it like I was proud and glad, which I was.

"Sooo..." she said, like I was supposed to explain.

"So I don't have any more sins because I went to confession and I don't have any more purgatory time because I did the plenary indulgence. So Jesus doesn't need to die for me because I'm OK."

"What makes you think the plenary indulgence is for you?"

"Because I told God I wanted it for me." Now I was worried.

"You can't do it that way. You have to give plenary indulgences away. You can never do them for yourself or your own selfish purposes. The only way you could get a plenary indulgence for yourself is if someone else gave you one." Mom looked like she was feeling better.

I could feel all the sins come swooshing back onto my soul like black, ashy ghosts. I didn't want any more of that thick fuzzy green soup either. I just wanted to go lie down and pretend I was as dead as Jesus was by now. Now I'd probably have to go to purgatory for at least a million years.

That night when I went to sleep, instead of bad dreams, I dreamt about an angel who was kind of like a real nice Mommy. She was all soft and light and didn't say one thing. Her hands were warm and knew everything. The wings were just for decoration. When she touched me, I got so limp I just molded into where she moved me. Everywhere she touched me I just fell into her, like she was candy and I was the sweet tooth. When she was all done, I felt good and clean and like I was strong but not mean. The dream felt like the realest, truest thing ever. It even lasted a little while after I woke up.

My bed felt cold, and pee smell was coming from the bunk below where my little sister, Francie, wet the bed again. Maybe this was the dream and the angel was real. Maybe I hadn't woke up from a dream at all but was just starting to have one again. And this one wasn't a very good one either. But if everything here was a dream, I sure didn't know how to wake up from it.

At breakfast, which was Cream of Wheat, I said, "Maybe this whole world is the real dream and the dreams are the real world."

Sonny said, "How do you figure that?"

I didn't know how I figured that, I just did, but I couldn't say that to him. So I said, "How do you figure it isn't?" He just looked hard at his cereal and slurped it up so it sounded like slop.

Since he didn't say anything, I felt even more like maybe what I said was true. I kept blabbing. "So I guess this is all just a dream. It probably doesn't matter what we do here because you can do anything in a dream." I knew I was on thin ice now, but I couldn't stop once I got started. "I can even commit all the sins I want to and it won't matter anyway because even purgatory is probably a dream." I got up from the table and danced around like no one could ever get me again.

Maureen was listening to the whole thing and said, "It's sacrilegious to talk like that, you know." Like she was the queen of what's right and wrong and I was an idiot sinner.

"It is not! I can think anything I want. And maybe it's true. You don't know anything anyway." I stuck my hip out at her and made a snotty face.

Sonny, who was still shoveling down the Cream of Wheat, looked up and said like he believed me, "You know I think you're right, I bet this is all just a dream." He got up and came over to my side of the table. He came real close. "And it doesn't matter what any of us does." Then he slugged me as hard as he could in my arm. It jolted the milk and cereal in my stomach so hard some of it bubbled up. "So it doesn't matter if I keep pounding on you or not. It's just a dream, right, runt?" He slugged me again. "Unless of course, it's not a dream and then maybe it hurts, right?" Then he stopped. I watched him walk to the bathroom where he'd probably stay locked up for an hour. I hoped.

Mom came in from the laundry room and when I told her Sonny pounded on me just for thinking dreams might be real, she said, "When you start questioning what's real you're on dangerous ground. You go too far and you might not get back again."

I thought hard about what could be so dangerous about questions. Then I said, "But Mom, what if it's true?"

"If it's true, then we're all crazy, but if it isn't true, then it's just you who's crazy." Then she looked at me kind of worried and touched my hair, but not the way the angel did. "And we don't want that, do we?" I didn't feel anything warm or soft anymore. Then Mom sort of swatted me on the butt and told me to go help Maureen sort the laundry. We had to get church clothes ready for Easter.

After the little kids went to bed, I got to help color the Easter eggs. We always started with the solid colors first, then we put oil in the colors so we could swirl them. I loved the swirled colors the most, but my stomach was hurting. It was like a fight inside between the angel dream and the gray ashes that were in my soul for keeps.

The next day was Easter Sunday. Mom told us we were going to the eleven o'clock mass and to remember that we had to stop eating our candy and eggs by eight o'clock, which was three hours before communion. And no liquids after ten o'clock, which was one hour before communion. That's because it was a sin to go to communion if you didn't fast for the right amount of time.

I put on my Sunday dress, which had a matching blue jacket. It made me look almost as old as a teenager. Except for my hairy legs. I was almost nine years old and didn't even notice how hairy they were until I saw how smooth and shiny Georgina's legs were after she shaved. She was sixteen. Mom didn't want any of the girls to shave their legs. She said if we didn't ever shave our legs, the hair would all be gone by the time we were forty or so. She showed us her legs to prove it. But who would want to wait until they were ancient to have unhairy legs?

Nicky still needed someone to get him ready. I put some Vaseline in his blonde hair and rubbed it around so I could comb it straight up in the front. He looked so cute with his white little teeth and his red wool bow tie. He was done. Francie was next. I ironed her baby dress that was wadded up and wrinkled.

Pretty soon everyone was lining up for Mom to check how we looked. We were supposed to look like our house did when we had company. But Luann couldn't find her shoes, Billy's socks didn't match, and Dean hadn't washed his face.

Mom kind of hissed at Dean, "When are you going to act like you're made out of something? Do I have to wash that filthy face of yours for you?" Dean turned and slunk into the bathroom. His face didn't look clean to me either, but maybe it really was, and it just **looked** dirty. Why was Mom was so mean to him?

Meanwhile, Dad was yelling, "We're almost late for church again, goddammit! This is the fourth Sunday in a row. What have all of you been doing all morning anyway?" Then everyone was running around screaming and yelling because we were going to be late.

I wondered why Mom and Dad could still go to communion after saying goddammit so many times. But they did. I bet if I said goddammit just once and went to communion after, I'd go to hell for it. Maybe that's because I'm a kid. It's a lot easier for kids to make mortal sins than adults. Because our sins are worse. Also, grown ups don't have as many interesting sins to make.

We all crammed into the car. It was a nine-passenger and could barely hold all eleven of us kids plus Mom and Dad. My stomach still wasn't feeling good. It was kind of bubbling. And right before we left the house I told Mom about it. She told me to drink some milk. I drank the milk right before we got in the car and now I was afraid maybe I drank it too soon before Holy Communion. I **had** to go to communion. Everyone had to. If you didn't, everyone would know you did a mortal sin. Otherwise, why wouldn't you go? So now I either had to go and maybe make a sin because I drank the milk too soon, or I'd skip communion and everyone would think I had a mortal sin on my soul.

It was mobbed at church. People were squeezed into every pew. That's why we usually went to the eight thirty mass, because it wasn't so crowded, especially on Easter Sunday. Mom said people came out of the woodwork to go to church on Easter because they felt guilty. She also said more of the alcoholics went to the eleven o'clock mass because they had to sleep it off from drinking on Saturday night. But no one there looked like an alcoholic to me. They were all dressed real nice and acted like they wouldn't ever do something bad. Mom said, "Looks are deceiving."

The ushers always made room for us to sit together, even if we were late. Dad knew them from the Knights of Columbus meetings. He always smiled, shook their hands, and looked handsome. We were supposed to be sort of a holy family because there were so many of us. It proved that Mom was doing the will of God. So when we all trailed in, even if we were late, it was like she was showing us off, especially to the priest.

I wanted to sit by Dad, but only the little kids got to sit by him. Francie held his hand and Jason got to sit on his lap because he was the youngest. I had to sit in between Maureen and Sonny. We were squashed together. Yuck. I could smell Sonny's greasy hair. And Maureen smelled like Mom's *To a Wild Rose* perfume. I wondered how she got it. Maybe Mom gave her some, but maybe she stole it. I wanted to catch her doing something bad, more than ever.

The yellowish-brown church windows were too dark to see through. If you stared at them long enough they made you think about God, saints, and sins. You'd forget all about the sun and since they only opened a few inches, you also forgot that there was such a thing as a breeze. It was always hot, and hotter than ever on Easter Sunday. The air was like a thick thing. When you breathed it in, it stuffed itself so far into your lungs you felt swollen inside.

We kneeled and stood and kneeled again and I tried to not think about how hard the wooden pews felt on my knees or how thick and gurgly I felt inside. I said the prayers in the missal, along with everyone else, and thought about how hard it was to keep anything clean. Especially your soul. Then I thought about the saints and how they had it good with God, but they got tortured all the time. Just for being Catholic. How they got their fingernails pulled out one by one. But they never gave in, even when their guts were all pulled out and they weren't even dead yet. That's why they were saints. I started to feel really sick.

We stood up again and I felt weak and wavery. The air was getting thick with holiness and went right inside me. Then it thickened up even more until I was filled with all the saints who were screaming from having their arms and legs ripped off. And God was too far away and too far inside at the same time. I couldn't breathe one more thing. There was no room left inside.

I started to feel a bad kind of dizzy. It was hard and sharp and slammed me down onto the wooden pews as hard as it could. Then someone must have carried me out because the next thing I remember I was laying on the grass outside the church. I wanted to suck on that green grass and chew it with my teeth, but I couldn't move. I sucked in the air instead and then the hard sharp thing grabbed my stomach and I was throwing up in the grass. Hardly anything came up, but it felt like the whole world was getting thrown out. Finally.

I was lying on my back on the grass. This time I breathed in and was OK. I was clean and empty inside. But I still couldn't get up. I could hear my brothers talking real quiet about me and saw them out of the corner of my eye. I looked straight up at the fluffy clouds and blue sky and wished I lived there like a spirit or an angel. I'd fly and live way up above the clouds with other angel spirits where the air is so thin it sparkles with the sun and we'd never come down to earth again. And my Angel Mommy would hold me tight all night long.

It was hard to stay in the sky for very long because of the noise from the church. Mass was over and people were coming out of church. Their voices sounded buzzy and it was making me shaky again. I felt Sonny trying to give me some water. I sipped some from a paper cup and it tasted good except for the throw up taste in my mouth. I drank some more and after a while I sat up. Just Dean, Sonny, and Luann were on the grass with me. It was nice of Sonny to give me water. Everyone else stayed in church when I fainted. I guess they didn't think it was any big deal because I had fainted in church before.

Mom, Becky, and Maureen came out looking holy-happy. Dad looked party-happy. Everyone else looked like they were just glad they didn't have to stay in church one more minute. Mom checked my forehead for a fever and said I was OK. Then Father Laughlin came over and put his hand on my forehead. He was the cute priest with the long black eyelashes. Even Mom agreed it was too bad he was a priest because his beautiful eyes were getting wasted on God.

I smiled at him and tried to look like a saint. Which was kind of hard because I never felt very holy, even after communion when you should be the holiest. How could you feel holy when the body and blood of Jesus Christ was in your mouth and one of his arms or legs might be stuck in your teeth and the rest of him was getting mixed up in your guts? Just the thought of God inside me made me feel a little sick again. The Angel Mommy, baby angels, the sun, or even thin air spirits would be OK inside. But that's all! I was really sorry to God, but I didn't want him or Jesus or any of his saints inside. I hoped it wasn't a mortal sin.

"Too bad yee missed communion. How are yee feeling?" Father Laughlin said.

I said, "A lot better." I started to stand up and he took a hold of my hand and helped me. It was embarrassing. He was so nice and was touching me.

"Perhaps yee can receive the Blessed Sacrament with yeer dear Mother sometime this week. We love seeing yee little ones." He smiled and blinked. His eyelashes were thicker and blacker and longer than any I'd ever seen. I started nodding and before I knew it, he said, "Aah good. The Lord loves yee." I sure hoped he didn't think I promised him something. Because I liked Father Laughlin. I just didn't like church, and there was no way I was going to go to church during the week with Mom.

I went over to where Sonny, Billy, and Dean were standing in the parking lot, kicking dirt and gravel. Mom and Dad always talked with the priest and some other grown ups after church so all of us had time to kill before we had to get back in the car. Sonny and Billy were talking about the engines in the cars that drove out. I was trying to be nice to Sonny for giving me the water before, so I acted like I cared about the dumb cars.

Really though, I was just feeling the sun. It was like it was alive and doing good things to me, to the weeds sprouting up in between the pieces of gravel, to the little ants that were carrying dirt packs on their back, and to the birds that you heard sing but never saw. Then I got the idea for the Big Trade.

I said to Billy, "I have a proposition."

"What is it?" He squinted like he thought I was going to pull a fast one.

"It'll be good. I promise, but we need to talk private." I didn't want anyone else screwing this up.

"OK." We walked over to where no one would hear us.

"You remember what Mom said about the plenary indulgences? How we couldn't give them to ourselves?"

"Yeah. And now the one I did on Friday is no good." I knew he was just as upset about it as I was.

"Yeah, but we can still give them away."

"But why would you want to give it away? Why do all that work for someone else?"

"Well, maybe because they'd do something just as nice for you." He stuck his tongue into his cheek so you could see it rolling around, and I knew he was thinking hard.

"Ohhhh. I get it. But if I give my plenary indulgence to you, how do I know you'll give yours to me?"

"Because I promise. Stick a needle in my eye. Besides, we'll both do it at the same time."

"OK...now?"

"Now." We both closed our eyes at the same time.

After a second or two I asked, "Did you do it?"

"Yeah, did you?"

"Yep."

We both smiled real big and purgatory was gone. I could start all over again with a clean soul. The sun **was** doing good things. And for just a few seconds we held hands while we walked, the way we did when we were real little.

16

Cleaning

NINE YEARS

WE cleaned our house about once a year, when it was Mom and Dad's turn to have the CFM meeting at our house. I think CFM stood for Catholic Family Movement. It wasn't really for families though, because only parents went to it. All they ever did was have meetings at each other's houses.

When it was our turn to have the meeting, we had to clean the house. Even though us kids never got to go to the meeting or even see any of the other parents, we still had to clean. The last time we had the meeting, it took us about a month to clean everything. Everything had to be scraped and scrubbed. Mom said it had to sparkle or else. She wasn't going to let her friends see how we really lived. See what slobs we were. "Or I'll never be able to hold my head up and look them in the eye," she'd say. I knew exactly what she meant. I didn't want any of my friends to know either. I couldn't even imagine asking a friend to come to our house.

We started cleaning the big stuff first, like washing the ceilings and walls in the kitchen. There was always grease and splatter there. Dried spaghetti sauce, soup, and grease splats were all over the wall behind the stove. The ceiling was dirty where the pressure cooker shot up applesauce and split pea soup.

Bacon grease splatters weren't too bad because they wiped up easy. But vegetable oil mixed with grease was so sticky when it dried that it didn't matter how hard you washed. It just stayed there and stunk its rancid stink, getting blacker and blacker the more you washed. There were always black oil smears left on the yellow walls after you washed the first time. Then you'd have to start all over again. Sometimes it took three washes with new soap and water to get them clean.

Mom did some of the ceiling, but then her neck got tired from looking straight up. She thought that was worse and more tiring than going on trips where you just had to sit for a bunch of hours. How could you get tired from just sitting or looking at a ceiling? She told Georgina to do the rest. "That's why God made you young and strong," Mom told her.

When Georgina griped about doing the ceiling, I said, "I'll do it."

Mom said, "Oh no you won't. You'll fall right off that ladder." Maybe she didn't care if Georgina fell off the ladder.

I begged Mom to do a big kid's job. She said, "You just keep on doing good work and we'll see." It was true that I did a good job. Not like most of my brothers and sisters. At least I knew what clean was. Clean is when there's nothing there that's not supposed to be there. How hard was it to figure that out? Not very, but try getting a born slob to see it that way.

Instead of cleaning the ceiling, I had to wash all the painted woodwork and the lowest part of the walls. I started in the kitchen with the baseboard. There was always more dried crud there than anywhere. On the baseboard by our dinner table there was so much gunk you couldn't even see the yellow paint. It was because of the way Sonny waxed the floor. He just pushed the dirt up on the woodwork and waxed it in.

The wall across from the dinner table had cherry pit stains all over it. That was where we spit the pits after Mom and Dad went into the living room after dinner. We practiced to see who could spit the farthest and if you could hit the wall. A lot of those pits were still stuck on the floor at the bottom of the wall.

There were also peach skins stuck hard on the walls. That was from the little kids who helped with canning. They'd slide the skin off the scalded peaches, and then wipe their sticky peach skin hands on the wall.

I scraped dried on corn flakes, cherry pits, noodles, and milk that was hard and polished from the wax. I used a butter knife for scraping, but sometimes it dug into the paint and scraped into the wood. It looked worse then, with the holes in the paint. I hated that.

We also had to wash all the kitchen and living room curtains, all the diapers, and all the dirty clothes. There were enough clothes in just the dirty clothes pile to fill up an entire bathroom from top to bottom. The only way to wash all those clothes at the same time was to take them to the Laundromat in town.

On Laundromat day, we started bright and early in the morning and sorted the clothes into colors. We spread big sheets all over the floor for the different colors. Reds, jeans, browns, blues, and mixed colors all went onto a sheet that was just for that color. There were also separate sheets for whites, dirty whites, and rags. Even a little kid could help with sorting, unless you were color blind.

I wished I was smell blind because those clothes stunk bad from being in the dirty clothes pile for so long. The whole room smelled like wet moldy cats.

Once everything was sorted into sheets, they were tied in a knot and stuffed into our car. We had to borrow a neighbor's car and filled it too. I wanted to go to the Laundromat with Mom, but only the big girls got to go. I was only nine.

By dinnertime, all the clothes came back clean. Mom, Georgina, and Becky had folded the curtains, diapers, and towels at the Laundromat, but everything else was thrown back into sheet bundles. All those clothes still had to be put away somewhere.

I helped put them all in a pile on the living room floor. They smelled so good I wanted to jump in the pile and rub my hair and face all over them. But instead, I picked out all of my clothes. I yelled at everyone, "Come and get your stuff or it's going into the Formosa pile!" All the kids were supposed to come and get their stuff. Because this was their chance to get any clothes that they hadn't seen since last year.

There was usually a lot of stuff left after everyone picked out their clothes, but most of it was junk or someone would have taken it. Mom picked out "good rags" and the rest we gave to the poor people in Formosa who didn't have anything but newspapers for shoes and it was below zero in the winter. Maybe they could tie the rags to their feet instead. But if it rained, their rags would get wet and they'd have ice cube feet. Then the rags wouldn't do much good. Unless they sewed all the rags together and maybe made a coat or something. But that still wouldn't help their feet. Mom said we lived like kings and queens compared to them. Maybe we did.

After everyone got their clean clothes, they were supposed to put them away in their rooms. The little girls, which were Francie, Luann, me, and Maureen, all had the same bedroom. It used to be the kitchen from Unit #4 so we had a long counter, and in the middle of it there was a sink with a window right above it. We also had shelves above and below the counter. The whole room was barely big enough for the two bunk beds that were almost squished together.

Each girl got two bottom shelves for their stuff but they were always filled up. The top shelves were too hard for us to reach and were always crammed full of junk too. So our clothes, homework, and other junk usually piled up on top of the counter or on the floor. When we had our fresh washed clothes, there was of course no good place to put them.

I decided I was going to figure out some way to put the clean clothes away. It was a really hard problem. I laid down on my bed and stared at the shelves until my eyes got dry from not blinking. I hated the way Luann had pushed her clothes into her shelf when it was already full. So everything fell right back out just waiting to get walked on. And Maureen was such a shelf hog. She took the biggest shelves just because she was older.

I kept lying there, staring, until I was like just a speck of dust on the windowsill, waiting for a breeze to blow me to the other side of the world. But then what if I ended up in Formosa? And I had only newspapers for shoes and had to wait for the next shipment of rags so I wouldn't get frostbite!

That scared me so much I jumped up and decided I was going to clean the room even if no one else helped. I'd get rid of everything that wasn't supposed to be there. I asked Mom if I could, and she said, "More power to you."

I told my sisters I was going to throw out any of their stuff that was just lying around, and this was their last chance to put it away.

They ignored me. They didn't think I meant it. I did though. I wasn't going to live like a rat anymore. I was sick of it and sick of being just like my slob family.

I got a sheet and spread it out on the floor in the area where we walked. Then I cleared a place to stand on the counter and took things out of the top shelves. I pulled out old towels, raggedy sheets we'd used for ghost costumes, old nightgowns, and ugly gray curtains with faded yellow flowers. I threw them onto the sheet. I dropped some blue plastic plates onto the sheet. Then I found the Parcheesi game we'd been looking for, some old Christmas decorations, some skunky cleaning stuff with labels that were falling off, and some old mouse-traps with crusty cheese that was sweating grease. All of it went onto the sheet pile.

After I cleaned the top shelves and cleared off the counter, I picked up everything on the floor, even from under the beds. I didn't touch anyone's bed because that wouldn't be fair. But if it was clothes on the floor, if it was junk, or I didn't know where to put, it went onto the sheet. If it was someone's stuff that I was mad at, I put it on the sheet too.

But if it was good stuff, **and** I knew where it went, I put it away. I also put away Francie's stuff because she was still real little and was never mean to me. If I saw something Mom might like, I put it back on my bed to give to her.

By the time I was done, the sheet was almost too full to squeeze out of the room. And it was also almost too heavy to pull. Even so, I knew I could do it if I tried hard enough. But where would I go with all of it?

I left the pile of stuff in the bedroom and brought out the things I saved for Mom. When I handed her the Desert Rose gravy boat that we only used for Thanksgiving and had been missing for over a year, she was so glad that she kissed me on the cheek. I was so proud!

Then I got an idea for a deal with Mom. I told her about the sheet full of stuff. I said, "Just tell me where it goes, Mom. And I'll put everything away."

She gave me her tired, *I can't lift another finger* look, got some coffee, and said, "OK, if you do all the running."

I said, "OK, all you have to do is sit." I was so glad because now I wouldn't get in any trouble from Luann or Maureen for what I did with their stuff. They wouldn't be able to do one thing to me.

I squeezed and pulled the stuffed sheet out from the bedroom and into the living room. I was already sweating but had more energy than ever. Mom laid on the couch while I asked her where things went. She told me, and I ran as fast as I could, because I didn't want her to get too tired and not be able to finish.

All the clothes went into the dirty clothes box, even though some of them were fresh cleaned. I felt bad about that because the dirty clothes box was already getting too full, too soon. But there was no way I was going to put away the other kids' clothes! Besides, Mom told me to do it.

After a long time, there was just Formosa stuff left. I dumped it into the huge Formosa box, which was the kind of box that refrigerators come in. Done!

At dinner that night I bragged to everyone that I cleaned the whole bedroom all by myself.

Maureen and Luann said, "You did not."

I said, "Oh yes I did. You'll find out," and smiled at Mom. They hadn't even gone into the bedroom yet.

When they went in there after dinner, they couldn't believe it. Maureen's clean clothes were still on her bed, but a lot of her stuff was gone. She was real mad but didn't say anything. She just looked at me like she hated my guts, and wanted to scratch my skin off. Then she walked out.

Luann threw a fit. "What did you do with my stuuuff?" She was howling like a sick puppy.

I said, "I told you what I was going to do. Your stuff is supposed to be in the shelf not on the floor or counter. It's your own fault."

"Yeah but..." She kept crying and looking for things that were gone. When she looked under the bed, there was nothing there. She cried even louder. "But I had stuuuff under heeeere." I could see she was really upset and felt like maybe she **was** too little and maybe it wasn't all her fault.

I tried to remember where I put her things and told her where to look. I said to be sure to check the Formosa box and the dirty clothes pile.

Luann cried, "Oh no! Not the dirty clothes! Those were all my best clothes. Now I'll never get them back."

I said, "If you go get them right away maybe they won't be too dirty from the other stuff." She came back with a huge armload of stuff and dropped it right on the floor.

I yelled, "You have to put your clothes away. They can't be on the floor or the counter. I told you!"

"I can if I want." She stood right on her pile and stared hard at me. Like that was going to make one bit of difference. I knew I shouldn't have been nice to her.

I yelled, "You'd better put that stuff away. You can ask Mom if you don't believe me." She started to cry again but started to clear out some space in her shelves for her clean clothes.

After Luann was done throwing her fit and the room was clean again, I went out to drag Mom into the bedroom and show her what I'd done. I wanted to surprise her. So when we got to the doorway, I told her to close her eyes. I knew she didn't want to because of the way she sighed and leaned against the wall, but she closed them anyway. When she opened her eyes and saw those empty cupboards and clean counter she said, "You're a darlin'. I can even see the floor now." Then she hugged me and I felt like I could clean the whole house all by myself.

While she was hugging me, she looked at our bathroom. The toilet in there was plugged up and piled full of poop. It had more and more flies every day and stunk like crazy. Mom sounded like a snake hissing when she said, "I don't know how you girls can live like that." Then she pushed me away like I was dirty too.

It made that dull achy spot in my belly that was starting to get quiet, get all buzzy, hard, and sharp again. I knew she was talking about the toilet. And I also knew I wasn't really her darlin'. I wasn't anyone's darlin'. It made me start to cry because I wanted something special from Mom even if it was stupid to try.

I was looking down at the floor when I said, "I hate it as much as you do, and it's not fair that Dad won't fix it."

She said, "I'll talk to him and we'll see."

About two months before this, the toilet got totally plugged up and had been that way ever since. It was always getting plugged up from bobby pins and other junk that fell in by accident. Then Dad had to snake it out. The last time he did, it flushed as nice as could be. I was so happy every time. Everything went down and there was beautiful clear water. But then something really bad happened. And it was my entire fault.

A friend at school gave me a big round chunk of petrified wood. I brought it home and thought it was so nice I set it on top of the tank part of the toilet, like a decoration. Then I peed and when I got up, I picked up the petrified wood to feel its round roughness and OOPS, it fell in the toilet. There it sat with pee and toilet paper floating around it. I thought I should reach in and get it, but I just couldn't stand the idea. I washed diapers in the toilet, but that was different. That was baby poop and this was almost big girl pee and it was mine and you weren't supposed to touch it.

So I closed my eyes and started praying to the Virgin Mother for purity. I flushed the toilet, hoping my rock would go down. I opened my eyes and saw that it **did** go down. But now the toilet was filling up with water. OH NO! I didn't know how to stop it. I ran screaming into the living room. "The toilet's overflowing! The toilet's overflowing!" Sonny, my older brother, walked in real slow while I yelled, "Hurry! Hurry!" He took the lid off the tank, reached in, and did something to stop it.

But pee water was all over the bathroom floor and it ran into our bedroom and onto some of the clothes that were on the floor. I was so scared I was shaking because I knew if Sonny hadn't come in, it would have kept overflowing forever and it would have been my pee all over the house.

I helped Georgina and Maureen get towels to mop up the water. I still couldn't stand to touch it with my hands so I pushed the towels on the floor with my feet.

Georgina asked, "Why did it plug up when Dad just cleaned it?"

I said, "I dunno. Maybe somebody dropped something in it." The buzzing in my stomach felt like huge flies hitting my insides. I started asking everyone if they dropped something in it. Nope, no one did.

When Dad came home, Georgina asked him real nice, if he'd look at the toilet and he yelled, "I just fixed that damn thing. I'll be god dammed if I'm going to do it again."

But later on that night, he came in the bathroom, flushed the toilet, and it started to overflow right off, but he stopped it in time. I wished I knew how he and Sonny did that, but it looked so ugly inside the tank I knew I'd never put my hands in there either. Then Dad got the snake, but it wouldn't go in. He said something hard as a rock was stuck in there and he'd have to take the whole toilet outside and it was too cold to do that kind of work outside and he was god dammed if he was going to do that and we could sit in our own shit, goddammit.

And we did just that for about two months. It started with one of the little kids, like Francie or Luann, or even one of the boys, pooping in there in an emergency because we couldn't use Mom and Dad's bathroom, and the living room and kitchen bathrooms were too far away. After a while, it didn't matter how much poop there was because it all stunk the same. It was the grossest thing in the whole house.

So that's what Mom saw when she hugged me after I cleaned our bedroom. And when she said she'd talk to Dad about fixing the toilet, I really, really hoped he would. I thought of all the reasons to try to convince him. At dinner that night, I talked about how it was getting warmer outside and how there were more blowflies in our bathroom than ever and that one tried to bite me. Neither Mom or Dad wanted us to get bit by them because they laid eggs under your skin and then you had to go to the doctor. I also said maybe us girls had finally learned our lesson with the toilet.

The next Saturday it was just a few days before the CFM meeting and Dad decided to fix the toilet. He scooped out all the poop from the toilet that he could, into a bucket. Then he put down a big heavy plastic sheet on the floor, unbolted the toilet from the floor, and laid it on the plastic. He pulled the plastic and toilet outside on the grass and hosed it down. With a hammer and chisel he hammered into the hard stuck place in the toilet and out popped my petrified wood. I was scared.

But I acted surprised and said, "Oh! My petrified wood! I was wondering where it went."

Dad said, "How in the hell did this get in here?"

"Maybe someone dropped it in by accident," I said.

Maureen said, "It's your fault for leaving it on top of the toilet."

I didn't argue.

Dad wasn't too mad, but he said, "The next time one of you girls plugs it up, you'll fix it yourself." I hoped he didn't mean it.

That same day, since it was nice and sunny outside, Mom decided to do something about the mattresses. The problem with the mattresses was the bed-wetters. I never wet the bed anymore. But Francie, Luann, and lots of the boys kept on wetting the bed. They peed almost every night, and after a while it rotted a hole right through the mattress.

One time I came into the bedroom after Luann and Francie went to sleep and saw Luann pee on Francie. Luann, who was about six, was in the top bunk and when she wet the bed it went in a pee trickle right through the hole in her mattress and down onto Francie who got soaked. No wonder Francie was always so wet in the morning. She was soaked, front and back, top to bottom. And it wasn't even her own pee.

I asked Mom why we didn't put plastic on the mattresses when they were brand new, but she said the kids might get chilled if they were sleeping in pee all night and it didn't get soaked up somehow. That's what the mattresses were for, to soak up the pee so they wouldn't catch a cold. It didn't seem like those mattresses were doing much good for Francie.

They were as ugly as a plugged up toilet. But the smell was the worst part. To cure the smell and the germs, we laid them on the grass and let them sit in the sun all day. Then we sprayed them with Lysol and Mom put about a cup of baking soda on the brown peed out spots. With new sheets, they smelled good enough for company.

Finally the day of the CFM meeting came and it was almost as good as the Fourth of July because all the kids got to go to the drive-in movie that night. It was the only time we ever got to go to a drive-in. Mom and Dad let us go because they didn't allow kids at the meeting, and they needed to get rid of us.

That morning, Georgina and Becky went to the potato chip factory and got five Safeway bags of potato chips. They also bought Cokes and stuff for dip. When she got home, Georgina hid a whole bag of potato chips from Mom just in case Mom changed her mind and said we couldn't have any.

Mom fried a bunch of chicken, and made potato salad and Jell-O with fruit cocktail, while Maureen and me made popcorn. We filled four Safeway bags full of popcorn. That was for us kids. Everything else was for company and we'd only get some of the company food if we did our work real good. If we did, we could eat it at the drive-in.

In the afternoon, Mom did the *finishing touches* on the house. We all made our bed, put our pillows and extra blankets into the car, and kept our hands and feet clean so we wouldn't mess up the house before company came. Then Mom got dressed with her nylons that had the black line on the back of her leg, and put on red lipstick. Her hair was already done from the day before. She looked like a regular Mom now, only nicer and not one bit tired. When Dad got home, he shaved and put on his suit. He looked so good I wanted him to dance me around.

I didn't want to leave our house. The red tile squares on the floor were as bright and shiny as Mom's lipstick and I wanted to touch all the new clean places and pretend I was a grown up. I'd sit with my knees together like a lady and eat chips daintily while they had their meeting.

But it was time for the kids to go. Mom scooted us out the door and Georgina told us to pile into the car so we could get a good spot at the drive-in. When we got there, it was still too light for the movie, so we ate and played on the swings in front of the movie screen. By the time the movie started, I was so tired I only saw the cartoons.

The next thing I knew, I was in bed at home and it was the next day and the house was still clean. I got up before anyone else and sat in the kitchen all alone. I ate leftover chips and dip and pretended Mom had only one kid and it was me and we lived like this all the time.

17

RATS AND BOYS

NINE YEARS

WHY do you think girls are better than boys?" Maureen stood in front of the bathroom sink parting her wet hair and looking for a fresh bobby pin while she talked.

I leaned against the doorway waiting for her to stop primping so I could use the sink. She was no example to me of a girl being better than anything. But since I was trying not to fight, I said, "Maybe because we're nicer." Then I looked at my arm. Just two days before, when we were fighting, she scratched the skin off my arms with her fingernails. The three long stripes already had scabs. She always won because she was a cat fighter with her claws.

So I had to say, "But maybe some girls just think they're better." I stared at her and squinted until she knew I wasn't on her side. Then I walked out of the bathroom. I hated that girl stuff. Especially the *I'm holier than you* snottier than snot attitude of Maureen's.

Mom said I was a tomboy. I didn't know exactly what that was. Was it just a girl who likes to do boy things and gets in trouble a lot? I knew Louisa May Alcott was a tomboy, and I liked her. But what if it meant I wasn't all the way a girl? All I knew was that I had a lot of catty sisters who acted like girls and a bunch of disgusting brothers who were about a hundred times worse than puppy dog tails.

I don't know why they never wrote a poem about what boys are really like. One of the girls at school who would swear sometimes said, "Boys are slug slime milkshakes and puppy dog poop butts." I had to agree.

Boys loved to kill rats and I didn't know any girls who liked doing that. Most girls are scared of rats. I wasn't that scared of them, but I didn't like killing them either. I thought maybe I was part boy and part girl. It was hard to say which one I'd rather be. It was the same with rats. I couldn't tell if they were actually good or bad.

We had them in our house once when I was nine and a half, and we didn't even know they were there until Easter morning. Us kids got up real early and ran to the kitchen table to get our Easter baskets. They weren't real baskets. They were little nests made out of yellow, green, and pink plastic grass that was soft and fuzzy.

We couldn't wait to get our eggs and candy, but when we came into the kitchen all we saw was a big mess. The nests were scattered all over the table and the floor. They didn't even look like nests anymore. In each one, there were a few yellow or green jellybeans, which none of us liked. There weren't any black ones, red ones, or orange ones. And there were **no** colored eggs. Instead, we found little scraps of aluminum foil, colored thread, some red wool, pieces of a plaid shirt, and a total of about three dimes. The dimes were the only good part. It felt like a real bad trick on us.

We went in the bedroom to get Mom and Dad and tell them what happened. It was a mystery to them too, until after Dad got his coffee. Then he figured it out. He lit his cigarette and said, "It was pack rats. For everything they took, they left something in its place." I wanted to ask Dad lots more questions, but I also felt like crying because I couldn't believe that I wasn't going to get any black or red jelly beans and I'd been waiting almost half a year.

I looked at the rat things in my nest and said, "It looks like junk to me."

Dad said, "Yeah. They like that kind of stuff. Especially shiny or red things."

We looked all over the house to see if we could find where the rats were hiding our candy, but we only found two eggs that were cracked. The rats probably dropped them because they were carrying a lazy man's load. I kept hoping that it was all a big joke and Mom would come out with a huge bowl full of jellybeans and eggs. She'd laugh and say, "Surprise!!!"

I gave up on that idea when Mom made us start getting ready for church. She tried to get us to think that church was the best part of Easter, but I wasn't that stupid. I was so mad at those rats I actually **did** want to kill them. Only we didn't know where they were.

Dad got a hunch though, about two weeks later, when a really bad smell started to spread through the house even when the door to the diaper bathroom was closed, the garbage was out, and there was no rotten food anywhere. He put on his helmet with the light on top. Dad had it since during the war when he was a welder. He pulled the nails out of the wooden door that went underneath the house and started to crawl in. Three of my brothers and I got to go with him. We all carried flashlights to help, since there was no light under there.

The dirt was really soft and dusty and it felt like it never had a drop of rain in its whole life. There was only enough room to crawl. Dad had to mostly lie on his stomach or he'd hit his back on the wood that held up the floors. We crawled a long time and meanwhile the smell was getting strong. I didn't know what we were looking for, but I knew it wasn't good. The smell and the dust almost choked me. I started to get scared, but I knew I'd better not say anything, since Dad was doing a favor to let me come along and I knew I'd better not start acting like a baby **or** like a girl.

Finally, Dad said, "There it is." We pointed our flashlights to where his light was pointed. There were lots of eggshells in different piles. Some of the eggs were part way eaten. That was where the stinkola smell was coming from. Dean found a couple of eggs that looked just fine. He accidentally broke one and the smell grabbed us so hard we started choking. Dad told him what a doomscheister he was and scooped up the rotten eggs into the bag he had in his pocket.

While Dad was scooping, we were gagging and looking at the rat nests. There were about seven or eight of them. They were made out of grass from our Easter baskets, straw, someone's red flannel nightgown, and a plaid shirt. In the nests were lots of aluminum foil, long colored threads, and fuzzy stuff from the dryer. In one nest, we saw two of Mom's dangly earrings that she thought Georgina had stolen. There were lots of shiny pieces of junk, silver paper from gum wrappers, a pretend silver ring, and gobs of black jellybeans. I guess the rats didn't like the licorice taste. We didn't get to eat any of them because of the germs.

I heard Dad say, "I'll be damned." He'd found his pocket watch that had been missing for more than a month. He was polishing it on his shirt and shaking his head with a smile on his face. I felt like smiling then too because those rats were not so dumb as you thought.

We got everything we wanted to save into another bag and crawled out. Dad said, "The rats aren't using those nests anymore. They went somewhere else." I thought it might be OK if the rats stayed there, even though they had stolen Easter. Maybe we could do interesting trades with the rats and try to figure out what they liked the best. But it didn't matter what I thought. Just to be sure the rats were gone, Dad went back under the house and put out some rat poison.

About a month later, we started getting another bad smell in the house. Dad told the boys to go down there where the nests were and bag up the dead rats. This time I didn't want to go with them. They collected about ten rats. When they came up, they wanted to show me, but I didn't want to see or smell any dead rats. When Sonny saw that I was really grossed out, he tried to shove the bag in my face. Boys are such pigs. After they were done showing off, they went up to throw the rats in the incinerator.

The only problem was, the incinerator was full. The garbage was piled so high you couldn't even start to close the lid on it. The boys knew that if they left those dead rats out where coyotes or some other animal got a hold of them, they'd get in trouble for putting out bait for more vermin. So they came back to the house and told Dad.

Dad said the garbage wouldn't go down because the incinerator was too full of tin cans. And why didn't they dig them out last week when he told them to? And now it was full of garbage again and he didn't care how they did it goddammit, but he wanted the garbage burned up and the incinerator dug out or there'd be hell to pay! This was exactly what they knew he'd say. The boys were mad because of all the work they'd have to do. I didn't care since I was a girl and it was boy's work and I had enough of my own work to do. And now they could pick on somebody besides me. They could go fight with the incinerator rats.

Since we lived outside the city, we didn't have garbage trucks. And since we had so much garbage from the family and the motel, we had to do something with it. That's why Dad built the incinerator. He did it when I was too little to remember anything.

The incinerator was like a huge brick fireplace pushed into the side of a real steep hill. The top part was a tall skinny chimney that went in the air. The middle part was where you could stand and open the heavy lid to throw in the garbage. The bottom part was where the garbage burned and where you could dig out cans and ashes after it cooled.

If you were a stranger and you dumped garbage in our incinerator you'd walk right over to where the lid was and drop it in, but you'd have no idea how far down that incinerator went unless you walked over to the edge of the cliff and looked down. Then you could climb down a steep rocky path that went part way down the cliff. That's where the bottom of the incinerator was. There was a big flat cement area to walk on, and a metal door at the very bottom. You'd open that door to scoop out the ashes and cans and throw them all the way down the cliff, where there was no more path and it was **real** steep.

When it was time to dump the garbage, we just lifted up the thick metal lid at the top and shoved in everything we never wanted to see again. Sometimes rats jumped out at us when stuff hit them on the head. So we had to open the lid, shove the garbage in real fast, and close the lid again as quick as we could. Before any rats could come up.

The boys opened the bottom door only when it was time to clean the incinerator. Rats always came out then. That's what made it such a good job for boys. Because those rats were fast and mean and there were lots of them. They actually lived inside the incinerator. There were probably whole huge rat families living in there with grandparents and everything because it was always plugged up with something and rats like that kind of stuff.

Everything got thrown in there. One of my older brothers even threw in a bed once. Its springs never burned up since they were metal. Those springs kept catching all kinds of other things that wouldn't burn either, like tin cans and clothes hangers. So the incinerator was never cleaned out all the way because it was plugged up right in the middle. Even if a grown man crawled in from the bottom and took a big stick to try and get the clogged part to come down, he'd end up swearing and smashing things and it still wouldn't do any good. The rats knew this. That's why they lived there.

After Dad told the boys to clean out the incinerator goddammit, we all climbed down the side of the cliff to the cement area at the bottom. Dean, Sonny, and Billy all started shoveling tin cans out of the bottom door. It was pretty boring and I was almost ready to walk back to the house with Nicky when a big rat ran out and stopped to bite Sonny's foot. Luckily, Sonny had work boots on. He kicked and swore, but that rat was long gone by the time Sonny started running after it. He was swearing to himself about how much he wanted to kill that damn rat and how he'd slam its puny face into the ground.

Then he got his idea. "Canned rats," he said. We knew he was making a plan because of the way his head was moving funny, like he was thinking. Sonny was in charge because he was the oldest, so everyone did what he said. Except for me. I didn't have to do anything since it wasn't my job. I was just supposed to watch Nicky, who was four and a half, and still too little for incinerator work.

They started lining up cans in one long row in front of the incinerator door. They pushed each can right beside the next one so the open end of every can faced the door and it was one solid can line. There were about twenty-five cans in the line. Right behind the first can line, they piled a bunch of extra cans.

Then it was time to light the incinerator. Everyone knew that if you lit the fire from the top, it would only burn part way down because of the stuck part in the middle. And if you lit it from the bottom, it would only burn part way up because of the stuck part in the middle. Sonny thought about lighting it from both ends at once, so that maybe the part in the middle would finally get burned out. That would make Dad whistle and smile at what a good job he did.

But Sonny liked his canned rats idea more. So he closed the door at the bottom. There was just a crack for air to come through, but no room for rats to come out. Then we all climbed back up to the top. He and Dean smashed the garbage down to make room to close the lid. Then they lit the incinerator. After the fire started to leap really high and the lid was getting hot, Dean used a long stick to slam it closed.

In just a few minutes, black, black smoke came rolling out from under the top lid and galloping out the chimney. A growling boiling sound came from way down in the incinerator. It burst up through the chimney and huge arms of fire were leaping out the top. Fire wasn't supposed to come out the chimney! The top lid was starting to shake. I grabbed Nicky and screamed to everyone that the lid was going to explode right off. He started to cry and I covered his head and face with my hands so he wouldn't be so scared.

Sonny told me to go home with the babies if I couldn't stand it. But then he yelled for everyone to back away from the fire. He and Dean laughed and jabbed at each other like idiots. They wouldn't ever admit it, but I knew they were as scared as me, maybe more. Dean said he sure was glad Dad had gone to town and wasn't around for this one.

The metal lid was glowing red. That whole incinerator was so hot it was like hell screaming at you. Right in your eyeballs. I hoped my eyebrows weren't singed. The long wavery heat waves made the whole chimney start to shake. If it exploded, the whole cliff would catch on fire. And before we knew it, our whole property and everything would be scorched to death. We'd all have to run away screaming because it would be like hell getting loose and no way to stop it.

After we were all almost toasted, the fire stopped coming out of the chimney and you could hear just the regular fire sound. The boys could hardly wait to can the rats. So we went down to the bottom of the incinerator again and waited about ten more minutes, just to be safe. Then Dean, Sonny, and Billy stood behind the can line while Nicky knocked open the bottom door with a stick.

Rats came pouring out like bullets and ran straight into the cans. When one of those rats ran into the open end of the can and hit the closed end, it was stuck for a second or two before it figured out how to back out. That's all the time it took for one of the boys to smash the sharp end of the shovel down hard on the can. The shovel bent the tin can all the way down into the rat. And that rat was canned. Sometimes it died quick when the shovel slammed down on it, but most of the time its squishy rat body was still alive and it would die slow while its tail and back feet wiggled like crazy. It made you sick to watch.

The boys moved fast because there were more than a hundred rats streaming out of the incinerator. They threw the canned rats down the cliff and lined up empty cans quick so there weren't any holes in the can line where one could get through.

Sometimes a smart rat saw the cans and tried to run to the end of the line and down the cliff. Nicky stood at one end of the line and tried to scare the rat back into the cans. He stomped, screamed, and even ran after the rats. He almost got bit when a rat tried to run up his leg. I yelled at Sonny that Nicky was going to get bit, but Sonny just yelled back at me to block the other end of the line. That's where the rats ran when Nicky scared them away from his side. Then they ran on down the cliff. No way was I going to help. Besides I didn't know whether I was more on the side of the boys or on the side of the rats. After I saw enough dead rats to make anyone sick, I was going to leave, but I was still afraid for Nicky. If he did get bit, I'd have to take care of him.

I couldn't see why the boys were having so much fun canning all those rats. They were laughing like it was the best thing since Christmas. The rats were just trying to have a family inside the incinerator. They had a right to get mad and jump out at you if you dropped things on them, or lit a fire or pulled out their ash beds. I don't think they deserved to be canned. The boys thought different. They were as proud of their canned rats as they were of their dead pack rats. It made me feel like I had a fever. I knew then, I didn't want to be a boy. But I still wasn't sure about being a girl. I wanted to run down the cliff with those smart rats who got past the can line.

When most of the rats were either canned or had run away, Nicky came over to sit by me. He was tired from helping so much and I let him sit on my lap. He was my favorite little brother even though he was getting bigger. I could see how excited he still was. He was telling me all about what he did to those bad rats and kept asking me if I saw when he kicked that big one and scared the other ones and how he wasn't scared even once and did I see him? I told him I saw everything he did and that he was so brave.

His eyes were shining like blue ice water that made you think about snowy mountains on the hottest day of the year. I loved him so much I forgot about how sickening boys were. I felt his warm blonde hair slide through my fingers and kissed his sweaty head. Then I remembered he was a boy. And all of a sudden I felt like a girl. It was weird, but I liked it. I kept my arm around him while we looked to see if he had gotten bit anywhere.

18

BUTTER

NINE YEARS

MAUREEN and me were supposed to make a pineapple upside down cake for Dad because Mom and Dad had a fight and Mom was trying to make him not mad anymore. Almost every night after dinner he'd start yelling and swearing. Sometimes he'd throw things. I sure hoped he wouldn't throw the cake after we made it. But at least there'd still be the goop on the bottom of the pan. And the cooks got that part right out of the oven.

I got out the yellow cake mix while Maureen got the canned pineapple. It was Betty Crocker that made me wonder what other people would think of our pigsty kitchen. You knew Betty was really clean even if you didn't know exactly what she looked like.

Maureen got the eggs and told me to get the butter. It was on the kitchen table where it always sat, in a yellow lump beside Aunt Jemima. Was there really an Aunt Jemima? I liked her best because I bet she wouldn't mind how bad our kitchen was. She probably had a ton of kids too and everything was a disaster. The only thing is, she never changed the look on her face once. She just sat there with that big scarf on her head and never said a word.

The butter had black crumbs on it from someone making toast. You can tell a lot from butter. Like how hot it is in the kitchen. Or what kind of sandwich the last person had. If there was ketchup or mustard in the butter, they had some kind of meat sandwich. Or if there was jam and peanut butter in the butter you knew that it was one of the little kids. When someone was baking, there was usually flour in the butter and finger swipes because you had to butter and flour the pans.

There was something a lot worse. It's what you never want to see in the butter. When you see blackish-brown things in the butter, usually it's just toast crumbs. But if they're a little too long and round you better look again. So I did. I looked real close to see if it was just toast crumbs. Nope. There were at least three perfect little mouse poops. I looked so close my nose almost got in the butter and I could even see little mouse licks, right beside a mouse paw print. Those mice must have liked our butter. But it was a bad sign. It meant there were too many and they were taking over the whole house.

Mostly they stayed down under the oven in the drawer with the baking pans. It was warm there because of the pilot light. And food was always dropping down for them to eat. Anyone could see it was mouse heaven.

Sometimes they made little nests in the pans. The babies were really cute except for the fact that they were mice, which was gross and the fact that they left mouse poop everywhere they went. There were always mouse droppings in the pans. You were supposed to rinse the pans before using them, but I know we sometimes forgot. And once you blew the mouse poop out it was easy to pretend there never had been any poop in there anyway. It made me kind of nervous, but Mom said not to worry because the heat would kill the germs. I hoped so. None of us had died yet.

There wasn't any good way to get rid of the mice under the oven. You couldn't set a mousetrap in there or someone might get their fingers snapped when they reached in for a pan. And we never used poison or those dead mice would get rotten behind the walls where you couldn't get them out.

They ran fast when they were running from one mouse hole to another. You'd barely see a mouse out of the corner of your eye. Then when you turned your head to look, it would have already run into one of its little holes in the wall by the floor. Those mice could squeeze into holes that were a lot smaller than they were. Because they were so squishy. You hardly ever saw a mouse. But you knew they were everywhere.

I don't know why they were scary. They didn't do anything except chew on things, make nests for their babies, make little squeaky sounds inside the walls, and run around fast. Maybe it's because we knew they weren't supposed to be there.

I wasn't that scared of mice, but Maureen was. In fact, I wasn't scared of mice one bit when Maureen was around. And it felt good because she was older than me but only a little older.

I picked up the butter and got a real good Maureen mouse poop idea. I brought it over to the sink where she was opening the pineapple. "Look.'" I showed her the butter.

"What." She was saying it like I was the stupid one.

"Do you see anything in it?" I was going to give her a chance.

"Like what? There's just toast." Then she looked at me with squinted eyes, the way Mom sometimes does and said, "Why don't you just butter the pan like you're supposed to. You haven't done one thing so far."

OK. She asked for it. I was real careful to use only the butter that was underneath the mouse licks and on the other side of the poop. But Maureen wasn't ever going to know that part. I greased the pan good. Then I hid the butter.

Maureen was breaking the eggs and mixing the batter while I was putting down brown sugar. I was arranging pineapple slices in the pan when Sonny came into the kitchen.

"Makin' more butter." He grunted. Sonny was supposed to make butter every Saturday, but he didn't. He waited until we were almost out and then did it all at once. Making butter took a lot longer then, because there was so much to make.

Sonny took the big jar of cream from the refrigerator that we'd been collecting for the last few weeks. He said, "Get out of my way," while he pushed me away from the sink. Then he poured that thick chunky cream into a big stainless steel bowl.

"Bully." I said real quiet, and sort of pushed him back with my hip. I didn't look at him.

He was just lifting his fist to slam my arm when Mom walked in and said, "Sonny, haven't you made that butter yet? I told you to do that hours ago." She shook her head and said, "You're going to be a total waste of a human being if you keep up like this." He already was a waste, if you ask me. He carried the bowl of butter over to the table real slow like he was trying to make Mom even madder.

Mom went over to where Maureen was pouring the batter onto the pineapple. Maureen smiled and said, "I'm almost done making the cake."

"Me **too**," I said.

"She hasn't done one thing, Mom." And shook her head like I was a total waste.

"Yes I did too. You liar." I said it real loud. Too loud. I was probably screaming.

"Stop your shrieking. You sound like a shrew." Mom was covering her ears and shaking her head.

"But she's lying!" I was still saying it way too loud and Mom gave me a look like I better not say one more word or she'd slap my face.

"Don't worry, Mom, I'll finish everything." Maureen said it while she smiled her sick sweet smile that made me want to tear her hair out. I was still screaming. But it was all inside.

Mom looked at me and said, "You help Sonny wrap the butter when it's done." Then she left. Maureen won again.

She won from the very first. When I was real little, I remember trying to go into Mom's bedroom after my nap. I was gray and sleepy inside and wanted to lie down where she was and make the sickie feeling in my tummy that you always get after a nap go away. But I had to open the door to her bedroom and my hands were too little to go all the way around the doorknob. I had to reach up high and I started crying when my fingers kept sliding off the knob. Then when I wiped my eyes with my fingers, they got even more slippery until I was bawling so loud Mom was going to wake up for sure. So Maureen came over and told me, "Shut up and leave Mom alone."

"Don't want to," I howled back.

"You better not get us in trouble. So just shut up."

"Want to go in."

"You can't. She's taking a nap."

"I want tooooo." And started crying all over again.

"You can't get everything, so just shut up." Now she was saying it with her teeth and was grabbing my arm.

"Stop it. Pig!" I screamed and yanked my arm away because it hurt.

"**You** stop it." She dug her nails across my arm and left little red trails that oozed blood. That blood was from inside me, and now it was coming out and it made an electric feeling all up and down me. Then it started to hurt.

"Ooowww!!" I was sobbing now and it felt like everything was getting swollen inside and hot. So hot I was getting dizzy and burning. I just slumped down on the floor and everything went even darker than gray.

Mom finally came out because of all the howling and yelled at me, "What's wrong with you? Can't you see I'm trying to get some peace and quiet?" All I could do was lie on the floor and cry and feel how cold the floor was on my hot skin.

Maureen said, "I tried to stop her, Mom."

"Thanks darlin'." Mom put her arms around her and hugged her.

She came over to me and said, "Why don't you stop your blubbering now and give me a hug." I didn't have a hug in me anymore. So when she yanked me up to hug me, I was kind of limp and felt as cold and lost as the gray specks on the floor.

Maureen wins all the time and it's not just because she's older and that she fights dirty. It's because she knows how to make me the worst. That's why I hate her. I can't help it, even though it's a sin.

So Maureen put the cake in the oven and Sonny sat at the table swishing the cream in the stainless steel bowl back and forth. He used the big wooden paddle that was only for making butter. It took a long time. I don't know why Sonny was the main one who made the butter, but it made sense because he could sit at the table and stare at nothing for hours anyway. He might as well make butter while he was at it.

After a long time of pushing that wide wooden paddle back and forth, the cream started to curdle. It was practically a miracle, but it happened every time. It was sort of creamy white in the beginning, and then when it was time to curdle, it was like the butter part and the buttermilk part were trying to get away from each other. Butter took all the yellow, and buttermilk took the white. Then when the butter was as yellow as a dandelion it was time to wash it with cold water.

Sonny drained the buttermilk down the sink and poured cold water into the butter and pushed the butter around until the water got milky again. Then he poured it out and put in some new water. You were supposed to wash the butter that way until the water stayed clear even when the butter was pushed into it. But Sonny never washed it all the way, and you could tell because it always tasted as sour and spoiled as buttermilk. I've heard of people who actually drink buttermilk and like it. They're probably the kind of people who also eat cow brains and pigs feet. Buttermilk was too sickening to me to even try.

I liked the way butter looked, but didn't want to eat it either. No one did. It wrecked the taste of toast, unless you put on lots of jam to cover it up. Margarine was the best. It came in tidy little cubes. Not the way we did it. Our butter was dropped in huge glops onto aluminum foil and thrown in the freezer where it got even more wrinkled. But margarine was just for holidays.

This time Sonny only rinsed the butter two times and then started scooping it in globs onto the aluminum foil. I could see white drops of water, rolling in little balls all over the butter. I knew it would turn out bad.

So I told Sonny, "You're supposed to wash it some more."

He told me, "I'm supposed to make butter, and there's the butter. Do it yourself if you don't like it." He shoved the bowl over to me.

I tried to stir that yellow butter, but it was really hard to push. It was so solid from the cold water and you had to push with all your muscles to make it give up its buttermilk. I stopped. Sonny said, "See, runt? It's not as easy as it looks, is it?"

"Yeah, but it's gonna taste bad."

Then I got an idea. I asked Sonny, "Can I have some of the butter for an idea I have?"

"You can flush it down the toilet for all I care."

I scooped a big gob of the butter into a bowl and then helped him wrap the rest of it. After we put his butter in the freezer, Sonny disappeared and I got to be alone for a while. I poured some cold water into my butter and washed it. I washed that butter over and over again until there wasn't a drop of buttermilk left in it. It was easy because there was only about two cups of it. I wrapped it up into a nice big aluminum ball so it wouldn't get mixed up with the rest of the butter and also so it looked nice. Then I stuck it in the freezer.

The timer was buzzing to take the cake pan out of the oven. Maureen came back in the kitchen and she held the pan while I held a plate on top of it. We turned the whole thing over and there I was holding a golden gooey cake that would be good enough for a birthday cake. Maureen was holding the almost empty pan. She knew we were supposed to share the pan. I looked straight at her with my head turned a little and she knew I was daring her to try and grab more than her share. I drew a line with my finger down the middle of the pan and she picked her side.

We sat beside each other eating the pineapple goo with our fingers. When she was almost done with hers, I said, "You know there was mouse poop in the butter."

"Which butter?"

"The butter I greased the cake pan with."

She stopped licking her fingers. "Mice poop in this pan?" She sounded kind of jumpy.

"Well, not mice poop but mice poop butter. Deeelicious." I smacked my lips and smiled so big I showed my teeth.

"That was a stupid thing to do. Now the whole cake is ruined. Now we'll have to throw the whole thing out. Now I'll probably get sick and die of some rat disease. I'm telling Mom on you. You brat." She was holding her stomach and did look kind of sick. I started laughing and then yelling.

"You go and do it and see if I care. I asked you if you saw anything, and you said no. And besides, you told Mom you did it all by yourself and that I didn't do one thing. Liar!" She stopped, like she was thinking about what I was saying. I kept talking. "And she told Dad she'd make him some cake. Now there's no time to make another one. And how do you think Dad's gonna like it if we wasted all of our ingredients? You go tell Mom. You snot."

She came over to me like she was going to pull my hair. Then she stopped again and said, "I know you're lying. You're just trying to get me and it won't work." She smiled like she was the smartest person in the whole world.

"Well, I can prove it." I went over to where I'd hid the butter in the cupboard and pulled it out. I showed her. "Three nice little poops. You want to taste another one? Oops, better wait till it's cooked. You don't want to die."

"You're sickening." She looked like she was going to retch.

"I know. I can't help it." I got her good this time. I walked out of the room like I was the queen of everything.

I found Lady, our dog, waiting outside by the door, waiting for someone to pet her. I sat down on the dirt and she rolled herself on top of me and onto her back so I could scratch her belly. She was so pretty there, where her long reddish-blond hair was even lighter and softer. I scratched her while she licked my feet until I laughed.

Then I remembered my butter in the freezer and ran to check on it. It was solid but not frozen yet. Perfect. I went back into the kitchen and no one was there. I put a piece of bread in the toaster and slowly unwrapped just an edge of the butter. Lady followed me into the kitchen and I let her lick the mouse poop butter until the plate was clean. She loved it and didn't care one bit about mouse droppings. Because she was a dog and germs don't kill dogs. Germs don't even make them sick.

The toast popped up and I cut off a piece of my butter to put on the toast. I took a bite real careful, like I was a scientist or something. It didn't taste like butter at all! It was good!! It was way different and even better than margarine. So **that's** why some people think butter is better than margarine. I knew I had something good. I couldn't wait to do something with it, but I didn't know what. I hid my butter in the refrigerator.

Dad came home at about four because it was Saturday and he didn't work as long on the weekends. He was in a growly mood and now everyone was jumpy because of it. Even after he had a nap and after dinner, we knew to be on the lookout. When Mom came out with the cake, he smiled and we knew he liked it. But then he got mad because he said the coffee tasted like crap. "What do I have to do to get a decent cup of coffee around here? And why do I go to work all day anyway goddammit when none of you can do a goddamn thing right?" Then he drank his coffee.

No one could leave the table until Mom or Dad did. So when Mom got up, everyone else did too. Except for Maureen, me, and Luann. It was Luann's job to clear the table. Maureen and me were supposed to wash and dry the dishes. But we couldn't very well do that until Luann brought them over to the sink. Maureen got up anyway and started to fill the sink with water and suds. But since it was my turn to dry and there were no dishes to dry, I just sat there and stared at Luann to get the hint to speed it up and clear the dishes so we could all get out of there as fast as we could!

Then Dad said to me, "Why are you just sitting there?"

I knew I better get up right then and help Luann even though she was the one not doing her job and now I was the one getting in trouble. I put the milk in the refrigerator. But I guess the door didn't close all the way.

Dad yelled, "That's the way. Keep the refrigerator door open. That's why we pay the electricity, so we can keep the refrigerator open day and night." So I went over to the fridge and closed the door.

Then he yelled, "That's the way. Keep the goddamn door open. It doesn't matter what the hell I say around here anyway." I thought I closed it all the way the second time, but maybe I didn't. I went back to the fridge and it was closed. So maybe he really wanted me to open it. So I opened it.

"What are you doing with the goddamn door? Can't you close the son-of-a-bitchin door? Don't you have a goddamn brain in your head?" He was really screaming at me now. I was getting scared he would hit me. So I went over to the door and now it was closed. I guess it closed itself the way it was supposed to. Or maybe I accidentally closed it when I thought I opened it. I didn't know if I was supposed to close it or open it. I just stared at it while everything inside started to shake. The tears shook right out of my eyes. All I could do was stare at the fridge door while it got smaller and smaller. I didn't move one muscle, but it still got farther and farther away.

Dad screamed, "Are you going to leave that goddamn door open all night or do I have to knock some sense into you?"

I was so far away I could hardly hear myself saying it. "I can't tell what to do." I could almost feel his big hand smack me on the back of my head.

"Close the goddamn door!!" He screamed it so loud, the veins on his neck were popping out.

I knew I better do or say something even if I got killed for it. So somehow I said it out loud, "But, Daddy, I think it's already closed." I heard his heavy work boots walking over to where I was standing and I covered my head real fast.

He looked at the door and said, "Oh. Why didn't you say so in the first place?" Then he went over to the table and sat down again.

I walked over to where Maureen was washing the dishes and cried real quiet, while I dried the plates. We knew Dad was still watching us like a hawk. She stepped close and sort of leaned against me, and I could feel how warm she was. I looked over at her for just a second and felt something in her eyes I never felt before. It wrapped me up in warm honey and held me there for almost a second.

I felt better all of sudden, and then realized that there were still some dishes on the table. Luann went to hide when Dad started yelling at me, and now one of us would have to go over by Dad to get the dishes. I looked at Maureen again and moved my head a little toward the table. She knew. I made my eyes beg her not to make me go over there. She nodded OK. Then she went over and cleared the dishes. I could see her hands shaking a little, but after a few minutes we had all the dishes in the sink and we hadn't heard another word out of Dad.

We were home free until Maureen's hand slipped on a plate and it broke in the sink. Dad jumped up and said, "What the hell!"

Maureen said almost at the same time, "I'm sorry, Daddy. It just slipped." She was crying already.

"What the hell are you trying to do anyway? Break every dish in the whole goddamn house? " He came over to look in the sink.

"I'll pay for it." Maureen was sort of whimpering.

"With what? I'm the only one who makes any goddamn money around here and what is it for? So you can break dishes day and night. Clean up that goddamn mess and get out of here or I'll give you something to cry about." Then he stomped to the other side of the room where the table was. He was swearing in German now and we didn't know what he was saying. He wasn't talking to us anyway.

Maureen was trying to wash the dishes too fast. I was afraid she'd break another one or cut herself on the glass that was still in the dishwater. Then I remembered my butter. I leaned over to Maureen and whispered, "Don't worry. I've got an idea."

Dad kicked a kitchen chair. It flew across the room. We had to get out of his way, but if we ran out of the room, we knew he'd chase us and we'd get hit for sure. So we had to stay put.

I walked over to the fridge like I was the invisible kid. Dad threw a can of evaporated milk across the room. I knew he was trying not to hit us. The milk splattered everywhere. His swearing did too. I grabbed my butter and snuck back over to the counter where Maureen was and buttered some crackers. I knew Dad liked crackers. He was getting a little quieter now but was still stomping and swearing. I brought the buttered crackers over to the table by his coffee cup. Maureen wiped up the splattered milk and put the can back on the table. She poured him some hot coffee from the stove.

Finally, he came over to the table and sat down. I knew the coast was clear for now. Maybe he wouldn't get mad again tonight. I pushed the crackers over to him and said, "I made the butter special for you."

He put a cracker in his mouth and said, "It's good. It's like the way my Mom used to make it." I looked at Maureen and smiled.

19

THE MOTEL

TEN YEARS

THERE was a dust storm coming and it was almost noon. We had to close the windows in all of the units before it came, or we'd have to clean them all over again. You could see the storm coming like a thick brownish-yellow blanket. Even if you closed the windows tight, you'd get dust so thick on the sills that in just half an hour you could write words on them. Then after another half hour you couldn't read what you wrote, which was good if you'd written bad words and didn't want to get your mouth washed out with soap.

During a dust storm, the dust crept through your shirt and pants and onto your skin. It went all the way into the little cracks in your skin that you didn't even know were there. After a while, the cracks would get bigger and bigger with dust, and pretty soon you'd look like an old wrinkly dirt devil.

I was carrying some clean linens to the Tates in Number 24. They were renting weekly so we only changed their bed once a week. They had been staying almost all summer and never wanted us girls to make their bed, just hand them the linens and towels. They'd strip the bed while we waited. Then they'd help us stuff the old towels and sheets into a pillowcase. Since the Tates were married and didn't need us to come inside, Mom let just one girl go to change their sheets. Otherwise, it was a rule that none of the girls were supposed to go alone to clean a unit or bring fresh sheets or even talk to a tenant. Mom said, "It just isn't safe." She was mostly worried about men, especially the bachelors.

The wind was blowing hard by the time I got up to Number 24, which was part of the long building that Dad called the Suzee-Q. None of us ever knew why he called it that, but we called it that too, and it went from Number 17 to 26.

The linens were collecting dust in their creases and the towels were changing color. I was squinting as hard as I could, but the wind was blowing dust right through my eyelids and into my eyes. They were crying even though I wasn't. When I knocked on the door and Mrs. Tate answered, I pushed the linens toward her and said, "I'm sorry about the dust. Do you want me to help you shake them out?"

She said, "Don't worry about it. Why don't you come on in and get out of the wind?"

I said, "I'm not supposed to. Mom doesn't want us to bother you." This was true, but it wasn't the main reason. Mom was afraid one of the tenants would grab us and do something bad to us. And if I went inside, there wasn't anyone to run for help if I got hurt.

Mrs. Tate said, "You aren't bothering anyone. Come on in, while I gather up the sheets."

I walked inside just a step and looked around for Mr. Tate. He didn't seem to be there. I was hoping he wouldn't come out of the bathroom in his undershorts or something. My heart was beating fast. I stayed by the door, rubbing my eyes, which felt like they just got scoured. They were crying all over my face and making mud.

Mrs. Tate scrunched up her face and asked, "Is anything wrong?"

So she wouldn't think I was crying from feeling sad, I smiled at her and said, "It's just the dust storm. It got in my eyes."

"Do you want to use the sink in the bathroom to wash your eyes?"

I wasn't sure where Mr. Tate was. If he was in the bedroom, he could reach right into the bathroom and grab me, and it would be my own fault for being so stupid. I peeked into the kitchen and saw that he wasn't in there. I said, "Can I wash them in the kitchen?"

"Sure."

The water stung my eyeballs even worse, but it also felt cool, and after splashing water up into them, they felt better. I knew I shouldn't use any of her fresh towels to dry my face. I also didn't want any of the germs on her old towels, so I wiped my face and hands with my sleeves. I did it fast so nothing could happen to me while I wasn't looking. I knew I'd better get out of there as soon as I could. I picked up the pillowcase full of dirty linens and ran out. Probably just in the nick of time.

I still had to go into all the vacant units in the Suzee-Q and close them up tight before the dust storm got any worse. I had the passkey, but I couldn't remember which ones were rented and which ones were vacant. Number 17 had Mr. Willie and he was a permanent tenant. I knew Number 18 was rented for the week. Number 20, 23, and 25 had cars in front of them, so they were rented too. And I knew Number 21 and 26 were vacant. But I wasn't sure about 19 and 22.

I left the dirty linens on the walkway in front of Number 24, the Tates, while I ran into Number 21 and closed its windows. No one was renting it and it was so empty in there. There was just the quiet whistle scream of the wind that came through the window screens that sounded like someone wailing. Like a ghost girl who was so cracked and dry inside that when someone touched her she turned into a gazillion bits of dust. And then the wind blew on her and there she was, scattered all over the kitchen and bathroom, where the wind was blowing the hardest. I shuddered and slammed the windows down hard. Then I ran fast to Number 26.

While I was closing the windows, I tried to figure out what to do about Number 19 and 22. I sure didn't want to clean any more rooms than I had to because of the dust. And there was no way I wanted to walk all the way back to the house to find out which units were vacant, and then have to walk back up to the Suzee-Q, and then walk back home again. I'd probably be blinded from the storm by then.

I went over to Number 22 to peek in their front window, but the drapes were pulled. That told me nothing. The only thing to do was to knock, and if anyone came to the door, I'd say I was sorry and that I made a mistake. I knocked. No one answered. I yelled, "Is anybody home?" No answer. So I sneakily unlocked the door, peeking in to see if anyone was there. No one. It was vacant. After closing its windows I went to Number 19 and was glad I was almost done and now I could go home and watch *Lassie* on TV. I wasn't even spooked anymore by being up at the Suzee-Q alone.

I knocked on the door, said, "Is anyone home?" and unlocked the door with the passkey all at once. I swung the door open wide and didn't even look up until I was inside. Then I saw a naked woman on the bed and a man with a penis lying right beside her. I started screaming, "I'm sorry! I'm sorry!"

At first they were just laying there. Then they moved around fast, trying to pull up the sheets. The woman asked me, "What's wrong?"

I covered my eyes and tried to go out the door all at once. I ran my shoulder into the door-jamb. I kept saying, "I'm sorry. I didn't know you were home. I'm real sorry." Finally, I got through the door and ran down the hill as fast as I could.

I was still breathing hard when I came into the living room. Everyone was watching TV and no one noticed me. It was wall-to-wall kids. You couldn't even walk into the room without stepping on someone. I found Nicky, who was my favorite little brother, and knew he'd let me squeeze in beside him on the floor. I curled his blond hair with my fingers while he let me hold him, and we watched *Sea Hunt*. *Lassie* had just ended. I didn't even think about the naked man and woman. But I sure hoped they wouldn't say anything to Mom. After *Father Knows Best*, Mom came in and said we were turning into vegetables and to turn the damn TV off and find something to do with our God-given brains.

After a while of finding nothing to do with my brain, I went into the older girls' bedroom and laid on Georgina and Becky's double bed. They got a double bed because they were the oldest girls. It was soft and comfy. The sheets weren't crunchy either, even though they used motel sheets on their bed. Motel sheets were always starchy and crunchy for at least a week. Then they started to get nice and soft. I couldn't understand why the tenants wanted new sheets every week or every day. We only changed the sheets in our house when they started to smell really bad, about once every few months.

Then Maureen came in and said, "Get off the bed. We have to clean Number 6 and 7. The Canadians finally checked out and Mom wants those rooms ready to rent out again tonight." We got the sheets and cleaning supplies from Mom and Dad's room and started walking to Number 7. I was glad the dust storm had stopped.

Number 7 was only three units away from where we lived. The front of the motel was one long string of units and our house, which wasn't really a house, took up about half of that. We lived in what used to be Number 1, 2, 3, and 4. We rented out Numbers 5, 6, 7, and 8 for overnighters. It only took a minute to walk to Number 7 from the girls' room.

I was glad it was Canadians who had been there. They always made their beds and left the unit tidy clean. They must be real clean in Canada, but don't they know they don't need to make the bed? All their work went to waste when we stripped it. I bet no one would have ever known if we didn't change the Canadians' sheets because they never left any spots on the sheets and they always left them smelling like soap. We put on fresh sheets anyway because we were supposed to, and Mom would kill us if she found out we didn't.

The first thing we did was check to see if they left any food for us. We hit the jackpot! They left three slices of bacon, a grapefruit that was only partly rotten, four eggs, some margarine, two loaves of bread, some baby hot dogs, and a little canned ham that was just as big as your hand. Maureen and I got to keep all the food since we cleaned the room, but we had to share it with each other. We'd divide it up when we got back to the house. I couldn't wait to have some fried bacon and watch the other kids drool. And I wouldn't give them one bite unless they did something nice for me. Except for maybe Nicky or Francie. Jason was nice too, but he was still too little to care about bacon.

I cleaned the bathroom while Maureen did the kitchen. There was a lot more dust to wipe up than usual, because of the storm. Then we made the bed together. She did hospital corners on the sheets **and** blanket exactly like Mom taught us, but I didn't think the bed looked very good that way. I made hospital corners just on the sheets and tucked the blanket in only at the end of the bed. That way it looked smoother on the sides when the bedspread was on. We fought about it every time. Maureen thought I was wrong for not doing it the way Mom said, and I thought she was stupid to not see that my way was better. Those units needed all the help they could get.

I still don't understand why anyone would want to come to our motel when they could go on into town and stay at the Star Bright

Motel if they wanted to. It had a cement circle in front and green plants growing all around it. I thought that those rooms must have soft pillows and lacy curtains and maybe even pink walls. Would you rather go there, or to our motel, which had a dirt driveway, no trees, too many kids, and units that were just plain? The only thing pretty we had were huge boulders in a line in front of the overnighter units. They were all painted in real light pink, orange, and lavender. I helped Butch mix the colors so each boulder would be a different color and look like a sunset.

Mom worried a lot about not getting enough tenants. The Canadians were our most regular overnighters. She said they kept coming back because we weren't immoral, the units were clean, and we had kitchenettes. I never did understand the part about us not being immoral. I knew it had to do with having sins on your soul. But our whole family had lots of sins. Otherwise, why would we always be praying so hard to get rid of them?

Mom would never rent to someone she thought might be bad. Not even for overnight. You had to be over eighteen years old to stay at our motel. And if a man and a woman came to rent a room and she thought they might not be married she asked, "Are you married?" If they said no, she told them, "You ought to be ashamed of yourselves," and asked them to leave. If they said they were married, she sometimes asked them to prove it. But she only did that with tenants who looked kind of young.

Mom talked to Dad about how maybe people in town thought this was a red light district, which is some kind of immoral place. She was worrying about it ever since they bought the long red fluorescent light bulbs to go in the front of the overnighter units. I thought the red looked pretty and the red lights also had less bugs flying and banging into them than the white lights did. Mom thought those bulbs were a real mistake though. Even when Dad mixed white fluorescent bulbs with the red ones, she still worried. Why would red light bulbs make someone think we were bad?

Maureen knew something about red lights but wouldn't tell me. She said I'd find out when I got older. She was only one and a half years older than me! I hated it when she knew more stuff than me and then gloated. When we were done with Number 7, we did Number 6. They only left us an orange, but it was real juicy. When we finished cleaning and started carrying the dirty linens back to the house, I remembered that I left the Tates' linens in the driveway up at the Suzee-Q. I knew I'd better go get them before I got in trouble. I told Maureen that if she carried everything back to the house, she could have one of my strips of bacon. She said OK.

I started walking up to the Suzee-Q again and saw that the linens were still on the ground, but were covered with dust. Just as I picked them up, I saw Luann walking over to Mr. Willie in Number 17.

Mr. Willie was old and had a fat belly. He wore shorts and a white t-shirt when it was hot. You could see the hair on his stomach skin when it rolled out from under the t-shirt. He didn't even care. He liked to sit on the stoop, drink beer, and talk to us kids. We liked him too, because he was nice to us. Mr. Willie was our only totally permanent tenant.

He gave us stuff to eat sometimes if we stayed and talked to him. He was a bachelor and I guess he was lonely from not having any kids. Mom said to watch out for him because he might be a dirty old man. When she found out me and Luann were sitting on his lap, she said we were **never** to sit on a tenant's lap. I couldn't see why not. He didn't seem that dirty.

Mom said he might grab us and do bad things to us and we'd need to fight like animals to get away. She said to use our teeth and fingernails to bite and scratch his skin. We should use our knees to kick him in the crotch and then run like crazy.

She didn't have anything against Mr. Willie though. She said, "It's just that you never know." We were also supposed to be polite to the tenants and not act suspicious of them or make them feel bad about anything. She told me it was up to me to keep an eye on Luann because I was bigger than her. I was supposed to make sure she didn't get hurt by a tenant.

So when I saw her walking over to talk to Mr. Willie, I knew I'd better go over there too. I asked Luann, "What are you doing up here?"

"Nothin'," she said.

Mr. Willie said, "Why don't you girls come over here and sit on my lap and I'll go get you a Coke." He patted his lap.

Luann asked, "Do you have any potato chips?"

He went into his apartment and came out with two ice-cold Cokes. He said, "Sorry, no chips. Do you want a saltine?"

Luann said no thanks to the saltines, took the pop, and climbed onto his lap.

I said no thanks to everything and stood there watching her have all the fun while I made sure he didn't hurt her.

Luann knew she wasn't supposed sit on his lap. She knew she got something and I didn't and that I couldn't say anything to her in front of Mr. Willie because we weren't supposed to hurt his feelings. When we walked back down to the house after she was done slurping down her Coke and didn't save any for me, I pinched her arm. She howled, and I told her if she said one thing about it to Mom, I'd tell on her. She acted like she hadn't done one thing to deserve it, and that made me want to pinch her again. But I didn't.

When we got home, it was getting close to dinnertime. Maureen had already divided the food and left my half on my bed. I ate some of the ham and bread from the Canadians in front of Luann while she begged me for a bite. I finally gave her two crumbs and she was so mad, she stomped out.

At dinner that night, which was just barley soup and coleslaw, the doorbell to the motel rang and Mom went to answer it. When she came back, she was smiling. "I rented out Number 5 for two weeks and Number 6 for a week. They'll be paying the daily rate." It was good news because tenants paid a lot more money that way than if they paid weekly. But it meant room service every day.

Mom looked at Georgina, then Becky, Maureen, me, and Luann. She said, "You girls stay away from those men. And I don't want any of you running outside in your nightgowns while they're here." We all looked at each other and smiled, because now we knew it was the playboys who were staying in Number 5 and 6.

The playboys were the cute guys who were musicians for the tavern, which was only about a quarter of a mile away. They all knew each

other and stayed at our motel. Number 5 was right next to the girls'
bedroom and most of those guys were so good to look at that I couldn't
help but stare and sometimes even talk to them. Georgina and Becky
even flirted with some of them.

The thing about not going outside in your nightgown was always a
problem though, because of the way our house was made. Like I said,
it wasn't really a house. It was just the boys' room, which was also the
laundry and utility room on the end, plus four motel units all in a row.

Next to the boys' room was the kitchen, which used to be Number
1 before we started living in it. Then came the living room and the
office for the motel where tenants came to pay us. The unit that used
to be Number 3 was Mom and Dad's bedroom and was also for motel
supplies, ironing, and tiny babies. The last part of our house was the
girls' room which used to be Number 4.

The bad thing about the girls' room was you had to go through
Mom and Dad's bedroom to get to it. Either that or use the outside
doors to come and go. Mom hated the way we always *traipsed* though
their room. And we weren't supposed to go in and out using the outside doors after dark. But it was dark lots of times.

Mom especially didn't want us running outside in our nightgowns where the tenants could see us or grab us. But we didn't want
to get yelled at for going through their bedroom. And who wants to
change clothes just to go to the living room, when you're already in
your nightgown?

It was fun and scary running outside in your nightgown when
the playboys were next door. If they saw you they'd whistle and you'd
have to keep running so they wouldn't grab you. And you hoped
Mom wouldn't catch you either. Then later on, if you had to clean
one of their rooms, they might tease you because they saw you in your
nightgown. It was more exciting than finding yummy food in one of
the vacant units.

The next day Maureen and I went to change the beds for the playboy in Number 5. Georgina and Becky took Number 6 because they
thought the cutest guy might be there. When we all went up to clean,
both guys were gone. I was kind of glad and kind of not, because I
wanted to at least see what the guy in Number 5 looked like.

The next day, which was Saturday, Maureen and I knocked on the door, and we heard a man inside say, "Come on in."

Maureen and I looked at each other. We weren't supposed to go in the units when there was a man there, especially if he was alone, even if there were two of us. Maureen said to the tenant, "We're not supposed to."

Then he kind of laughed and said, "Then why'd you knock on the door?"

I said, "We just came to clean your room."

"Then you'll have to come in, won't you?" He still hadn't come to the door and opened it yet.

I whispered to Maureen, "You go in because you're older and I'll stay by the door and run for help."

She whispered back, "OK, but you better not leave me alone."

I said out loud to the playboy, "OK, we'll come in."

He said, "Then come in!" He sounded like he was getting sick of us.

Maureen opened the door a crack and then slowly opened it a little more. We saw him lying on the bed with one of his long legs hanging out of the covers and his chest all bare and tan. He was so handsome I couldn't help but smile. Then my face got hot, and I knew it was red too. That just made it even hotter.

He said, "You can start cleaning in the bathroom. And then finish up in here."

Maureen didn't even look at him when she walked by. She just pushed her chin up in the air and ignored him. I kept staring at him, and then looking at the floor when he stared back. He said, "Are you just going to stand there or come over here and keep me company?" He patted the bed.

I said, "I'm just going to stay here and wait for Maureen."

He said, "Why don't you at least close the door?"

I had to think fast, but my mind was as thick and lumpy as peanut butter. Finally, I said, "I have to keep it open a little so I can hear if my little brother needs me."

He looked kind of disgusted with me. I wished he was a Catholic who didn't have any sins, and wouldn't ever hurt me, and then I could go over and sit by him and touch his brown chest. But I knew he was a playboy, and they were immoral. And who knows what he would do to you after he grabbed you. I was so scared and embarrassed that my legs and arms were trembly. But he was still so cute. I smiled at him and then he smiled back. I kept shaking, smiling, turning beet red, and wiggling around by the door until Maureen was done in the bathroom and kitchen.

She came back into the living room where the bed was and said, "I'm done in there. We just need to make your bed now."

"Well then, I'll need to get out of it, unless you want to make it with me in it." He laughed.

Maureen just looked at him like he wasn't funny, and then he jumped up out of the bed. I covered my eyes but peeked a little. He had on little tiny underpants that didn't even cover his butt. He walked into the bathroom, and after a while, we heard the shower. We made the bed as fast as we could, and left before he came back.

The next day he wasn't there, but he left some girlie pictures on the wall near his bed. We didn't see him all week, but every day there were more pictures. Some of them were even on the ceiling. They were from magazines like *Playboy* and after a few days, they practically covered the walls. In the beginning, it felt like a sin to look at them. Then Maureen and I decided it was probably a sin for just him, because he was the one who put them there, and he was a man looking at naked girls. It couldn't be a sin for a girl to look at a naked girl.

We looked and looked at those girls with the naked bosoms and bikini panties, sticking their butts in the air. They acted like they were bunnies or kittens and dressed up in cowgirl outfits with only a hat, holster, and leather bikini bottoms. We laughed at the girls in the pictures for being so stupid, but I had to admit some of them sure were pretty.

When we came to the room the next Saturday, he was there again. When we knocked he said, "I'm busy. Come back after dinnertime." He sounded kind of hoarse, like he'd been yelling a lot. We came back at about seven and he said through the door. "Just forget it. I'll be gone tomorrow anyway."

Early on Sunday morning, Becky saw a girl with a pink scarf and red pedal pushers leave his unit. She said the woman was walking wobbly and looked kind of sick. He checked out a few hours later.

Later that morning when we came to clean the room, it was a disaster! There was shaving cream all over the walls, in the closet, around the bed, and all over the bathroom, even the ceiling. The bathroom floor was soaked, and there was a woman's bra in the shower, along with half a jar of maraschino cherries. I didn't want any of them. We found two empty bottles of vodka in the kitchen. What were they doing with all that shaving cream? And why didn't she take her bra off before she got in the shower? The maraschino cherries I could understand.

After cleaning up the shaving cream, we pulled the blankets off the bed and saw something that looked like blood smeared all over the sheets. I hoped it wasn't really blood. It went all the way through the mattress pad and into the mattress. Maybe it was just ketchup.

"Do you think it's blood?" I asked.

"Yep." Maureen looked kind of disgusted.

"How do you think it got there?"

"It's from the woman who was here with him."

"Do you think he tried to kill her?" I wondered to myself if she left early in the morning to go to the hospital.

"Don't be so stupid. It's because she was a virgin."

I knew a virgin was a girl who saved herself for her husband. But what did that have to do with blood? I said, "If she was such a virgin why would she come into a playboy's room?"

"I don't know."

"And what would make her start bleeding like that?" I hoped Maureen knew what she was talking about.

"It's from having sex if you're a virgin. That's how you know if someone's a virgin."

I wasn't exactly sure what sex was. I knew from Mom that it had something to do with having babies and that the sperm from the man's penis had to be planted in the woman's vagina to have a baby. But Mom never said how it got planted or what that had to do with sex. I got the feeling Maureen knew a lot more about sex than me. I said, "How do you know so much about this stuff?"

"I'm older than you."

"Not that much!"

"Well, I'm older enough. Obviously." She was smirking at me. There was no way I was going to ask her any more questions with her snotty attitude.

I figured out how the blood got there by myself. I told Maureen, "The blood wasn't from being a virgin. It was from having a miscarriage like Mom did last time. And I bet that's why she had to go to the hospital this morning."

"Did she have to go to the hospital?" Maureen looked surprised.

Ha! I knew something she didn't, even if I wasn't sure if it was true. I said, "Yeah. Remember how she could hardly walk this morning?"

After stripping the bed, we had to pull down all the girlie pictures that were on the walls. I wanted to save one of the pictures because I thought the girl was so pretty and I hoped I would look like her someday. Maureen said, "You'll go to hell if you save it. It's a mortal sin." I knew she was right, so we tore them all up and threw them in the garbage. I was glad they were gone because they were definitely immoral, but I didn't hate those girls the way Maureen did. I felt sorry that they were all ripped up and in the garbage.

We barely got done in time for dinner. That unit took about three hours. While we were setting the table for dinner that night, I told Mom about the shaving cream and the vodka. Becky told her about the woman leaving in the morning. And Maureen told her the woman was going to the hospital. Mom just shook her head and looked disgusted. When we were all sitting down and ready to eat I asked Mom, "Why do you rent to the playboys when they're so immoral?"

She looked at me hard for a minute. Then she put her head down and said, "There's only so much I can do. Let's say Grace now."

We said the dinner prayer and then the Hail Mary. The Virgin Mary was supposed to protect you from impure thoughts if you prayed to her, but I still thought about how cute that playboy was even while I said the Hail Mary. I hoped the Virgin Mary wouldn't mind too much.

20

BLACK ROSES

TEN YEARS

THE thing I wanted to do the most with Butch was paint. She was an artist and so was Mom, but Mom stopped painting a long time ago. "Too many kids," Mom said. They both did murals, but Butch's was the newest. One whole wall of Butch's living room showed a sunset in Aruba. It was of the beach, the ocean, and ming trees. Her sunset paintings always had ming trees. I asked her why they all bent over in one direction that way. She said it was the trade winds. I wondered if the trade winds had some kind of magic in them to bend those trees so far over. She put silver and gold sparkle glue on the water to make it look like sunlight. That was my favorite part. The whole painting was mostly a greenish blue color. "Aqua," Butch said. I guess she always wanted to remember Aruba.

Mom, Flora, Butch, and Grandpa all lived in Aruba when Mom was a kid. Grandpa worked for Standard Oil back then and wasn't retired yet. Mom liked to remember Aruba too. It was the sun and aqua water and coral reefs that she remembered.

The biggest freckle ever made lived on my Mom's arm and it came from Aruba too. It connected to other freckles and altogether they made a freckle family so big you couldn't find one place on her arm that was just regular. She said she had those freckles since she was about ten. What she really wanted back then was peaches and cream skin like Greta Garbo, even though everyone knew those movie stars had the morals of a guttersnipe.

After trying all kinds of goop to make her freckles go away, she bought some Freckle-B-Gone. Well, she got peaches and cream skin for almost a whole day, but when she went out in the sun again those freckles came back a **lot** bigger than before, and now they'd probably never go away. She said that even if you want to keep fighting some things, you also have to know when to stop. I knew I couldn't stop fighting. What if the things I was trying to get rid of would never go away?

When I talked to Mom about Aruba, I always tried to find out more about Voodoo or black magic, but she wouldn't tell me anything. I knew she sort of believed in it and sort of didn't. But was scared of it. She wasn't scared of mind reading though, and did it all the time with Flora, her twin sister. When they were kids, they cheated on tests that way. But it only worked if one of them knew the answer to the question. They always knew weird things about each other, even when they were grown ups. Like if one of them was sick or mad or having a depression.

They also saw things that no one else could see. Things like halos, crosses, and rosaries. "Mystical visions," Mom said. They both saw those things at the same time. That was supposed to prove that they weren't crazy **and** that they were really holy. Mom even did an oil painting of the Sacred Heart, which is Jesus with his heart all stabbed out and bleeding with thorns and a little knife going through it. That came from one of her visions back when she was getting converted and still painted. Father Laughlin thought it was holy. We had to look at that Sacred Heart every time we watched TV because Mom hung the painting right above it. So we wouldn't be brainwashed by everything we saw on that damn fool TV.

Butch didn't think Mom's visions meant anything holy. And everyone knew what she thought about Catholic stuff. She'd shake her head, click her false teeth, and walk away when Mom started talking Catholic to her.

Mom was always doing novenas for Butch. A novena was a bunch of prayers that practically guaranteed that you'd get a miracle. And Mom wanted the miracle that Butch would become a convert before she died. I could see why Butch didn't want to become any kind of convert, the way people are always praying for you. I was glad hardly anyone ever prayed for me. Because I hated it when they did.

What I hated worse, was having to do a novena the hard way, by kneeling down to do the rosary three times in a row and killing your knees. I wanted a miracle as much as anyone, but why couldn't we wait until Good Friday to do the novena and **also** get a plenary indulgence, just by saying one or two prayers? But when Mom wanted a miracle, we never waited until Good Friday. She also thought you got a better miracle if you did it with the rosary. And if your knees hurt, it was all the better.

When I was almost ten and Grandpa had already died, Mom and Dad went to visit Frank and Flora. The whole family had to do a novena first, so they'd have a safe trip, and also for Butch to be converted. We had to kneel and say those prayers over and over again for so long I didn't even want a miracle after a while. But I still hoped Mom and Dad would have a safe trip.

They were gone for almost three days. The older kids were in charge, but Butch got to come over anytime she wanted and keep an eye on us. Sunday morning after Becky drove us home from church, Butch came over to our house to do some painting.

She thought rose vines would look swell on Mom's pinkish-orange kitchen cupboards. Butch had rose vines on her own cupboards and they were as pretty as the sunset mural to me. I begged to help her, and to learn how to be an artist too. First she drew the pencil lines for the vines. Then she gave me black paint to go over the pencil and fill in the lines. I was real careful and did it just the way she said to. But when I stood back and looked at those vines, they looked snaky and not one bit like the pretty ones at Butch's house.

Meanwhile, Butch started to paint black leaves and black roses on my vines. I told her I wanted pink roses. But she said the cupboard door already had enough pink, and the black would show up better. I wanted to keep helping, so when I was done with the vines, I tried to make the best black roses and leaves I could. By the time I got the idea for red roses, they were all done. Butch still liked my idea for red though. She painted in tiny thorns on the vines with just a little drop of red on their ends. I didn't help with that part. I crossed my eyes a

hundred times to make those cupboards blurry, hoping some pretti-
ness could sneak through, but all that I saw was ugly and scary. I was
sorry about my idea for red.

I was all mixed up inside me when I went to bed that night. I was
so proud to help paint an almost mural, but the vines just didn't turn
out right and my roses were even worse than Butch's. When I started
to go to sleep, it felt like there were spider vines crawling up my legs.
Then I dreamt about an old native woman from Aruba with black
hair, who didn't have any teeth. She was holding a chicken with its
head cut off and was standing in the middle of a fire. She looked at
me with her shiny black eyes and started shaking the chicken until
drops of its blood landed on my face and on the inside of my legs.

Mom came back the next day and when she saw the vines she
didn't say anything. I could tell she was mad. Before she did one other
thing, she went out into the garage, found the pinkish-orange cupboard paint, and painted right over those vines. It made me almost
cry because it was my first time as an artist. But I had to admit they
looked better gone. The black spidery feeling was creeping around,
way down inside me, making me scared for what I did. Scared for
almost everything. I hoped it wasn't there for good.

Mom didn't let any of us kids visit Butch for a long time. When we
did go up to her house, Mom would ask us what we talked about. Mom
said Butch was getting senile, which I guess just meant old and crazy.
But she was also kind of mean, mainly to Mom. When Mom made a
mistake like putting the salt in the refrigerator, Butch would whisper
so everyone could hear, "You're slipping..." Or she'd make a joke about
a woman who lost her salt first and then her mind. Then she'd laugh,
or click her teeth. Mom prayed hard those times and sometimes cried.
I also saw the way her jaw got hard and she clamped her mouth closed
like she was going to break her own teeth even while she was crying.

A few months after Grandpa died, Butch started getting sick with
heart attacks. Sometimes it was just indigestion, which looked like
heart attacks. She got sick so many times that she had to come and
live with us since there was no one else to take care of her.

Butch didn't seem that sick to me, except when she was having
one of her indigestion heart attacks. Then she sat up and coughed a

lot. We were only supposed to call an ambulance if she went uncon-
scious, because Mom thought she might be faking it. One of the kids
had to be with her all the time, even at night. We took turns sleeping
with her in case she started to die.

She told me lots of things when I stayed with her then, but she
couldn't grab me as hard with her voice as she could when I was little.
And I didn't believe her stories as much as I used to. It was more like
they just gave me things to think about.

She said Dad was a thief and that he stole Grandpa's carpenter
tools when Grandpa died. Dad had a million tools already. What
would he need Grandpa's tools for? Besides, Mom said Dad was the
most honest man she knew. Even though I knew Butch was senile,
I still couldn't help wondering where some of Dad's new tools came
from. She also said I should stop sitting on Dad's lap because he was
still a man and you can never trust any man and you can never tell if
he'll do bad things to you. I wondered a lot about that.

One weekend Mom went away to a Catholic meeting called the
Legion of Decency, where they talked about indecent exposure, girls
who wore tiny bikinis, and bad movies. Mom had to go see a lot of the
bad movies so she could see for herself how indecent they really were.
Then when she came home she'd go on and on about us girls showing
too much damn flesh around the house. Anyway, she was supposed to
be gone all of that Friday, including overnight, and all day Saturday.

Dad worked on Saturday so Butch got to be in charge that day. I
was eating breakfast at our big kitchen table and stared at the mural
that Mom painted a long time ago. It covered the whole dining room
wall and was of another sunset in Aruba. Mom did it with oil paints
so you could wash it easy. It wasn't as pretty as Butch's and there was
only one ming tree in it. Mom liked palm trees more. There was also
a beach with a native woman who had a big basket on her head and
was naked on top. You couldn't see any bosoms though because she
just showed her back. She was walking away from the water and into
the palm trees. That native woman had been carrying that basket on
her head my whole life.

That's the morning that Butch got the bad idea to fix up Mom's
mural and surprise her. I knew we were in for trouble. Becky told her

that Mom would get really mad if anyone messed with her mural. But Butch had that look, like she didn't hear a word Becky said.

Butch went right ahead and got out her paints. She looked like a cat chewing on a mouse tail with the paintbrush in her mouth. After a while of chewing the brush and clicking her teeth, Butch started in. She painted the yellow, orange, and pink sunset a dark blue except for about three or four red streaks where the sun was setting. The light blue water turned into medium dark blue. Mom hated blue because she said it made her think of depression. Then Butch put just a few red streaks into the water. The native woman became a huge black ming tree as tall as me with branches crawling all over where it used to be green forest. The ming branches looked like black rose vines and the palm trees looked like big spiders, which Mom was scared to death of.

The worst part was the new cactus that Butch stuck right in the middle. It was pitch black and even bigger than me. I didn't think it looked like any kind of cactus, but that's what she said it was. It was like a tall cylinder that was rounded and only slightly pointy on top. And it didn't have any stickers. You couldn't ignore it, no matter how hard you tried. I sure didn't want to eat in front of that mural anymore. And I was glad I'd given up being an artist.

When Butch was done, she announced to all of us kids that Mom wasn't ever coming home again and not to worry because she was going to marry Dad and take really good care of us. We looked at each other and wrinkled up our faces while we tried to figure out what she was talking about. It didn't make any sense to any of us. After a minute or two we started to laugh, roll our eyes and make koo koo sounds. It wasn't very funny though, because even though what Butch was saying couldn't be true, she wasn't kidding and **none** of us knew what was going on,

We waited for Dad to come home. When he came inside, he and Butch went into her bedroom together for about half an hour. What was happening? When he came out, he looked as scared as I'd ever seen him. He called Mom on the phone and told her, "Come home right now goddammit."

Mom didn't seem that upset when she came home. I think she liked it that Dad was scared. Now she had proof for him and everyone else that she wasn't the crazy one. Now she was the cat and Butch was the mouse. She stood back to look at the mural and said, "That's such a sick mind. It's like blood streaked all over the sky. And that cactus is a phallic symbol, plain and simple."

The next day, Sunday, Mom called Flora. They talked for a long time. The day after that, Flora and Frank came to our house. Mom and Flora drove into town and stayed all day. They were doing their hush hush talking the whole visit and us kids were wondering what was up. Butch didn't notice anything. She was mostly staying in bed from indigestion.

On Wednesday afternoon, all of the grown ups took Butch for a drive and came back without her. They left her at the Colonial Mansion nursing home. It was where some old governor used to live in the summer time.

Dinner that night was weird. Butch's new mural almost crawled its way into our salmon loaf and peas. Even though Dad and Frank laughed, made jokes, and talked in German, I kept looking at Mom and Flora. They didn't say anything. They just ate.

I was thinking that Mom was being a rat fink to trick Butch that way, even though Butch probably deserved it. But Mom was mean to her, too, even though she wouldn't admit it. So maybe they both deserved it. But Mom won. For good. And somehow it didn't seem fair. But maybe it was.

That night, when everyone else was gorging themselves on the new five-gallon tub of strawberry ice cream that Frank bought for all of us, I got to talk to Flora. She and Frank were staying in Number 7. She needed something from her suitcase and when she started to walk up to the unit, I grabbed my bowl of ice cream and walked with her.

I asked her, "Did Butch get mad when you left her?"

"Oh yes. It's a good thing Karl and Frank were there. She was spitting mad. But they sweet-talked her into the nursing home. And the nurse gave her a tranquilizer. She'll be all right."

We went inside Number 7 and Flora shuffled through her suitcase while I slouched on the bed and licked ice cream from the spoon.

"Flora, will you promise to answer me something if I ask?"

"OK. If I can."

"Did Butch ever do Voodoo?"

She sat down on the bed with me and said, "That's a long story. And I'm not sure you..."

"I'm old enough. And you promised."

Flora gave me an almost smile and took a bite of my ice cream. Then she said, "I don't know the whole story. No one does. Because I was young and Butch never said much and your Grandpa only told what he wanted to and...."

"That's OK," I said, and gave her another bite of ice cream.

"Butch was always interested in the occult, mainly astrology and sun signs, before we ever went to Aruba. Then she started reading tea leaves. That's how she entertained when we lived there – doing tea readings for her friends. She didn't know much and it was just for fun. Then one day she read tea leaves for Maria, the maid. Maria was a native. The next day, another native woman, this one really old, shows up and looks at Butch's palm. She says she has the mark. This scared Butch, but since she was superstitious and curious as a cat, she asked, 'What mark?'

"'Never mind. Just come to my place tomorrow. Maria will show you the way.'

"Well, Butch goes there once a week or so for months. She learns how to throw shells from that old witch woman and make circles for all kinds of things. When she came home making circles to ward off evil spirits, your Grandpa got spooked. It got him thinking too much about what kind of evil must be lurking around if you have to set up a circle to be protected from it. They never needed a circle before, but now Butch couldn't go to sleep at night without making one around the bed. Butch even admitted she was getting in over her head and the witch woman made her swear on her grave and the grave of her children and her children's children to say nothing about what she learned in that hut.

Butch couldn't stay away. It was your Grandpa that made her give it up. I think she was glad when he went to the witch woman's hut and told her Butch wasn't coming back and to keep her spells and circles to herself and to leave them and their spirits be. I don't know what happened after that."

"Oh."

"Now don't you start asking your Mom a bunch of questions about all this or I'll never hear the end of it. OK?"

"OK."

We walked back to the house. For once, I didn't have five hundred questions ready to jump out of my mouth.

About a week later Mom brought a bunch of us kids to visit Butch. The mansion was right by the river and had a big willow tree in front. Even though it smelled like pee inside, it wasn't as bad as our house. So I thought Butch might be happy since they gave her all the food she wanted and made her bed and everything. But Butch didn't seem to be anything. She just sat in her chair, staring out the window at the river.

Butch looked at Mom like she was a dirty rat but didn't say one word. I gave her a pedicure while Mom talked to the nurse and the other kids played outside. Her toenails were almost an inch thick and had lots of toe gunk, but I was real careful and she only said ouch a few times. Otherwise, she was just staring out the window. I wanted to paint them red for her so she wouldn't feel so bad, but she said maybe next time.

Even though we never hugged in our family, Mom hugged Butch good-bye. Butch didn't hug back and I could see her face while Mom had her arms around her. Her eyes were just black muddy puddles. There wasn't even a speck of magic. I kissed her fingers like she was the Pope or a Bishop and she rubbed her hand on my face. I promised I'd do her toes or her fingers every time I came to see her. She said, "You're my girl." But I didn't know whose girl I was.

Mom didn't paint over Butch's new mural for a long time and I thought about Butch every time I saw it. I wondered why she made it so ugly when the one in her house was so pretty. Did she really learn Voodoo from the witch woman? And how did you do it anyway? And was it always bad? I knew I wasn't supposed to even think about those things because Mom said it brought evil into your mind. Maybe she was right because it made the bad spidery feeling crawl all over me when I wondered too much about Butch.

Every time I stared at Butch's mural for too long, that feeling crawled up my legs. Mom couldn't help staring at it either. I think she liked trying to figure something out about Butch's sick mind. She even took a picture of the mural to show her psychiatrist. They saw each other every week again like they did after her breakdown. She got all kinds of new ideas from him about what that mural was saying.

I begged her to paint over it, but she wouldn't. I even told her it was gross and made me want to puke. I didn't tell her about how it made the black crawly feeling inside get bigger and bigger. Red blood drops were there too, always down low in my belly, and inside my legs. And there wasn't one thing I could do about it. Not one thing. I couldn't help wishing I had a black magic machete to chop out everything I felt.

Mom knew I was upset. Probably because I didn't eat hardly anything and I was already skinny. I told her it was because my stomach hurt. A few days later she did something nice. It was after dinner, when I was clearing the table, and she was cleaning jars for canning. I said, "I bet I could make a better cactus than the one Butch did."

She said, "Maybe you could. Do you want to see some of the drawings I did when I was in the Famous Artist's school?"

"Yeah!"

She finished the canning jars and took out a bunch of old pencil drawings that she did on onionskin paper. There were even naked people drawings. I said, "Isn't it a mortal sin to draw naked people?"

She said, "No, not when it's art or done in the spirit of art. Art changes things. It brings beauty to even the ugliest things." I'd never heard her talk that way before. Then she showed me a drawing of a fat old bald man who was naked and running. It was so realistic! How did she know what old fat guys looked like naked?

I wished I could draw like that! But I didn't know if I could ever be an artist again. Even so, there was something about all those drawings and what Mom said that made my stomach stop hurting so bad. It's like the spider inside just yawned, laid down, and went to sleep. I couldn't figure it out.

21

HALOS

TEN YEARS

W**HEN** I was a baby I had a halo, but it didn't do me much good because it scared Mom and she was the one who saw it. I didn't even know I had one until a few years ago when Georgina told me. That's when she said, "You know, Mom thinks you're going to be a real problem someday because of that halo you had." She thought I already knew about it, but it was a surprise to me. I couldn't get her to tell me anything more.

Georgina just bit on her fingernails like there was nothing in the whole world as important as getting them even shorter than they already were. I wondered if I'd start chewing my nails when I was her age. I wanted to be just like her when I got to be a teenager and almost grown up. Her hair was red, not too curly, and she had **no** freckles, which was like a miracle in our family.

Georgina also had grown up bosoms. I thought she looked like a movie star when she wore her orange-gold baby doll pajama top that was see-through. I used to lie on the bed and watch her put curlers in her hair and walk from the bedroom to the girls' bathroom while her bosoms bounced. You could see them soft and clear as could be through the nightie. I could hardly wait until I got ones just like that. It was like thinking that someday you'd get all the candy you ever want. If I had bosoms like that, I'd roll around on the floor and kick and smile all over just from feeling good.

Mom thought Georgina and me were alike because we both pushed her away when we were babies. I don't remember that, but I

179

remember once when I was still real little that Mom slapped me just for feeling good. I was lying there in my crib feeling so good that the biggest big smile ever was coming out of every speck of me. I was so happy I just knew everyone felt the same way. Then she slapped me and shook me until I stopped the smile feeling. Maybe she was trying to shake off the halo that she was so worried about. I wondered if she did that to Georgina too. But I wasn't sure if Georgina ever had a halo.

Georgina was worse than me any day. But I have to agree that of all the girls we were the worst. The rest of the girls were so good it made you sick. They'd all go to the seven in the morning mass with Mom during Lent and sometimes even Advent. Just the boys, Georgina, and I stayed home. Why would anyone want to go to a mass at seven in the morning? The ten o'clock one on Sunday was bad enough to last a whole week.

Besides, it was warm in bed and too cold everywhere else. When you got out of bed, the hard floor slapped your feet, and the cold air snatched all your warm spots away. You'd get so tired from shivering that all you wanted to do was go back under the covers again. It was better just to stay in bed. But then everyone would know that you were one of *those people* who wouldn't make a sacrifice for God. I knew it wouldn't do any good to go to church anyway. Praying and acting holy would do me about as much good as that halo.

One of the good things about staying in bed instead of going to church was trying to figure out infinity. I'd close my eyes and go part way back to sleep but not all the way. Then I'd think about infinity. Infinity is where you go when you die, and it's what was there before any of us were born. It's what heaven and hell are and it's something that is going to last so much longer than forever that you just **have** to figure it out because you're going to be there a **long** time. Just when I almost had it figured out, it felt like my brain bit itself, and I'd have to start all over again.

I tried to talk about infinity with Mom. I asked her, "Mom, if God is infinite, how did he get there in the first place?"

She looked at me for a second with her sharp yellow-hazel eyes and said, "Why are you thinking so much about that? You can't question God." Then she started peeling some potatoes.

I told her, "I can't help it."

She looked at me again and pushed one of her fingers into my shoulder and said, "You know, you can open your mind too far and you won't know what kind of evil will come in and fill it up." Then she shoved the potato peelings into the garbage.

Mom never was any good for asking questions about God, or anything I thought about when I was in bed. Georgina wasn't too good at it either, but at least she didn't make me feel bad about it. She also didn't get spooked by anything. I don't think she thought too much about infinity. She was too busy thinking about boys and how to sneak.

Georgina snuck all kinds of things. When she did the cooking, she always hid the best food for herself. If you wanted any of her food, you had to be her slave and do everything she said. Then when she hid some yummy food she'd share it with you. I was her slave lots of times because she never cheated you. Everyone knew she snuck food, but we never caught her, and when you were a slave you couldn't say anything or you'd lose your bribe.

Steak was the best bribe. It was everyone's favorite, and the only way you could get extra bites was to do Georgina's work. When we made steak, it always needed to be pounded with a hammer until you could almost see through it. When Georgina was cooking, she got me to do the pounding. Then when it was cooked she hid some of it in the bedroom and shared it with me after dinner. That's when we would sit on her bed and eat it under the covers. It was when we were hiding and eating that she told me about the halo. I asked her if she ever had a halo and she said, "Maybe, but I sure as hell don't anymore." Then she started telling me teenager things.

Boys were almost as good as food to Georgina, maybe better. I guess that's what happens to you when you get to be a teenager. Rod was Georgina's sweetie pie. He hardly ever wore a shirt. He was so tan and tall my chin just came to his stomach. You could punch him as hard as you wanted in the stomach, and your hand would hurt worse than his stomach ever did. He was so cool. I was too little for a boyfriend, but I still liked him a lot. He gave me a happy tingle feeling all over when he came to visit.

Mom thought Rod was a good for nothing hood. She also said he was dumb, like the worst thing in the whole world is to not be a genius. I couldn't tell if he was smart or not, but I knew he wasn't a hood. He was a famous baseball player at school. This didn't matter to Mom. No more Rod. Period.

Mom didn't want Georgina going out with any other boys either, unless **she** liked them. Maybe this was Mom's sneaky way to make sure Georgina didn't get too much of the tingle feeling either. Why did Mom hate us feeling that way?

It didn't work for Mom to try to stop her because Georgina was born to make trouble. She was also mad at Mom, and I don't blame her one bit. What she did was get some other guy at school to come to the house to go out on a supposed date, and then he'd take her to go see Rod. She never told me or anyone about it. We only found out about it later when she got caught, and Mom told us the whole story of why Dad beat Georgina up.

Mom and Georgina didn't like each other even a little. Georgina would sometimes act like everything was hunky-dory for a while. Then she'd bring something like a bowl of ice cream to Mom. Ice cream was one thing Mom couldn't stop eating even if she tried. Georgina would act happy and pretty until Mom took a few bites. Then she'd whisper to Mom, "You'll never know if it's poisoned." Sometimes Mom started crying and threw the bowl down and sometimes she just kept eating like it didn't faze her. But we all knew it did. I felt sorry for Mom then.

When Georgina acted like that, it reminded me of the Bible woman who danced with her glitter bra and see-through skirt. Then John the Baptist got his head cut off. Georgina was really mean to Mom but she told me she wasn't actually going to poison her. She just thought it was funny.

Mom called it psychological warfare when Georgina scared the bejeezus out of her. Georgina had lots of ways to do it too, like drawing and cutting out pictures of spiders, which scared Mom to death. Then she'd put them around the house where Mom would run into them and jump about a mile out of her skin.

One time Georgina brought home a big hairy tarantula from biology class. Mom tried not to act too scared and made her take it back the next day. Then Georgina found a black widow spider. She trapped it in a canning jar and decided to keep it for a secret pet. It lived on the shelf on top of the girls' toilet. Georgina fed it flies and mosquitoes that were still buzzing and after a while it had babies. Then when they were just beginning to crawl around, they all magically disappeared.

Mom didn't even know about the black widow, until its babies disappeared. Everyone was scared of where they were. We didn't know if they were in the house somewhere growing into big spiders. Georgina just laughed at all of us. We never found those baby spiders.

Mom got back at Georgina by grounding her and not letting her go anywhere even with guys Mom liked. This didn't seem like such a smart thing for Mom to do since we all knew that Georgina was probably the only one who knew where the baby spiders were. What if she put spiders in Mom's bed? But Georgina probably wouldn't do anything like that. What she did do was start to sneak out. I knew it was true because I caught her when I was on a hike.

Us kids used to go on hikes into the hills behind where we lived. The only thing you saw was sagebrush, the irrigation ditch, rattlesnakes, grasshoppers, jackrabbits, and a coyote, if you were lucky. We heard about cougars, but none of us ever saw one.

We always hiked just a couple of miles along the irrigation ditch to the canyon. When you got to the canyon, the irrigation ditch turned into a trestle. It crossed right over the top of the canyon with its little river down below. Dean said the trestle was about a quarter of a mile long. There was nothing on top of the regular irrigation ditch, but the trestle had railroad ties on top.

The ties were just close enough so you could step to the next one when you walked across trestle. If you fell off the trestle onto the ground, which was about a half a mile down, you'd be dead instantly. You'd have to be a real idiot to die that way. The other way you might die was if you tripped and fell in the ditch and drowned. Sonny said the water moved at about 50 to 60 miles an hour there. We dared each other to walk across the whole trestle. And then you'd have to walk back again.

I have to admit it was really scary. Because some of the railroad ties wiggled or were rotted out. If one was missing, you'd have to jump to the next one. And you could lose your balance real easy. Sometimes you'd chicken out part way through and start crying because you almost fell and might die.

One day me and Billy were walking on top of the irrigation trestle counting the number of rotten railroad ties. When we looked down, we saw Rod's car parked in the dirt by the river underneath us. We almost fell off from trying to look, so we went back to where we could get off the trestle, climbed down the canyon, and snuck over to where the car was. Georgina was sitting real close to Rod. We saw them kissing and making weird sounds. It was so funny we started giggling and making smooching sounds too.

They got out and caught us hiding behind the car. It looked like they were kind of mad, so we covered our mouths to try to stop laughing. I didn't want Rod to not like me, so I said I was sorry. Georgina knew if she wasn't nice to us we'd tell on her. So she gave us both a bottle of Coke and told us to shut up and not tell anyone we saw her with Rod.

The green Coke bottle was so cold in my hand, and I was so thirsty and hot that I just had to have a sip. That's all it took. One sip and I was bribed. It was wrong, but the Coke tasted better than the bribe felt bad. Then she told us to get on home.

We started walking back with our Cokes. I turned around and saw them kissing again. He had his hands on her rump. They looked nice with her all molded into his bare chest. I knew she'd get killed if Mom or Dad found out. I also knew I'd get killed if Mom and Dad found out I knew and didn't tell them. I never did tell, but Georgina got caught real bad just a little while after that. It turns out she'd also been sneaking out of the bedroom at night to see Rod. Mom and Dad found out somehow and the next day there was hell to pay.

It was Saturday afternoon and Dad was home from working that morning. Mom and Dad were in the bedroom, and you could hear Mom talking real fast and mad to Dad. The whole house felt like something was going to jump out of thin air and explode right in your face. Mom never talked that fast. It was like Dad was some tired old racehorse that she was whipping, like she wanted him to get up and run as hard as he could.

They came out into the kitchen and got Georgina. Mom started screaming at Georgina and grabbed her by the arm. When Georgina yanked her arm away, Mom slapped her across the face and called her a tramp. Then Mom asked her if she'd been sneaking out at night. Georgina said no and Mom slapped her again.

Then Mom yelled at Dad, "Are you going to let your daughter lie to us like this?" Georgina looked at Dad like maybe she'd get some mercy. Mom said, "Ask her where she was last night."

So Dad did ask, and Georgina said she was out with Rod. Mom started in on Dad again, "Are you going to let her get away with that? She's making you look like a goddamn fool."

Dad started yelling at Georgina, "Who the hell do you think you are?" Then Georgina made the biggest mistake of her whole life. She yelled at Mom and said, "You're just jealous!" and then tried to run away.

Mom grabbed Georgina and shoved her at Dad. Mom's throat was making a weird rattling sound when she said, "What kind of a man are you? Are you going to let her treat me like that?"

Then Dad hit Georgina in the face. She was screaming, but it didn't do her any good because when Dad loses his temper it's gone for a long time. Georgina was as good as dead. He slapped her so hard she fell and then he yanked her by her red hair until she was on her feet gain. She was sobbing and screaming. He was swearing and screaming that she was nothing but a goddamn tramp and when would she ever learn a goddamn thing. Mom was gloating. She kept shoving Georgina back to Dad, who would hit her again.

All of the other kids, including me, were hiding underneath the table like little statues. I knew this would be me in a few years if I wasn't careful. He hit her so many times she couldn't get up even when he pulled her hair. Then he kicked her in the stomach and in the back. "That'll teach you a lesson, you little slut." I started to cry even though I knew if I made a sound he might hit me too. So I stuffed my arm in my mouth and made the sounds hide inside. I was almost invisible. My eyes still cried though.

I couldn't stand to see Georgina's beautiful face with blood on it and her red hair with chunks of it torn out. She was as broken as a china cup on the floor. Finally, Mom and Dad left her alone. Everyone left, except for Maureen, Becky, and me. We helped carry Georgina to the bedroom.

I secretly kissed her arm where it was already swollen up and starting to turn into a bruise. I felt so sad for her that I started crying again, but she looked at me like she didn't want my sorriness, so I stopped. I watched every move she made as she tried to crawl into bed. We helped her get her clothes off and saw the red marks and bruises starting up all over her. Her stomach hurt real bad where Dad kicked her. She threw up. We washed the blood and vomit off her face. Then we gave her some water, and she said she was OK but had to go to sleep. Becky said she hoped Georgina didn't have a concussion. I hoped so too.

I asked her if I could lie there with her for a while. That was OK with her if I didn't move or make any noise. I was as quiet as a mouse. I waited until she went to sleep and then I got to stare at her all I wanted. I just kept looking at where her eyes were swollen and red, and at the purple marks on her cheeks and at the blood still around her nose. I thought about infinity while I did all that staring and after a while I saw a glowing sort of light around her beat up head. It was really there. She **did** have a halo. It was still there even after I blinked my eyes. It was there even when I stopped thinking about infinity. It was just there. I looked in the mirror to see if there was any light shining on my head too, but I couldn't see any. When I went back to look at Georgina, her halo was gone. But I knew it had to be there somewhere. Maybe mine was hiding somewhere too.

It took all summer for Georgina to get better since she had two broken ribs and a broken collarbone. I still don't know what halos mean, but I know you don't get them from being holy. And I also know they're good, even if they are mainly on people who are trouble.

22

BOY TROUBLE

ELEVEN YEARS

L UKE came to live in our motel for the summer in between sixth grade and junior high. He was about the same age as me. The first time I saw him I figured he was a beach boy, since his mom wrote, "California" on the motel registration card. You could also tell by his hair. It was bleached and blondish just on the top and was dark underneath. It came down longish over his forehead and almost covered his bushy black eyebrows. Later on, I found out he even knew how to surf.

He was wearing tight Levi's the way Mom thought was obscene. Mom talked with his mom about how long they were going to stay. Two months! He was too cool to look at me. I was too scared and excited to look at him. I stared out the window while they talked about what unit they would be staying in. All I could think about was how hairy my legs were and how baggy my shorts were. Mom never let any of us wear tight pants or shorts.

A few days later Maureen, me, and a bunch of the little kids went for a hike to the canyon. On the way, we walked by Number 11 and saw Luke sitting on the stoop while his Mom was lying on a towel in the sun. He looked at us, but no one said anything.

After we went by I said to Maureen, "Isn't he cute?"

She said, "I guess, but his hair is too long. Besides, Mom doesn't like him already." Good. I could tell Maureen didn't like him either, and even if he never liked me, at least I didn't have to worry about him liking her. The rest of the hike I thought about how I could ever get the nerve to look at him. Or smile.

A few days after that, when it was just me, Billy, and Luann going on a hike, I asked Luann and Billy, "When we get to Number 11, why don't one of you ask the new kid if he wants to go with us on the hike?"

Luann said, "Yeah, but you know we're not supposed to go places with tenants."

I said, "But he's just a kid, like us, and anyway we're not going anywhere with him. He'd be going somewhere with us."

So Luann asked him to come on the hike and he did. He didn't even ask his mom. She didn't care anyway. She just laid in the sun all day long and drank beer. When the sun went down, she sat and smoked cigarettes. Mom thought she must be an alcoholic. And that she must be trying to get over a divorce and tan her skin into leather all at once.

After that, he went with us every time. We hardly ever talked to each other in the beginning. And we never walked beside each other. Luke never said much at all. He was tough. I used to be just as tough, but something weird was going on inside me. I was feeling too gooey and there wasn't anything I could do to stop it. Usually, when you like someone it's fun to hit them, but I didn't feel like hitting Luke. And he didn't hit me either. We made sure that we never touched one hair on each other.

It was the same at school with John Washburn before school got out for the year. Every day I stared at the back of his head, looking at the black hairs growing out of his scalp. Because he sat right in front of me. I waited for him to turn around and look at me when he was passing papers. When he did look, I was too shy to look back. Sometimes I had to bring papers to the front of the room and walk right by him.

The only way something might happen with John was if I fainted. I could see it all. How I'd stand up and walk real slow. Then right when I got past his chair I would suddenly faint. I'd fall back in slow motion and he would catch me in his arms. I would be like a lacewing butterfly falling into his hands. He would breathe air into my mouth and I would fly away. It would be all I ever wanted for the rest of my life.

I never did smile at John and now the same thing was happening with Luke. I figured the best thing to do was not talk about it with anyone, since when I talked about John with my girlfriend at school, those feelings inside came out and went everywhere like spilled milk. After that, every time I was around John, all I could think about was how scared I was of him ever finding out. It was like trying to wipe up the milk when the sponge was already sopping wet.

The first time Luke and me went on a hike with just each other, it was by accident. We started out with Billy and Nicky. But then Billy started to get a stomachache and Nicky was tired because it was too hot and neither one of them wanted to go all the way to the canyon. So they went back and it was just Luke and me. We **had** to walk by each other now. So anything we said about rattlesnakes, or tumbleweeds, or the fuzzy lint from the cottonwood trees that was flying in the air, was to each other.

After we got to the canyon, we sat down in the dirt where we could see the little river below us and throw rocks in it. I could smell his clean sweet sweat. It was better than Dad's. I wanted to sit closer to him. And I knew I shouldn't even think about being his girlfriend, but I couldn't help it. My stomach was full of sparks and swirls.

Don't ask me how I ever did it, but I actually started talking to him. I asked him, "Do you miss California?"

"Yeah."

"Did you have lots of friends?"

"A few." He didn't seem to mind talking to me.

"Did you have a girlfriend?" I almost hit myself for saying that out loud to him.

"Yeah."

"Do you miss her?"

"Yeah, but we broke up." I was glad to hear that.

The only thing left to ask was did he kiss her and what did it feel like and did he ever want to kiss any other girl since then. But I would die before ever asking anything like that.

I wondered though, what it would be like if he kissed me. If it would taste salty or sweet. Or if it would be so scary I'd faint, or even throw up. Yuck! He'd never want to kiss me then. And if he found out I was thinking anything about kissing, I wouldn't be able to look at his brown eyes ever again. Or go for a hike or say one word to him. So I just acted the same, like I didn't really care about anything.

We didn't say anything else and sat together for a long time. I noticed every time he moved, to see if it was closer to me or farther away. Finally, we walked back.

After that first time with just each other, Luke and I went hiking together a lot because it was a rule with Mom that no one could go hiking by themselves, and most of my brothers and sisters didn't want to go every day. That way if you got bit by a rattlesnake or got kidnapped, there would be someone to run for help.

All those hikes started to build up inside and after a while I ended up blabbing to Luann about how much I liked Luke. She of course thought I was stupid for liking a boy. Even so, she said, "If you want someone to like you maybe you should act nicer. Hint hint." I knew she was just trying to get me to act nicer to **her**, but I didn't want to act nicer to anyone. That was the whole problem! I hated it when I acted nice. It felt way too goopy inside already. It didn't make any sense, but I had to act mean, just to feel regular again.

Luckily, I had lots of good ways to be mean. Like playing *Witch*. When I was the witch, I scared all the little kids. They begged me to do it. Because I was the scariest witch they'd ever seen. Even including the one at the beginning of the *Wizard of Oz*, who gave everyone nightmares. I didn't even have to dress up. All I had to do was get so mad I wanted to kill someone and then hold it in tight, tight, tight and then stretch that mad feeling so far out that it started to shake and then start screaming. Which I did at the kids. And start chasing them. I never said words. I just shrieked and shot knives out of my eyes. I always surprised them, even when they were ready for me to start. Because I really was the best witch ever.

I always felt better after *Witch*, but sometimes the real little kids were still scared. I just laughed at them and told them it was their own fault for being so stupid to ask me to do it, when they knew what a good witch I was.

I never wanted Luke to know I did *Witch*. Even if I only had the tiniest minuscule chance of him ever wanting to kiss me, I knew it would be gone if he ever saw me do *Witch*. Because I knew it would scare him too. Even though he would act like it didn't. I knew *Witch* would scare anyone, even if they were tough.

I also knew *Witch* would be as revolting to Luke as Mr. Alton was to me. Mr. Alton was my sixth grade math teacher. And an albino. Last year I tried hard to imagine him having sex. Because that's when we found out about how grown ups actually did it. Mrs. Terry showed everyone in the sixth grade a drawing. The penis goes all the way **inside** the vagina. You did it on purpose. How could anyone do something so disgusting and totally embarrassing on purpose? Mrs. Terry said it's what adults do. I asked, "All grown ups?"

"The married ones mainly," she said.

And I knew that Mr. Alton was married so he must do it too. When he walked up and down the aisle, talking about powers of ten, his gray slacks made that scraping sound that made you want to either scream or scratch your nails on the blackboard, just to get even with him.

I figured he probably took his clothes off when he had sex. First he'd take off his shirt. Then you'd have to see all that pinkish-white skin on his scrawny bones. Maybe his wife was an albino and skinny too so she didn't think he looked that bad. But maybe if she was normal she would make him keep his clothes on so she wouldn't have to look at him. But she probably still had to kiss him. His teeth were yellow and crooked and his nose was bony. He had almost no lips. So how could you kiss that? You couldn't. So you'd have to look at just his eyes, which were like no pink you've ever seen except on albino rats and rabbits.

I tried to look like I was listening when I stared at Mr. Alton's eyes. Like I was really interested in base numbers. Then his white eyelashes blinked really fast and he started lisping so bad that you couldn't understand what he was saying, even if you did know what the difference was between base two and base ten. I figured he probably never had sex even though he was married. But maybe Mrs. Alton would kiss his eyes when he stopped blinking long enough.

They told us about sex right before school was out so we'd have all summer to be grossed out. Which I was. And Mr. Alton being so repulsive didn't help one bit. I felt sorry for Mr. Alton because he was so ugly and he couldn't help it. I couldn't do anything about that, but I could make sure that Luke didn't see things about me that would gross him out. Like finding out that I liked him.

So I had a problem, which of course I have never solved. How do I get someone to like me without ever letting him know that I care one bit? Luann's idea to act nice was the worst idea ever. There was no way I could do that, even if I felt like being nice.

Mom told us girls that the way you get a man to like you is to comb your hair and look fresh as a daisy even when you're a wrung out dishrag. That was the only way you were supposed to get a guy to like you. I figured it wouldn't hurt to at least comb my hair and wash my face once a day, even though it was summer. I also tried the almost empty tube of Tangee lipstick that Becky gave me. I hoped Luke might think I was a little bit like a daisy, even though I wasn't.

I wanted to talk to someone about what to do, but we couldn't talk to anyone from school because it was summer, and we never got to talk to friends in the summer. Georgina couldn't help because she was gone. She eloped with Rod. Now she was married and they were going to have a baby. She probably couldn't remember what it felt like before you got to be pretty anyway.

If I talked to Maureen, she'd probably tell Mom I had a crush. You weren't supposed to have a crush because that made you boy crazy. Then Mom would treat you like there was a mortal sin just waiting to pop out of you.

Maureen could like anyone she wanted and no one ever accused her of being boy crazy. But I always got in trouble for even looking at a boy. Mom said it was flirting if I looked at any man in the eyes.

I said, "Why is it flirting if I look at a boy, but when Maureen does it you don't care?"

"Because you have bedroom eyes. And Maureen doesn't. And don't you tell her I said that, either."

"So is it good to have bedroom eyes?" I asked. I hoped I had something good that Maureen didn't.

"It'll get you in trouble. It's like you're giving the man a *come hither* look. You better be careful with who you're asking to come hither. You know how men are."

"Yeah, but I'm just talking about boys. And anyway, I'm not asking anyone to *come hither.*" I said the come hither part kind of snotty.

"So you think you know all about it, do you? Do you want to end up like Georgina? She's a smart girl too, who has nothing now. Nothing! Except a husband that's so stupid he doesn't know how to tie his own shoelaces."

"Yeah, but he's cute." I knew right after the words popped out, that I shouldn't have said anything.

"You listen here, Miss Sassy Pants, you're never going to leave this house until you learn how to behave."

That didn't sound good at all, even though I didn't get to go anywhere anyway. But if Mom let me, maybe someday I'd be able to go out on a date and drive around in a car with some guy who'd be resting his salty golden-tanned arm around my shoulder. I told her, "OK, but I can't help it if I have bedroom eyes. I still don't even know what that is."

"All you have to do is not look at any boy, or any man, in the eye."

"How can I see a guy if I don't look at him? "

"Just look at his mouth."

"OK."

It was tricky to learn to look at a boy's eyes and not get caught looking **in** his eyes. But after a while I figured it out. I would look at his eyes, and the second he saw me looking, I'd just slide real smooth right down to his mouth. I knew this was exactly right.

The only other person who could maybe help me with Luke was Becky. I knew she wouldn't tell Mom. Partly because she knew what it felt like to get in trouble when you haven't done anything wrong. Becky got in more trouble for stuff she didn't do wrong than anyone. And it always had to do with boys. Mom was afraid she would turn out like Georgina too. But they were way different. Georgina did stuff that was wrong on purpose. Becky never did.

One time Becky brought a record home. It was just music and no words. Everyone liked it, even Mom, because it made you want to dance. Becky could dance real good because Dad taught her. She swished around the house and looked as pretty as Georgina. The whole house felt dancey-happy. But then Mom found out the record was called Scarlett O'Hara. And Mom hated Scarlett O'Hara, who was some kind of tramp from the South.

Becky had the music playing while she was frying sliced potatoes for dinner and was dancing while she flipped the spuds. I was copying her as good as I could, and trying to push my hips up in the air like the belly dancer I saw on TV.

Mom came in and saw Becky swishing her hips around. Then she looked at me. I stopped doing anything, but she'd already caught me. Mom asked Becky, "What kind of example are you setting? Has that music made you lose all decency? You're acting more and more like Scarlett O'Hara all the time."

Becky said, "I am not, Mom. I'm just dancing."

Mom said, "Like hell you are. You're idolizing a woman who was no better than a prostitute. And she got everyone to think she was an innocent flower when all the time she was just a worthless selfish little tramp."

Becky started to cry. "Mommm. It's just a record. I don't even care what it's called."

"Well, you should care. You're seventeen years old for God's sake. And if you don't care, you're not old enough to buy these things on your own." Mom grabbed the needle off the record. You could hear it scratch.

Becky screamed, "Mom!!! You scratched my record! And I paid for it with my own money!"

Mom yelled back, "What's more important? This damn record or common decency?"

Becky just cried and didn't say anything.

"Well?" Mom waited for Becky to say something. And when she didn't, Mom slammed the record hard against the edge of the table and it broke in two.

Becky screamed, "And you wonder why Georgina couldn't wait to get away from home!"

"That's it, young lady! You're grounded for the next month," Mom snarled. You could tell that she was finally done with Becky. Becky just ran crying into the bedroom. She never did fight as good as Georgina. But she also didn't get beat up.

What Mom did to Becky's record wasn't one bit fair. All I could do was go into the girls' bedroom where Becky was crying and tell her, "Just think, Becky, pretty soon you get to leave home for good. And you don't ever have to come back if you don't want to." Becky didn't say anything.

That same summer she also got in trouble for something one of the tenants did. It started when Becky and me found a big brown paper bag full of magazines and books that was resting against the outside door to the girls' bedroom. Inside the bag, there was a note to Becky from the playboys in Number 7, saying, "We thought you might like these."

They were girlie magazines where the girls were part naked and partly wearing nighties and baby doll pajamas. The weird part was they were all real loungey and cozy with each other. Some of them were even kissing. We looked at picture after picture. After a while I said to Becky, "Why would a girl want to kiss another girl?"

"I have no idea, but that's why Mom won't let any of us ever go to slumber parties."

I said, "Really? I thought it was because she was afraid there were lesbians there who would do bad things to us."

"Well, what do you think lesbians are, anyway?"

"I dunno," I said.

"It's girls who have sex with each other."

I thought hard about that. It made no sense to me. I asked, "How can they have sex when there's only girls?"

"I don't know. They probably just kiss and hug a lot," Becky said.

"But they're probably real bad anyway."

"Yeah, they'll probably go to hell, but they don't look mean the way Mom said they were. Do you think they look mean or nasty?" She pointed to a picture of three naked girls all cuddled up together in bed. They were all wearing fuzzy pink earmuffs.

"Not really. They look nice to me. Are you sure they're lesbians?"

"I think so."

After a while, we'd seen all the pictures and Becky started putting everything in a pile to go back in the paper bag. "You know we probably shouldn't look at this stuff anymore."

"Yeah, but what else is in there?" I looked over at the bag. She dumped out some paperback books with more girlie-girlie pictures on the front. They didn't look that interesting.

Becky said, "I'm going to hide this stuff and throw it out before Mom finds out. Don't you tell anyone, OK? Because if Mom finds out, she'll kill us."

"Don't worry about me." And then I forgot about them. Because even though they were fun to look at, they didn't make too much sense. I thought Becky probably threw them in the incinerator.

It turns out that Becky threw out the magazines but saved the books. And Mom found them a few weeks later. She screamed at Becky again. This time about making the guys in Number 7 think she was a slut. Otherwise, why would they give her those books? I sure was glad Mom never found the magazines, or Becky might have gotten grounded for the rest of her life, instead of just the rest of the summer.

About a month later Becky decided that she was going to go into the convent when she graduated from High School. Mom thought becoming a nun or priest was the best thing anyone could ever do with their God-given life. Mom even wanted to be a nun herself. So once all us kids left home, she and Dad were going to become a nun and priest. Mom was so glad about Becky's vocation that she ungrounded her from then on.

So now when I talked to Becky about Luke, I was afraid she'd be no help at all, since she was on the holy side now and everyone knows that boy feelings aren't holy. Because it was like she'd already given up. And I was just getting started. But she did give me some pink lipstick and showed me how to put curlers in my hair. She also taught me how to wash my face better and practice looking in the mirror. Then I didn't look so much like a scrounge. Becky figured all that would help some. I hoped so.

After the summer went on long enough for the tomatoes to get red, Luke and I got used to each other. We hung around outside every day, even when we weren't hiking. I still had a crush on him but didn't feel so bad about it. Because we actually talked together. It was weird because I really **liked** him, even though he was a boy. The whole thing with Luke was like blue sky. You don't know why it's there, but it is.

I even started to feel like some of the sky was inside me again. Like when I was real little. Maybe even before I was born.

One day after a really long hike, I told him he could come inside our house to get some water. Then after that he came over all the time. I knew Mom would throw a fit if she knew. Because no one came to our house, especially tenants. So Luke only came over when she was gone.

One day we were playing our old music on the record player. Everyone liked *Love Potion Number Nine*, but we'd all heard it a million times. Then Luke came over with his new 45, *The Twist*. Pretty soon everyone started dancing: Luke and me, Billy, Luann, Francie, and Nicky. Then the little kids wanted me to get up on the table and dance wild for them. I only did that when no one else was around and wouldn't ever have done it in front of Luke, but the music made me want to, and he kept saying, "Come on, I want to see." Then he smiled real nice.

I got up on the table and told Billy he had to turn the music up even louder and everyone else had to promise to keep dancing when I did. Then it was like blue sky, *Witch*, fuzzy earmuffs, and lightning all at once. I was waving my shoulders, throwing my head, shaking my hair, and wiggling my hips better than I had in my whole life. Luke whistled at me and it went right into the music and up my legs. I wasn't thinking about anything. My brain was just music and dancing and Luke looking at me and whistling with sparks in his eyes. And I wasn't one bit embarrassed.

Suddenly the music stopped with a "rrrrrrrriipp" sound coming from the record. I looked up and saw Mom glaring at us from the record player. She was carrying a package that made her look bigger than ever. My heart thumped to a standstill. It was dead silence.

She didn't have to say it very loud, "What in the hell is going on here?"

Nicky and Francie ran away. I was shaking and stumbling off the table. I said, "Just dancing. The little kids begged me."

She walked over to me and yanked the back of my shirt hard. It pulled up just as hard against my throat. I felt like gagging but tried not to make a sound.

Her hand was coming down toward my face. The wild feelings must not have all gone away yet because I put my arm up to cover my face and accidentally hit her hand away.

She screamed, "How dare you hit me like that!" And then slapped me across the face.

I screeched a loud, wailing, witch sound that shot through me before I could stop it. Then I remembered Luke. I looked over at him and felt hot red rush over my face. He was slowly edging toward the door.

Mom let go of me but she was still way too close. She practically spit the words in my face, "What has gotten into you, anyway? And I thought I could trust you." She whirled around and looked at Luke. "And who is **this?**"

Luann said, "He's in Number 11. He's Tracie's boyfriend." I looked at Luann like I was going to kill her after Mom was done killing me.

"Boyfriend?" Mom looked stunned.

"Out with it, Luann," Mom said.

"Yeah, they go together every day. On hikes and stuff." Luann was such a rat fink tattler!

Mom was shaking her head like she couldn't believe it. I hoped I wouldn't get beaten as bad as Georgina. She said real calm to Luke, "You are not welcome here. And I don't want to see you with Tracie ever again." He left.

I begged her, "Mommm, he didn't do anything wrong."

"But YOU did! You deliberately disobeyed me, letting some good for nothing kid, a tenant for God's sake, in our house, sneaking around behind my back and swishing your tail around in front of him like some cheap tramp!"

"But he's a friend more than he's a tenant."

She looked hard at me. "Since when have you been having boyfriends?"

I was getting more tangled than ever. "I haven't. I mean, he's not really a boyfriend."

"Then why are you defending him like that?"

"Because he's nice to me."

"Is that all it takes? Are you so easy that all someone has to do is give you a little something sweet and you follow them like a puppy dog? Where in the hell is your self-respect?"

There was nothing I could say. Maybe it was true. I just pushed my back against the wall, held my stomach, and cried. Mom went into the kitchen and started putting groceries away. Everyone else made themselves scarce.

I only cried for a little while. I couldn't give up on Luke. After a few minutes, I went into the kitchen where it was quiet except for Mom. The sun slanted in and mixed with the sound of the rustling paper bags and cans and boxes going into the cupboards.

I said to Mom, "But I'm still your best worker. I wash all the dishes, and do the laundry and ironing better than anyone. I take care of the little kids when you're in bed, and you know I can fix them if they get hurt. So you know you don't ever have to worry when I'm around. So can I at least still go for hikes with him?"

"No."

"But Mommm, he's my only friend for the whole summer."

"And he'll be your last."

"But Mommm..." I was starting to cry and wail again. She ignored me. I couldn't give up. I begged, "I'll do anything you want."

"Good. But it won't make any difference."

"Mom, you just don't know how bad it feels."

"Yes, I do," Mom said.

"But if you know how bad it feels, then why are you making it so I can't see him anymore?"

"Because it's time for you to get used to it." She looked hard at me, like she really **did** know, and really **didn't** care one bit.

My stomach turned over and chewed on itself. I felt like throwing up. I was shivering and bit my fingers. I wished she would just hit me instead, beat me up until I didn't feel anything.

But I knew she was done with me. Finally, she walked toward the kitchen door. On her way out she looked down at me and said, "Get over it. We all do." I sat at the table and stared at the bite marks on my fingers until Becky came in to make dinner.

Becky said, "Luann told me what happened." Then she whispered in my ear, "Don't worry, we'll figure out a way so you can see him again at least once, and not get caught."

I looked at Becky's soft eyes and was glad she wasn't a nun yet. But I wasn't sure I could stand being around Luke again after the way Mom treated him. And after he saw her hit me and heard my witch scream. It was all too gross. Maybe, though, I could write him a letter. I'd hide a secret kiss inside the envelope that no one would ever see.

23

TWINS

MOM started wearing her pregnant clothes again just this last year. Another baby. Finally! I'd been waiting for more than two years. The last time she got pregnant, was back when I was finishing the fourth grade. That one turned out to be a disaster miscarriage.

She'd been pregnant almost six months when she went to the hospital. I thought it meant we'd get the baby sooner and it would be like an extra surprise for it to come early. But she didn't come back with any baby. It was just her and Dad. She was spooky gray. No lipstick, no rouge. Just reddish-purple around her eyes. Her stomach was flabby and soft in the front like some old worn out balloon that lost all of its air. I asked her where the baby was and she said, "There isn't any baby. There never was any baby." Then she started crying and went into the bedroom. She stayed in there for the rest of the day. And hardly came out of the bedroom after that, for a bunch of months.

I asked Dad where the baby was and he said, "It died. It was too little. The priest baptized it before it died so it didn't get stuck in limbo. It went straight to heaven." I looked right at his blue eyes and they scared me for just a second. They were too blue and I wasn't sure if I should be looking in them. Then I felt so sad I started to cry, and pulled and chewed at my fingers. Dad said, "Don't worry. We'll have another baby real soon."

But it wasn't real soon. It was forever. And all Mom did was stay in bed and sleep and take pain pills that made her even sleepier. She only got up a few times a day and hardly ever left the house, except to see the doctor, the priest, or the psychiatrist. She saw Dr. Lieberman, the psychiatrist, on Wednesdays.

Dad didn't really like the idea of her seeing the psychiatrist since it cost so much money. And also because she was in a bad mood after her appointments. One time she came home and helped Maureen and me make dinner because she was too mad to lie in bed.

She rolled biscuits out on the Formica and said, "That damn Dr. Lieberman. I don't know why I keep going to see him. He argues with everything I think. Why can't someone just agree with me for once."

Maureen cut out round circles of dough with a kitchen glass and said, "I agree with you, Mom." Of course, Maureen would say that. And she probably did agree. I didn't say anything.

Mom said, "He thinks I should get away from the whole family and have some fun. But how the hell can I do that?" I knew Maureen didn't like the idea of that any more than me. Why should Mom get the fun when we were the ones doing all the work anyway? Becky, Maureen, and I did all the shopping, cooking, cleaning, and the whole motel by ourselves while she just laid in bed.

We knew not to say much when she was griping about Dr. Lieberman. She didn't like him or say one good thing about him or do one thing he told her to do. But she kept seeing him. I guess all that fighting was supposed to be good for her. Anyway, after the miscarriage Dad never yelled about how much money the psychiatrist cost. I think he was just glad she wasn't having a breakdown.

So that's why it was the best news in the world when Mom put on her pregnant clothes that I hadn't seen in over two years. It meant we were having another baby! I wanted the new baby to be all mine. It was only fair since Becky had gotten Francie for her special baby and Maureen got Jason.

Mom was getting ready to go see Dr. Meyer, the baby doctor. She took off the house smock she was wearing and I could see where the new baby was pooching out her belly. She had to wear her old girdle because the new one squeezed her too much.

When she pulled the dressy blue smock over her head, I asked her, "Can I be in charge of the new baby? It's my turn and you know I can do everything."

"Are you sure you can be that grown up? They're not playthings, you know."

"Yeah. I know that. And I wouldn't let anyone else hurt it either. I know how to make the formula just the right temperature and I'll feed it at night so you won't have to wake up. You know I can burp babies real good. And my diapers are as good as Becky's any day. Please?"

"We'll see." She clipped on the sparkly silver earrings, made a perfect pink lipstick kiss onto the Kleenex and stuffed it into her bra. She was ready to go. Mom never took any of us kids with her to her appointments, even though we begged. It was her best way to get rid of us for a while.

When Mom came back, she looked tired. That was the bad part about her being pregnant. She was always tired. Even more than usual.

I asked her, "Did the doctor say the baby was good?"

"Yeah. Both of them. Twins." She said it like it wasn't the most exciting thing that ever happened.

"Twins? We're getting twins? Do I get both of them? I can do it, Mom. Please?" She just looked at me. But didn't say no. "Oh boy!! Twins!" I ran out of the room yelling to everyone in the house. "We're getting twins! We're getting twins!"

When Dad got home and Mom kissed him hello, she whispered in his ear and he sat down right there in the kitchen. He wanted a beer right then too. Before he took off his work boots. Even before he washed his hands. Then he had another beer. Dad almost never had two beers, but Mom didn't yell at him for it.

Mom and Dad were kind of quiet at dinner. I was too, even though inside I was screaming and dancing upside down from happiness. I knew that from now on, I had to act like a good Mommy or she wouldn't let me have the twins. And I wanted them more than anything in my whole life. More than all the presents on Christmas.

I knew I could do it. I was big enough now and it was going to be the best thing I ever did. I even started to feel a little fat, like Mom. But I was too excited to eat very much.

Every day when I didn't want to come home from school, I remembered the twins. They made the icky feeling at our house go away. I could even run up the hill to our house and feel happy even though there was always more work, work, work to do. Every day I felt Mom's belly and it was weird how hard it was compared to fat. They were definitely in there; sweet little blobs of baby that were waiting for me to hold them and coo them to sleep and rub pink baby lotion on their bald little heads.

Even when Dean and Sonny both picked on me at the same time, I could float away and ignore what low life rats they really were. Because all that baby love was inside and no one could make me feel bad. They were all mine. I could see my twin babies in my mind, all rosy pink. I cuddled them up against my face and chest, and they were so warm and snugly they melted right into me.

Then one day when I came in from playing outside and Dad was carrying Mom by the shoulders while Sonny and Becky carried her legs. Her bottom was sagging down and almost scraping the floor. She was wrapped up in sheets and you could barely see her face. She was totally limp.

Dad yelled to Dean, "Come over here and help us goddammit. Can't you see she's falling on the floor?" Dean helped them carry her out of the house. We all watched while they pulled her into the car. Meanwhile, Becky slid a whole bunch of diapers under Mom's bottom. What did she need diapers for?

I kept asking, "What's wrong with her?" But no one was answering me and after awhile I knew I'd better shut up. Dad got in the front seat with Sonny and Dean. His hands were moving fast when he rolled down the window to tell Becky, "You clean up that mess before **anyone** goes in there." The tires spun gravel before the car even started moving.

I ran inside to see what it was that I wasn't supposed to see. In Mom and Dad's bedroom. Blood. Soaked all over the sheets and blankets. And on the floor, a big pile of wadded up sheets and diapers with more bright red blood. I started screaming, "Why is it...?" when Becky came in and pushed her hand over my mouth.

She said, "Shut **up**." Like she was yelling real quiet. "And don't you dare scare the little kids. Now get out. Right **now**." She turned my shoulders, pushed me, and closed the door behind me.

I was in the living room staring at the little kids who were staring at me. Luann said, "What's wrong with Mom?"

I knew I better act like a Mommy and do what Becky told me. I said, "She got kind of sick, but she won't die. Don't worry. It's just a little blood."

"Blood?" Luann asked. Then she tried to push past me and into the bedroom.

I stood in front of the door like I knew everything and told her, "You can't go in."

"Why not?"

"Yeah. Why not?" Billy added.

"Because you're too little. And there's nothing in there anyway. And besides I won't let you."

I sat down in front of the door to block it and didn't say one more thing. Billy and Luann could've pulled me away from the door if they both tried hard enough, but they didn't. They knew I was doing what I was supposed to.

When they decided to leave me alone, I plopped my chin down into my hands and thought hard for a long time about what must be wrong with Mom. And where all that blood came from. But it was more like thinking about infinity than really figuring anything out.

When Becky came out of the bedroom, we all went in to see what happened. The bed was made, and everything looked like usual. Except that there were about ten pillowcases on the floor crammed full of sheets and blankets. I stared at the stuffed pillowcases. Where was the blood? How could Becky clean it up so fast? Wasn't the whole room full of blood just a while ago? Where was it all? It felt like my head was loose and not quite stuck to my neck. Maybe there wasn't really any blood there before. Maybe I was the only one who saw it.

Becky started to haul the stuffed pillowcases to the big motel laundry bag that went to the cleaners every week. I picked one up too and followed her out of the room. When we were away from the little kids I asked her, "What's wrong with Mom?"

Becky looked around to see that no one was listening. Then she said in an almost whisper, "She started hemorrhaging."

"What's hemorrhaging?"

"It's when you almost bleed to death from between your legs."

I felt like she just stabbed something all the way down my throat and into my stomach. It felt empty between my legs. "Why?"

"It's probably a miscarriage."

"A miscarriage? You mean the twins? Our babies? Will they die?" I was scared and that thing inside me was stabbing farther down now. It was hot. Even my eyes were stinging hot and wet.

"We don't know. We have to wait and see." She went back into the bedroom to carry more sheets.

I sat on the floor by the big laundry bag that could hold hundreds of filthy sheets and kept crying. It felt like I was losing everything.

I didn't really want to see any more blood, but I couldn't help it. I waited until Becky was done with all the sheets and no one was in Mom and Dad's bedroom. I closed the door and started looking. None on the floor, or under the bed. No drips to the bathroom and none in the sink. I went back to the bed and pulled back the sheets to look at the mattress. None.

Then I knew, even though I was scared to know. I reached my hand under the mattress where it was wet and cold. I pulled my hand out and Mom's blood from between her legs and from the baby twins was streaked brownish-red on my hand. It was bright red before. I wondered if part of a baby was smeared there too. It wasn't something you should ever think and it was so wrong. I knew it was a sin or maybe crazy and I couldn't tell which. But I knew I lost. And those babies were dead.

They were too. Dad told us the next day. Mom had to have lots of transfusions but was probably going to come home in about a week. Since she almost died.

When she came home, I told her, "They were going to be my best thing." And I started crying again even though I hardly ever cried.

She said to me, "I'm sorry, darlin'. I know you wanted them almost as much as me."

"More. More than anyone ever wanted anything."

She took the warm Kleenex from her bra and wiped my eyes.

I asked, "Will you get pregnant again real soon?"

"The Doctor says I shouldn't ever get pregnant again. We'll have to see. Maybe you'll have to have your own babies when you grow up."

I **did** want my own babies, but I wanted Mom to make them for me. It was her job. She even said so. That it was the Will of God to have so many babies. And besides, it was too long to wait until I was all grown up. I'd have to be a teenager first and then have a boyfriend. Then some guy who might be cute would say he wanted to be head of the house so I'd have to marry him. Then he could boss me around worse than two older brothers ever would. And who knows how he'd get that sperm inside me. I just didn't want to be stuck with some creep just to get a baby.

I wanted my own baby right away, but I knew Mom was still kind of sick, and she couldn't get pregnant again until she was better. So I waited for over a month, and when she still wasn't pregnant, I asked her. I waited until we were alone in the bathroom and she was putting on her face. I knew it would take at least fifteen minutes and we'd have time to talk.

She was scooping cold cream onto her face and wiping it off with Kleenex. That was her way of washing. It was supposed to keep her from getting wrinkles. But her face was still a little wrinkly and real white, like she was getting more tired every day. So tired that pretty soon she might not be able to get out of bed at all. I put the seat cover down on the toilet and sat on it with my knees pulled up to my chest. Then I asked her, "When are you going to have another baby?"

She looked at me and said, "I don't know if you're old enough to talk about this or not."

"You know I am, Mom. I'm almost twelve now. I can talk about anything. Are you going to have another baby real soon?" I tried to look really strong and old.

"I may need a hysterectomy."

"What's that?"

"It's when they take out your uterus. Then you can't have any more babies."

"Why?"

"Because I'm not getting better since the miscarriage. I keep bleeding and there's too much pain."

I could still feel her cold blood from the mattress on my hands. "But what does the doctor say?"

She gave a big sigh. "He doesn't believe me. The rat." The Kleenex looked kind of soppy and see-through from the cold cream. She threw it into the wastebasket and got a fresh one.

"Why not?" I asked.

"He thinks I'm imagining the pain. That I'm making it up so I can get out of having more kids. Maybe I am, but I don't think so. I'm sure as hell not imagining the bleeding. But he thinks he can judge me just because he's a Catholic too. Those damn doctors." She wiped away the rest of the cold cream and started slapping powder on her face. It puffed out into the air.

Then she looked right at me but like she didn't see me. "I'd be happy to leave the judging to Father Laughlin. But he won't give me his opinion. What the hell kind of a priest won't tell you what's right and what's wrong for God's sake?" She sighed loud. "But even if he did, what the hell difference would it make? What do priests know about women anyway?" Now she was looking at the mirror again and putting on red rouge. It made her look even whiter.

"And my psychiatrist isn't any help. He doesn't know a thing about living with faith." Then she slumped over the sink and said, "I just don't know anymore."

I didn't know either. But I knew that just about everyone liked babies and one more would probably make everyone happy. So I said real quiet and nice, "Mom, just have another baby. Everything always gets better when you have another baby. Don't worry. I'll take care of it."

Then she burst out crying and slumped against the bathroom door. It was so weird for her to cry like that in front of me and not even try to cover it up. She looked like she might slide down all the way to the floor. So I took her hand, which was limp and pulled her over to the toilet seat so she could sit down.

I didn't know what else to do. I sat on the bathroom floor while she sat on the toilet crying. The skin on my thumbnail was torn and bleeding from where I was picking at it. I told her everything was going to be OK.

After a while, she was just sniffling. She looked as soggy as a pancake, but she got up and stood in front of the mirror and stared for a few minutes. She started slowly nodding her head. Then her head just dropped and I could see more tears leaking out of her eyes. Finally, she looked right at me and this time she saw me.

She said, "I don't know about the hysterectomy. But whether I have one or not, there's one thing you better get used to. There aren't going to be any more babies. I can't go through it one more time. No matter how much you want one. Fourteen pregnancies are enough. One more would kill me. I know that much."

"But Mom...." Now her tears were coming over into me and out my eyes. I felt like falling over. I didn't want her to die, but I had to have my own baby. That baby was everything I ever wanted. I was even going to have two! And now none? What was I going to do? The bottom was coming out of me and my insides were snarling. I was dizzy and felt like I was going to throw up. All at once. And there was nowhere to go. Mom filled up the whole bathroom and it was too small in there. I had to run.

I ran out of the house and felt the chilly wind shoot through my shirt onto my sweaty skin. It helped me keep running. I ran into the pasture where I saw the cows and chased Molly, our Mama cow. I screamed at her, "We're just going to kill your next baby anyway so why not start mooing now and get it over with?" Then I threw a rock at her. Hard. She galloped. She never galloped except when we were going to butcher. I threw another rock at her. I ran after her and threw rocks until she did start mooing and I got too tired to keep chasing her. Then I walked.

It was cold and I could see fog coming out of my skin. I sat down on the grass by the salt lick. It had a nice shape from all that cow licking. I picked it up and licked it. Even though it was full of germs. Then I licked my arm, which was also salty. I wondered about all the other things that were salty. Blood was salty too. I walked to the far end of the pasture where Dad kept some old lumber that had been there for about a hundred years. I sat on the pile of wood and kicked one of the two-by-fours that was laying crossway. I didn't know what to do with either my hands **or** my feet now.

Then I heard a little squeaky sound. It was coming from somewhere in the woodpile. At first I thought it was the board I was sitting on, but the squeaks came even when I stopped wiggling. I looked underneath the top boards, where the wood was making kind of a tent. It was mostly dark, but I could see a little nest of grass. Inside the nest were six teeny little rats with long tails. They were only about a half inch long. The Mama rat was gone. I hoped. I picked up the tiniest one, the runt, and brushed it on my face. A baby rat was better than no baby.

I thought about Mom's twins that were dead and how Dean said they probably got flushed down the toilet in the hospital. And now I'd never have any! I still couldn't stand it. I wanted those babies so bad that the tears came burning back and I hated my crying worse than anything right then! Even worse than being hit by Sonny. I looked at the little rat in my hand and wanted to pull its tail off and squish its soft pink little body into the ground. I felt stabbing sick again for even thinking such bad things. I had to stop everything.

I did. It was like a law. That nothing inside gets to move. Not even one tiny bit. Everything stopped. And suddenly I was as hard as the salt lick and strong. I was smart too. I knew that the dead babies were way better off up in heaven where everything is pink and sweet. They'd have to stay up there forever, along with all my baby love.

I looked at the little rat that was still in my hand. I lifted it by its tail and said, "Too bad." I dropped it on the ground and started walking back to the house.

24

THE INVISIBLE WOMAN
ALMOST TWELVE YEARS

O N school nights after dinner there wasn't that much to do because Mom wouldn't let us watch TV or listen to the radio or talk on the phone. None of us could visit friends because we lived so far out of town and no one ever came to our house. It was kind of like jail with no more new babies to make it better. That was a fact, since Mom's hysterectomy.

School was better than home because I did what they told me and got A's and B's for it. The school counselor said I was smart. I wanted to know how smart. He said if I worked hard maybe I could get a scholarship for college. That sounded OK with me, but he still didn't tell me how smart I was. I asked Mom. She said she wasn't telling any of us that stuff anymore because of the way Georgina and Sonny were turning out.

Georgina, Sonny, and Becky all had official IQ tests when they were little because the teachers thought Georgina might be really smart. It turns out Sonny was between 165 or 170 and Georgina was way smarter than that. Becky was the dumb one because she was only between 130 and 135. The weird thing is that she's the one who got A's and B's. Sonny was getting C's and D's, and Georgina practically flunked out of school before she eloped.

Mom figured it did no damn good telling kids their IQ's because of what happened to the *geniuses*. She told the rest of us we were all plenty smart, but not to get any big ideas about being special. We still had to work hard because it was how hard you worked that made all the difference.

I wished I was **really** smart. Then I could figure out all kinds of things. Maybe I could finally figure out infinity. Or stay awake when I fell asleep and find out what dreams really were and what they had to do with real life. Because if you ask me, I still think dreams are sometimes the most real.

Real life was boring and made you feel like a blob. There wasn't anything to do at our house. I almost never had homework and didn't want to play with any of my slob brothers or sisters. All of our babies were growing up. Jason was already five and he was our last baby.

I was in a quandary. That's what Mom called it, when I griped about nothing to do and feeling like this house was a prison. She also told me what The Bird Man of Alcatraz did about his quandary. Even though he was in a **real** prison, he found a hobby that made him famous for feeling like he wasn't in prison at all.

I don't really like birds that much, but I decided maybe I'd get myself a hobby like The Bird Man did. I tried stamps. How could **anyone** get excited about a stamp? Coins were better, but I still wanted to spend more than save and I got tired of looking at every coin I ever saw to see if it was worth more than it was. And bugs took too long to die with that pin stuck through them.

I decided to make a monastery out of toothpicks and glue and get extra credit for school. I copied it from a picture in the encyclopedia. It was cloistered, which meant that once you went inside, you couldn't ever leave again for the rest of your life. Even though it was the most boring thing I ever did and took forever with all those walls, I could think about anything I wanted and no one bugged me when I was working. I especially wondered what those monks did all day. I bet they didn't just sit around and pray! What did they do? And why?

Even though I never wanted to make anything with toothpicks again, I liked putting things together. So Mom got me the Visible Eye for Christmas. I painted and put together a huge eyeball with big muscles pulling back from the front of the eye. You could take it apart and look inside. Then I got the Visible Ear. Then the Visible

Man, who was clear plastic. You could see through his skin into all his organs, which were colored.

The best one ever was the Visible Woman. Because you could make her pregnant. She never got as big as Mom did when she was pregnant, but there was still a baby inside. Then you could make her un-pregnant again. And then pregnant and then un-pregnant as many times as you wanted. I spent more time on her than I did the monastery. I wanted to make her perfect.

She was the *Invisible* Woman to me because you could see through her skin. I wondered what it would be like to be see-through and have your organs see-through too. You'd be like a ghost or spirit. I wanted to be an Invisible Woman all the way through. Then I could go into the sky or anywhere I wanted. I could fly right into infinity.

One night when everyone else was busy watching something stupid on TV, I sat at the kitchen table and painted all of her veins and arteries. It took a long time because those veins were so tiny you had to get them right up to your eyeballs to paint them. The paint got on my nose and the smell got so strong it made me feel sleepy and dizzy.

I was tired anyway and just felt like laying my head down on the table. I stared at her feet. They were begging me to paint their toenails. I decided I would, but I wanted to close my eyes first, for just a few minutes.

I put my hands under my head so the table wouldn't feel so hard. When I closed my eyes, it was like my brain was floating. I thought about how sick I was of my family, how it would be six more years before I got to leave home and how hard it would be to not get in any big trouble before then. I was also thinking about how long infinity was and how I'd rather have everything horrible in my whole life to happen all at once and get it over with. Because I could stand anything for a little while. But I hated waiting for things that might happen.

Then the wobble in everything happened. It happened inside me, but it happened **everywhere** inside. And you can't tell me it was just a dream.

It felt like Rainbow Ghost from my dream a long time ago was right in front of me again. She took her invisible hand and slid it over my eyes, and instantly I was right in the middle of a swirl. Everything in the whole world was swirling around me, including my whole family, everyone's feelings, the motel, the teachers, and kids at school, the priests and nuns and all their ideas. It was a BIG HUGE swirl. None of it was new stuff, but I never saw it that way before and all at once!

There was too much of it and even though I could stand it, I felt dizzy. I floated up out of the big swirl and could see it from the outside. That felt a little better. And having Rainbow Ghost with me was nice.

Then the scariest part happened. I looked around and saw Mom, with everything swirling around **her**. Then I could see that it was her own swirl and it had a lot of the same stuff as mine but way different too. And I was just a **little tiny** part of hers. My stomach was falling down inside me. It was like when Mom came back from after her breakdown and I knew she didn't miss me that much.

My brain was hurting from trying to figure out which one was the main swirl. Hers or mine? Then I looked around and saw Becky. She was in her own swirl too. It was kind of mine and kind of like Mom's, but it was also different and I was just a little part of hers too.

Then everyone's swirls all whooshed around me all at once. Georgina's, Dad's, Butch's, Luann's, Sonny's, Billy's, Nicky's and everyone in my family and lots of other people too. I was just a little speck of nothing in all their swirls. I knew that everyone thought theirs was the main swirl just like I thought mine was. But none of them were. There wasn't any main swirl anywhere. It was harder to understand than infinity.

I got smaller and smaller looking at everyone's swirl and the way they thought theirs was the main one. I got so tiny I felt like I was just a spark that could be blown out by a big puff of anything. It was scary to think I might just disappear, when I was pretty sure I didn't want to.

That's when Rainbow Ghost pointed me back to my own swirl. I knew I had to go back there, even if it was just my own and was just one stupid little swirl and wasn't the main one and there never was any main swirl anyway.

Rainbow Ghost said, "Re-**mem**-ber. Remember **you**. Remember **me**." Her voice sounded like wind chimes. She kissed my forehead and both cheeks and her breath was like the sweetest, cleanest, baby breath that tingled through my whole body. Then she disappeared.

My arm jerked, my eyes popped open, and Invisible Woman's liver fell off the table. It rattled across the floor. When I went to pick it up I knocked over her spare belly, the pregnant one. My hands were shaky. It felt like everything had poured out of me, and something new was poured back in. But I didn't know what any of it was.

There was a big wobble in everything. Nothing was like it was before, and I had the sneaky feeling it would never change back ever again. I could still feel some of Rainbow Ghost and her tinkling voice that smiled at me. I knew the Wobble didn't scare her one bit. And I knew she loved me. And I would always remember her. But nothing else made any sense.

I also knew Invisible Woman needed the rest of her organs put back in before I went to bed. I put in her intestines and heart. My hands were fumbly and it took a long time because I was still scared and excited and swirling. Her un-pregnant belly was the last piece. I'd wait until the next day to do her toenails.

When I was brushing my teeth before bed, I remembered the banshee from a long time ago. Was she going to come screaming back for me after all those years and grab my spark? I knew the banshee was real the way Rainbow Ghost was real. But if I remembered Rainbow Ghost, I wasn't so scared of the banshee.

When I laid in bed, I tried to stay awake as long as I could, and wondered how it could be that there isn't really a main swirl. After a while, I fell asleep and didn't have even one nightmare. I was in the sky with the clouds and turned into a lacewing butterfly that flew from cloud to cloud while we all floated around and around together.

25

Manifesto
TWELVE YEARS

I WAS on my way to get my new diary. Mom gave it to me for my twelfth birthday and said that I could even draw in it. That what I did with it was up to me. It was bluish silver and had its own silver key. I kept it hidden in the canning pot in the kitchen where no one would ever look.

I got as far as the living room. Sonny was blocking the doorway with his legs. He said, "You have to say the password." There probably wasn't any stupid password anyway. He was just trying to get me. I looked at the grin on his fat head and wanted to chop his whole head off, the way dictators do when someone does something they don't like. I didn't feel bad about it either because he deserved it.

I yelled, "Just move your stupid leg." He didn't. I pushed his leg too, but it was way stronger than me. I shouted again, "Why don't you just leave me alone for once?" He was getting even happier.

I turned around, sat in a chair, and pushed my face into my hands, thinking hard. How do you get people to stop bugging you? Then I figured out one of the best things so far. I got the idea from Cleopatra. Even though Mom thought she was just a high-class tramp and wouldn't let us see the movie, I still saw pictures of her. She sat there like she was rolled in gold and was so royal no one would even think about messing with her or try to boss her around.

I went over to where Sonny was and tried out my new idea. I leaned against the wall with one hand on my hip and my head a little sideways just looking at him. I didn't say it out loud, but in my mind I told him he was the most pitiful pile of dog shit I ever saw in my whole life. I even said shit in my mind. It felt good and I didn't care if it was swearing. Besides, it was only a venial sin and you can't go to hell for that. He smelled like dog shit too and I could see that even the flies were grossed out. I could hear him saying some things to me, but I wasn't listening. I was concentrating hard.

After a few minutes he said, "What's the matter, you look like a spazz." I didn't say anything. The dog-shit smell was making my nose sick. I brushed the flies away from my head. Then he kicked my ankle and said, "You know if you keep staring like that your eyes are gonna dry up and fall out." I looked at him and blinked real slow like it was the stupidest thing anyone ever said to me. Then I just sighed and rolled my eyes, like he was the most dismal person in the universe, who should do us all a favor and just disappear.

Finally, he got up and slugged me in the arm. I didn't make a sound or act like I even felt it. Then he gave up and walked into the living room.

It worked!! I had won!! And I knew I could do it again anytime I wanted. It felt so good I wanted to do a jump-kick-scream dance. But I didn't. I sauntered into the kitchen, opened up the cupboard where the canning pot was stored, and tucked my diary under my shirt.

Then I went outside where it was hot and laid down on a patch of long grass. I looked up and there wasn't one cloud in the whole shiny blue sky. I could smile now. I'd finally figured something out. I stared at the sky and smiled all the way up. I let everything go wide open and didn't think anything. Even the grass that was itching my arms and legs melted away. Pretty soon everything was gone except for the sky. It was so blue I fell right into it. And it wasn't one bit scary. You can't get hurt falling up. I could even see the light that peeks and swims fast through the blue. Me and the sky were as close as you can get. And the sun was kissing us.

I had to blink after a while because there was so much light and my eyes were starting to hurt. When I closed them I could feel all my best dreams, especially the things Rainbow Ghost showed me.

I decided to try to remember everything I've figured out so far. I thought of so many things and knew I'd better write some of it down and save it. I took the key from my pocket and opened my diary. I wrote two lists, and here they are.

THINGS THAT ARE TRUE

No matter how hard you try to figure things out, some things just don't make sense.

But you still have to figure out everything you can because otherwise nothing makes sense.

You can't tell what's crazy and what isn't because what's real and what isn't are so mixed up.

I can't help it if I'm boy crazy. Besides, I can't stop it and don't want to. And Mom can't make me.

Sometimes you're bad for reasons that make no sense.

You have to try and be good even when you're bad.

Lots of things I think will probably be wrong, but there's nothing I can do about that.

Even if what I think isn't right, it might be true.

WHEN I GROW UP

I'm going to leave home some day and no one can stop me.

I can do whatever I want. I could be a dictator – but a good one – an architect, or a nurse. But I don't ever want to be a housewife. Or a nun.

I'm going to be so strong I can stand almost anything.

My house is going to be clean and I won't let anyone mess it up.

I want some cute boy that I really like to kiss me some day.

I'm not sure if I ever want to have any babies. But I love every baby that ever was.

I'm going to find out about Voodoo and mind reading.

That was all I wrote, but I was still thinking a lot. I decided as hard as can be, that when I grow up I'll never forget what it's like to be a kid, even when I'm all the way grown and it's past the year 2000. When I see a girl who's the age I am now, I'll look at her right in the eyes. I'll remember everything about what it was like and she'll know that she's not alone and that every bit of what she feels is real.

I was done thinking and knew I better hide my diary again before someone caught me with it. I hid it underneath my shirt and folded my arms. I walked past Sonny on the way in and smiled at him like I was the Queen of Blue Sky. I put my diary back in the canning pot. Then I went to hide the key in a new place. I put it on the floor behind the toilet in the girls' room where no one would ever look and there wasn't any boy pee to mess it up.

Falling into Blue is Barbara Bouchet's first novel. She is also the author of *The Enlightened Edge for Leaders: Ignite the Power of You*. Barbara is a leadership coach and organization consultant with many years experience as a psychotherapist. She is a facilitator and teacher in the courageous work of transformation and creativity. Barbara works intensively with individuals, groups and organizations. She lives in Seattle, Washington with her husband and family.

Go to the website, http://fallingintoblue.com for more information. Barbara's blog is there, and you can follow her on Facebook and Twitter.